SIBLINGS and SECRETS

A Brenna Wickham Haunted Mystery

---

by

Kathleen J. Easley

This book is a work of fiction. Names, characters, places, and incidents are either the product of the author's imagination or are used fictitiously, and any resemblance to actual persons, living or dead, business establishments, events, or locales is entirely coincidental.

All rights reserved. No parts of this book may be reproduced or transmitted in any form or by any means, electronic or mechanical, including photocopying, recording, or by any information storage and retrieval system, without written permission from the author, except for the inclusion of brief quotations in a review.

Copyright © 2023 by Kathleen J. Easley

Published by Ames Lake Press

ISBN-13: 979-8-86421-162-5

Cover art by Dar Albert, Wicked Smart Designs

Dedication

To Kathy Elling, my best friend and writing buddy since seventh grade. The help and support you've given me all these years is immeasurable. Thank you for everything.

And to James H. Cobb, dear friend and immensely talented writer. You always said, "just keep writing." I did, and here I am. You left us too soon and I miss you.

Chapter One

A warm feeling of déjà vu enveloped me as I pulled up to the old house and got out of my car. A tired 1950's bungalow, the place hadn't changed in as long as I could remember. The same faded green paint still clung to the wood siding, the same split-rail fence encircled the small front yard, and the same rhododendrons sprawled beneath the kitchen window, bigger now and less tidy.

To me, this would always be Grandma's house, the home where my mother and Aunt Peggy had grown up, and where I had spent many happy summers visiting as a child. Thoughts of my grandmother stirred up pleasant memories of gingerbread men, taffy pulls, and stories at bedtime.

But Grandma was gone now. My cousin Connie had inherited the house and had been living here for the past three years. Today I was moving in with her.

"Brenna! Welcome to Shoreline!" Connie bounded down the front steps and nearly bowled me over in her rush to greet me. Face beaming, she embraced me in an enthusiastic hug, squashing me against her ample bosom. My cousin was two years older than me, but we'd always been close.

"Thanks, Connie," I said. "I don't know what I would have done without you. I know this is an imposition."

"Not at all," she said, waving a plump hand in the air. "I love having you. It'll be fun, just like when we were kids." She grinned. "Besides, it gave me a great excuse to stay home from work today. Here, let me help you with your bags."

She looked over my shoulder and grimaced as her eyes lit on the rust bucket that passed for my car these days.

"Really? That's your car? You couldn't have found anything uglier?"

I gave the dilapidated old PT Cruiser a fond glance. "Hey, it's well broken in and it runs great."

She narrowed her eyes. "I thought you had a Bimmer."

"*Had* is right. That thing was worth six mortgage payments. I got this one for practically nothing."

Connie sniffed and gave a nod, embarrassed perhaps at inadvertently drawing attention to my current state of penury. She gave the car another quick once-over. "It *is* kind of unique, I guess. I like the color. What do you call that, maroon?"

"I think it's called *plum*. One thing's for certain, I never have trouble finding it in a parking lot."

She snorted. "I'll bet."

I pulled two large suitcases out of the back. Connie took one and I took the other. I followed her up the steps to the porch and into the front room of the house.

Directly to the right lay the living room. Like the rest of the house, it hadn't changed. I could still make out the stain on the olive green carpet where, at age seven, I had spilled a glass of chocolate milk; the tatty orange and brown afghan Grandma had crocheted years ago still draped the back of the lumpy old couch. Built-in shelves on either side of the fireplace were cluttered with a mix of books, framed photos, and bric-a-brac.

"It's not fancy," Connie said, "not like your condo." She uttered a quick laugh. "I keep saying I'm going to remodel, but I never seem to get around to it."

I shook my head and smiled. "I like it the way it is." The beauty of this home was in its memories, not its décor.

I followed her through an archway into the hall. To the far right was the master, and next to that a room that had been converted to a study. The spare bedroom was to the left. I could have found it blindfolded.

Stepping through the door, it hit me that I had come full circle. Not only had this been my mom's room growing up, but it had been the room where I'd spent the first three years of my life. I'd heard the story so many times. After my father's untimely death, my mother had moved back home to take advantage of the free babysitting while she finished her associate's degree and found a job to support us.

I took a deep breath and looked around. The room was good sized, furnished with a twin bed, a dresser, and a small desk and chair. A closet took up one wall, and a large window overlooked the backyard. There were no adornments, no knickknacks, no pictures on the walls. A blank canvas awaiting my personal touch.

"Feel free to decorate it any way you like," Connie said, reading my mind.

I spun to face her. "Connie, it's wonderful. Really. I can't wait to get settled. And I promise I'll try not to disrupt your life too much." My throat tightened. This was a big step, but I knew it was the right decision.

"Hey, no worries," she said. "Disrupt away. It's been too quiet around here for way too long. I've been wanting to get a roommate for ages, and I'd sure rather have you than some stranger. Besides, Buster likes you."

Buster was a pudgy black and tan beagle who was at this moment examining my suitcases with intense interest. Grateful for the distraction, I reached down to rub him behind the ears. He turned blissful eyes up to my face while his tongue lolled wetly from a toothy grin.

"If you don't want him in your room," Connie warned, "be sure to keep your door shut. He does tend to get into things."

"Curious as a cat, eh?"

She chuckled. "And twice as much trouble."

I pulled my phone from my pocket and waved it at her. "Now then, stand over there by the dresser and smile for the audience. My mom expects to see pictures."

"*Ugh.*" Connie made a face. "At least let me go comb my hair and put on some makeup. I look like a dumpy old hausfrau who's been cleaning all morning—which I *have*, by the way, but it's very unlike me."

"You look fine," I said. "I just need a picture to show my parents that I made it here and everything's okay. You know how my mom worries." In fact, my mother was the dictionary's definition of a worrywart. To say she fretted when Jason and I announced we were moving to Seattle would be an understatement. Lately, she had begun campaigning for me to move back to Phoenix where the rest of the family lived.

Connie sighed and gave in, picking up the beagle and hoisting him in front of her. She peered over the top of his shoulder. "All right, but I'm hiding behind Buster."

I moved in beside her and held the phone out at arm's length, snapping a picture. The results produced, if not a glamour shot, at least a decent photo of my cousin and me with Buster. Connie grunted as she examined the picture over my shoulder. She had a pleasingly round face with a slight double chin, ash blond hair cut short and tapered evenly to just below the ear, and bright hazel eyes that peered through gold wire-framed glasses.

Next to her, the camera captured an image of me striking a goofy pose: coffee-colored eyes crinkled at the corners, wide lips stretched in a crooked smile, and a narrow face framed by my best feature—wavy, shoulder-length nut brown hair.

Buster's adorableness went without saying.

"Good enough," I said, sending the picture off to my mom. I would text her a few words later when things were more settled. I stuffed the phone back into my pocket. "Well, I guess I'd better get unpacked. Why don't you give me an hour, and then I'll take us out to lunch. Is there someplace close by that you like?"

"You betcha. I call it the *kitchen*." She grinned. "Best place in town. Just ask Buster."

She saw me start to protest and put up a hand. "No, seriously," she said. "I love to cook. It'll be a pleasure to have someone to cook for besides myself."

"Okay," I said, "but I'll make the next trip to the

grocery store."

"Nope. I've got that covered too. Brubaker's up the street delivers my groceries every Monday. I have a standing order for certain things and I just give them a call if I want to add anything."

I stared in amazement. *"What?* How'd you manage *that?* Isn't Brubaker's just a 'mom and pop' place? I didn't think they did deliveries."

The small family-run store had been in the neighborhood forever, or at least since I was a kid. My mom and I used to walk there occasionally to pick up the odd loaf of bread or quart of milk my grandmother needed.

Connie cracked a sideways grin. "I'll let you in on a secret. They only do it for me and my weird neighbor." She jerked her thumb toward the house immediately to the south.

"Your weird neighbor?" I shot her a feigned look of reproof. "Connie Kestler, I'm surprised at you."

She laughed and threw her hands up. "Can I help it if my neighbor is weird?"

"Weird how?" I cocked an eyebrow. "If I'm going to live here, I ought to know what I'm getting into."

"Right. Listen, Brenna, forget about unpacking for now. Come have some tea. I'll give you the lowdown on all the neighbors while I fix lunch."

I followed her to the kitchen. Even the tiny flowers and teacups on the faded yellow wallpaper evoked memories of my grandmother. I took a seat at the kitchen table, leaning my elbows on the smooth Formica surface. "Don't forget," I said, "I used to live downtown. Every other person on the street was weird. It'll take a lot to impress me."

"Oh, just you wait." She crossed her eyes and stuck out her tongue. "Downtown's got nothin' on the *'burbs*."

We shared a comradely laugh, and I felt an unexpected wave of sadness as an image of Jason's smiling face rose unbidden in my mind. Together we had laughed so often—as best friends, as soul mates. The finality of what I was doing suddenly hit me.

Tears welled up. I turned and fixed my gaze to a spot on the wall, sniffing and wiping at my cheek, but not before Connie had seen.

"Ah, sweetie," she said, handing me a tissue from a box on the counter.

I let out a heavy sigh as I dabbed my eyes. "I'm sorry. It's just that selling the condo is hard." Absently, my fingers toyed with the ring on my left hand.

"Don't be sorry," Connie said, all sympathy. "I understand."

"I know it's time to sell," I said, combing a hand through my hair, "but somehow it feels like I'm letting go of the last little piece of the man I loved." I gave a hiccupping little sob as the words caught in my throat. "When we bought that condo we thought we'd live there forever, maybe have a baby or two. Dying never even crossed our minds. Who dies at thirty-two?"

"It wasn't fair," Connie said. "They should have thrown the book at that guy."

"He said he never even saw Jason. It was dark and Jason was crossing in the middle of the block wearing dark clothing. The judge called it comparative negligence—Jason wasn't watching where he was going."

"That driver should have been watching where *he* was

going. I'll bet he was texting."

My mouth pulled tight and I shrugged. These arguments had been hashed and rehashed, investigated, disputed, argued, and reasoned to death. I didn't feel like dragging it all out again.

"It's been two years," I said, straightening my shoulders. "Time to move on. I signed with a realtor this morning." I gave my cousin a warm smile. "Thanks for being here for me. I mean it. You'll never know how much I appreciate it."

Connie's offer to rent me her spare bedroom at a pittance of my mortgage payment had been a godsend. Since my husband's death, I'd been struggling to make it on my own, trying to convince myself that I was happy living alone. But ten-hour days working in a high-stress office to maintain an expensive downtown Seattle condominium had taken a toll on my nerves and my health. I had barely been holding on by my fingernails to an increasingly joyless existence. The end had finally come two weeks ago when the venerable old attorney for whom I'd been working announced his retirement, convincing me it was time to give in and start fresh.

"Hey, that's what family's for, right?" She took off her glasses and wiped them with the hem of her shirt. "Anyhow, this place was always too big for just one person. Grandma would be thrilled knowing her old house was being lived in by her two favorite granddaughters."

Her *only* granddaughters, but who's counting? I smiled and took a deep breath, then pushed my unruly hair back behind my ears. "You're right. Now, didn't you say something about lunch?"

"Yep," Connie said, becoming all business. She turned on the oven to preheat. "Just give me a minute. I'm going to make my famous chicken crepes." She reached into the refrigerator and pulled out a large covered bowl. "I cooked the chicken this morning and made a Waldorf salad to go with it."

"Sounds yummy." I was always impressed by people skilled in the art of cooking since I'd never developed the knack myself. Other than one or two basic recipes, following instructions on a package was about the extent of my talent. "What can I do to help?"

"Plates are up there and silverware is in that drawer. Careful—don't trip over Buster."

While I set the table, Connie filled a large ceramic mug with water and a tea bag, nuked it in the microwave, and handed it to me.

I took it gratefully and sat once more at the table. "Now, why don't you tell me about your weird neighbor."

"Oh, right. Maureen Moreland." Connie talked while she mixed chopped chicken with various ingredients in a bowl. "She never leaves her house. *Literally*, she *never* leaves her house."

"That's not weird, it's *sad*."

"Not even to go to the store? Or sweep the *porch?*"

"I think it's called agoraphobia. It's a kind of mental illness."

"Well, she doesn't seem to mind hanging out her window and yelling at Buster."

"What for?"

Connie ran her tongue over her lower lip, then sheepishly confessed. "He may have gotten into her yard a couple of times and dug up her flower beds." She began spooning the chicken mixture into thin crepes, rolling them up, and placing them side by side in a baking dish.

"Connie! No wonder."

"I know. But it's not like he does it every day. And I always go over and fix her stupid flowers."

Hearing his name, the beagle in question positioned himself at Connie's feet, giving the bowl of chicken his rapt attention. Connie looked affectionately down at him. "Yes, you're a naughty boy." He responded with a hopeful twitch of his tail.

She poured a can of cream of chicken soup over the crepes, topped them off with a handful of slivered almonds, and popped the dish into the oven. "There—thirty minutes."

I was struck with a thought. "Wait a minute. You said her name is Maureen Moreland? Isn't that the same girl who lived there when we were kids?"

Connie nodded. "Yep, same girl. A few years older than me. I wasn't sure you'd remember. She was a teenager back then, and she didn't hang out with us kids that much."

"Sure, I remember. She was nice. I always liked her. She babysat me a few times. There was a brother too, and a younger sister about my age. What was her name? Anna? No—*Hannah*. I used to play with them when we came to visit Grandma."

"Uh-huh. Maureen was the oldest. She lives alone there now. The brother still comes around to check on her every couple of weeks or so. His name is Gage. You'll probably run into him one of these days. I've talked to him a few times, but he's not the friendliest guy in the world."

I laughed. "Yeah, he was kind of a jerk when we were kids—typical boy—but I would have thought he'd grown out of that by now."

I remembered Gage. He was three years older than me, and as a kid he'd had a wild, mischievous way about him, teasing us girls and chasing us with his water pistol. But he'd had a fun side as well, often joining us in games of tag or hide-and-seek. I also recalled that he had an affinity for animals, rescuing a kitten stuck in a tree, prodding a garter snake out of the road with a stick so it wouldn't get run over, and romping with the neighbor's dog because his dad wouldn't let him have one of his own. At nine years old I had been thoroughly smitten with him, though I would have stuck needles in my eyes before admitting it.

"I don't imagine he's too happy about being tied down to his weird—sorry—*sick* older sister," Connie said.

"At least he checks on her. You've got to give him that."

"Sure, until you realize he arranged the delivery with Brubaker's to keep from having to come by so often himself. I don't think he and Maureen get along very well. Andy Brubaker, the grocer's son, went to school with Maureen a long time ago. He always had a crush on her, which is why he was so quick to agree to deliver her groceries at no charge."

"And where do you fit into all of this?" I asked. "How did you talk them into delivering yours too?"

"Gage arranged it. I get my groceries delivered the same time as Maureen in exchange for agreeing to be available if she ever needs help in an emergency."

"Seriously? What a deal." I narrowed my eyes. "So,

has she ever had any emergencies?"

"Sort of. She sometimes has these nightmares or hallucinations or something. She's woken up the whole neighborhood a couple of times screaming bloody murder in the middle of the night. I've rushed over there and found her trembling and hiding behind the bed, but she always insists she's fine and refuses to let me call anyone."

"*Geez.* Does her brother know about this?"

"Oh, yeah, I've told him." She frowned and gave a shrug. "He just gets annoyed. He's had all sorts of doctors and therapists visit her. They have to come to the house because Maureen refuses to step outside. Nothing they've done has ever helped for long. So now he just makes sure she's comfortable and her needs are taken care of."

An uneasy thought occurred to me. "You don't suppose she's dangerous, do you? She sounds a little schizophrenic. Do you go over there by yourself? Has she ever done anything that made you feel uncomfortable?"

Weren't most murder victims killed by people they knew? *Gosh, officer, she seemed so harmless—a little eccentric maybe...*

Connie waved a hand carelessly in the air. "Oh, no. She may be weird, but she's not dangerous. Besides, she's a tiny thing. I could knock her over with one finger if I had to. The only issues we've ever had were those couple of times when Buster got into her yard and dug holes in her garden. Other than that, we haven't had any problems."

I sat pondering this and sipped my tea while Connie set out the salad. A moment later, the timer went off on the oven.

"Mmm, this looks delicious," I murmured as I helped

myself to a large portion of the savory dish. "I didn't realize how hungry I was."

She laughed. "Take lots. You're way too skinny."

As we ate, I said, "It's funny how things turn out, isn't it? They all seemed so nice and normal back when we were kids. I wonder what happened? I mean, agoraphobia doesn't just come on for no reason. Is Gage the only one taking care of Maureen? Where's the rest of the family?"

Connie shook her head. "All I know is that the parents moved away. I've lived here for three years and I've never seen them."

"What about Hannah?"

She bounced her shoulders in an exaggerated shrug. "Don't know. Maureen isn't what you'd call *talkative*."

"I thought you were friends."

"Well, yeah, but it's not like I spend a lot of time over there. She doesn't exactly confide in me."

I nodded, chewing thoughtfully as I visualized just how isolated the poor, disturbed woman must be.

"Wait a minute—" Connie's face worked as she concentrated. "Actually, now that you mention it, I *did* hear a rumor once that the younger sister ran away, or was kidnapped, or something. Just disappeared without a trace."

Chapter Two

My eyebrows shot up, my fork poised halfway to my mouth. "What? *Really?* That's awful." I only had sketchy memories of the girl—I couldn't have been more than nine years old the last time I saw her—but I remembered playing with her. We had both liked horses, and spent hours every day neighing and galloping around her yard like a couple of wild two-legged mustangs.

Connie's mouth twisted uncertainly. "I'm not really sure about that. It's just something I heard. But it was a long time ago. I don't know if anyone really knows what happened." She placed her hands on the table. "Would you like anything else? I have some cookies."

"No, thanks," I said, feeling unsettled. I put my fork down and shoved my chair away from the table. "I think we've gabbed long enough." I gave my cousin a good-natured smirk. "Aunt Peggy would be *scandalized*."

Connie's mother had always been a stickler for propriety and never missed an opportunity to remind us of how she disdained women who sat around all day gossiping.

Connie rolled her eyes.

"I'd better go get my things unpacked," I said. "It's getting late. Then I think maybe I'll go for a walk and check out the neighborhood. I'll take Buster with me."

The little beagle had parked himself beside my chair in hopes, I suspected, of intercepting any food that might find its way to the floor. I reached down and caressed his velvety head. My fingers were rewarded with a slobbery lick.

"That's a good idea," Connie said. "You'll probably run into Nancy Chumley, the neighbor on the other side." She pointed north. "She's usually outside working in her garden this time of day. She's a *real* wealth of knowledge. She and her husband Oliver have lived in this neighborhood forever. They knew Maureen's parents. Same with the people who live on the other side of Chumleys', Bill Prescott and his wife Sylvia. She can be a bit prickly. Doesn't talk much, but she's nice enough once you get to know her. Hey, maybe I should throw a party and invite them all so you can meet them."

"Oh, my god—please *don't*." I pressed my hands to my face in horror.

Connie let out a loud laugh. "All right, all right. I get the message."

An hour later, I attached Buster's leash to his collar and made my way outside to the front of the house. I couldn't get over how *green* everything was. What a contrast to downtown: no tall buildings, no throngs of people, no hard angles or rigid lines anywhere—simply a narrow walk from the porch steps to the asphalt driveway. The lawn unfurled toward the fence and petered out at a gravel parking strip adjacent to the blacktop road. Up and down the street, trees spread branches in all directions, heedless of boundaries. I took a deep breath—everything smelled so fresh and *leafy*.

A sprawling bedroom community on the edge of Puget Sound, Shoreline was settled in the early 1900s as Seattle spread northward. While a few modern developments have sprung up here and there, most neighborhoods still consist of older homes set in tidy yards crammed with rhododendrons, hydrangeas, and rose bushes.

Other than the occasional chirping and rustling in the trees overhead, everything was amazingly quiet. How would I ever be able to sleep at night without the soothing din of traffic in the background and the comforting glow of lights from the city?

I had once heard a saying, *fences make good neighbors*. If that were true, I thought, then this neighborhood must be chock-full of good neighbors. Split cedar rails, chain link, and white pickets existed here in abundance.

Having no desire to run into any Chumleys or Prescotts, I turned and headed south. The way was clear and the sun shone brightly in the early autumn sky. So far, the summer weather lingered, but here and there the leaves were turning and I knew it wouldn't be long before the ground was carpeted in drifts of russet and gold. I started off at a brisk pace with Buster pulling ahead as he snuffled noisily at clumps of grass growing in the gravel verge.

Siblings and Secrets

As we neared the front of the Moreland house, I happened to glance up and see a little girl in pigtails standing on the other side of the street. I smiled and gave her a friendly wave, then was nearly pulled off balance as Buster made a sudden dash toward her. I did an ungainly pivot and yanked on the leash, dragging the dog back from the road. As I did so, I reeled backward and collided with a man unfortunate enough to be walking behind me at that moment.

"Watch out," he snapped irritably.

"Sorry," I said as I regained my footing. I turned to apologize and found him juggling a large grocery bag and a pink cardboard bakery box. The box was threatening to topple so I made a grab for it. My fingers had barely touched it when Buster chose that moment to run between us, wrapping the leash around my legs and pulling me once more off balance.

The man uttered a curse, and I watched in horror as the flimsy pink box tipped and slid from his grasp, landing upside down on the ground with a splat. Before I could stop him, Buster made a gleeful dive for the carton, flattening it further with his front paws and ripping into the frosting-smeared cardboard.

"Buster, *no!*" I yanked on the leash. "Oh, my god, I'm so sorry."

I pulled the beagle away from the ruined confection. He stood at my feet happily licking pink frosting from his muzzle, heedless of the wreckage he had caused. "I am *so* sorry," I repeated, gripping the end of the leash. I was mortified. This had obviously been a cake intended for a special occasion.

"Get your damn dog under control," growled the man.

His face had turned a vivid red. I could practically see steam rising from his collar.

"I'll buy you another cake," I said. It sounded lame, but I didn't know what else to say. "Buster got excited when he saw that little girl across the street. If you could just tell me where..."

"Forget it," he said hotly. He shifted the bag of groceries in his arms and began unceremoniously shoving the cake box with his foot toward the shrubs at the edge of the yard. "Just leave it there. I'll come back and get it later." He turned his back and began to stomp up the driveway toward the Moreland house.

Suddenly, it hit me. "You're Gage," I called, "aren't you?"

He stopped and spun around, a look of surprise on his face. I hadn't seen him in over twenty years, but now as I studied his features, I knew I was right. As an adolescent boy, he'd had a long narrow nose, big ears, and a lanky frame. His shaggy brown hair had hung perpetually in his eyes. I had delighted in calling him "donkey face," and he had retaliated with a well-aimed water pistol. But I had been nine years old at the time.

In the intervening years, he had matured from an awkward twelve-year-old into a reasonably attractive adult: tall, broad-shouldered, and well proportioned. He had grown into his ears, and his long nose now appeared straight and strong, set squarely in a firm, masculine face. His dark hair was neatly cut and combed, and he was smartly dressed in an expensive sport jacket with a sky-blue shirt and gray wool slacks.

"Do I know you?" His look was stern, his features taut with annoyance.

"You used to, a long time ago. I used to come here as a kid with my mom to visit my grandmother." I waved a hand in the direction of Connie's house next door while struggling to maintain a grip on Buster's leash with the other. The dog kept pulling toward the smashed cake box, now lying abandoned beneath the low-hanging bough of an ornamental juniper bush. "My cousin lives there now. I just moved in with her."

"What's your name?" His brow furrowed as he scrutinized me curiously.

"Brenna Wickham, used to be Price."

"Brenna," he repeated, rolling the name around on his tongue.

"I used to come over and play with your younger sister when my mom and I visited in the summer."

His frown relaxed a little. "Hannah's friend. I remember."

Yes, Hannah's friend. It had been so long ago. As children we had sworn to remain best friends forever, promising to write each other every week while we were apart, but it hadn't happened. I wrote a couple of times, but when no answer ever came back, I finally gave up and figured she had forgotten me. Over time, the hurt subsided and I moved on. Literally.

My mom, a widow since before I was born, remarried when I was ten, and my new dad moved us to Phoenix where he'd gotten a job as the marketing manager for a large retail company. Mom became busy with two new babies and a part-time job, while I got involved in school, sports, and new friends. Rather than insisting the whole family trek back to Seattle every year, Grandma had come to Phoenix instead, always saying she enjoyed the excuse to go someplace warm. As the years passed, thoughts of my childhood friend receded.

By the time I was married and moved back to Seattle, Grandma had gone into assisted living and the house had been rented out. Three years later she was gone, and Connie had moved in. Now both granddaughters were living in the old house. Strange how things worked out.

"Did you say you've moved in next door?" Gage said.

I couldn't tell by his expression if he was pleased by the idea or not.

"Yes. My cousin Connie inherited the house when Grandma died a few years ago. I'm renting the spare bedroom for awhile till I get things sorted out."

He nodded, his face impassive. "Guess I'll be seeing you around then." He repositioned the bag of groceries he carried. "I'd better get inside."

Without another word, he turned and strode toward the house leaving me staring at his back. A dozen emotions assailed me. Connie had warned me he wasn't very friendly, but somehow I had envisioned our first meeting differently. I guess I thought he would be pleasantly surprised to meet me again after all these years, that he would have happy memories of playing together as children.

A jerk on the leash brought me back to the present. Buster was still trying to get to the cake. I took a deep breath and sighed. The cake. I guess I couldn't blame Gage for being angry. I looked askance at the little beagle and muttered, "Buster, you *are* a naughty boy." His tail waved happily as he raised his head to look at me with bright, unrepentant eyes.

I looped the end of the leash over a nearby fencepost,

then went to kneel beside the crushed cake box. Gingerly, I lifted the cardboard lid. There, amid flattened chunks of chocolate cake, squashed red roses, and smeared pink frosting, the smudged words "Happy Birthday, Maureen" could still be made out.

I groaned and sat back, pressing my fingers to my face. I had to do something. I glanced at my watch. Not quite three o'clock. Plenty of time. I got to my feet, grabbed Buster's leash off the fence post, and dragged him protesting back to the house.

"Connie!" I hollered as I burst in the front door, "I have to bake a cake!"

Shortly after five o'clock, I knocked on the Morelands' front door carrying a chocolate sheet cake made from my grandmother's favorite recipe and iced with a smooth pink buttercream frosting. Gage opened the door and looked shocked when I presented the cake.

"You didn't have to do that," he said. His face creased as it settled once more into what I was beginning to see as a perpetual frown.

"I know," I said, ignoring his dour expression. "I wanted to. Besides, I'd like to see Maureen and wish her a happy birthday. It's been ages. And since we're going to be neighbors..."

He hesitated, and I could see him debating with himself. Finally, he shook his head. "It's not a good idea. Maureen's not well." He took the cake and started to close the door.

"I know," I said quickly, putting my hand against the

door. "Connie told me about Maureen's illness. But don't you think it would do her good to see a friendly face?"

"Maybe another time," he said. "Thanks again for the cake." With that, he gave the door a firm shove, closing it in my face. Once again I was left standing with my mouth open.

"I don't get it," I complained to Connie later that evening. "What's his problem?" My hands made frustrated gestures before finally clamping into fists. "What possible harm would it have done to let me say hi to Maureen and wish her a happy birthday?"

My sudden rush to bake a cake had demanded a recounting of the incident on the street with Buster and Gage Moreland. Now we were seated in the living room kibitzing over a glass of wine. Indignation had put a sour taste in my mouth, and I had barely done justice to the grilled salmon Connie had prepared for dinner.

She shrugged. "I *told* you he wasn't very friendly." She took a sip of her Riesling, her arched eyebrows just visible over the rim of the glass. Buster lay stretched out on his side in the middle of the room, his rib cage rising and falling rhythmically as he slept.

"I know, but it doesn't make sense. It's not like I was asking her to come outside or anything." I was peeved at being put off, and more than a little annoyed at Gage's uncalled-for boorishness. What had happened to the fun-loving boy I remembered? "Doesn't he *want* her to have friends?"

"Maybe he wanted to feel her out first, get her reaction

to having a visitor. After all these years, she might not remember you. Who knows how she'd respond? Sometimes the strangest things will set her off. Maybe he's afraid she'll get hysterical and have a stroke."

I stared at her incredulously. "Oh, come *on*. It *can't* be *that* bad."

"You haven't seen her," Connie said. "The last time she had one of her fits, she wound up practically catatonic."

"From a *nightmare?*"

"No. Get *this*—she said she saw..."

Suddenly, we were interrupted by a loud knocking at the front door. Buster leaped to his feet and started barking. Shushing the dog with a sharp word, Connie set her glass on the coffee table and went to open the door. A moment later, Gage entered holding out Connie's empty cake platter. Buster sniffed curiously at his pant leg.

"Thanks again for the cake," Gage said.

Connie took the platter and stepped aside, nodding in my direction. "Brenna made it."

He turned toward me where I sat on the couch in the living room. He tugged self-consciously at his jacket, then cleared his throat. "Thank you. It was good. Maureen appreciated it. I put what we didn't eat on another plate to finish later."

"I'm glad she liked it," I said, keeping my voice cool, "but you didn't have to bring the plate back tonight. It could have waited."

Connie looked at me, then at Gage. With an inscrutable expression, she pivoted and disappeared with the platter into the kitchen, leaving me to fend for myself.

Gage watched her go, then turned back to me. "I

wanted to apologize," he said. "I owe you an explanation."

I folded my arms and remained seated. I saw no reason to make this easy for him.

He shifted his weight from one foot to the other. "There's something you should know about Maureen."

"I know," I said. "She suffers from agoraphobia—she doesn't leave the house. And she has nightmares. Connie told me. Don't worry, I won't..."

"It's more than that," he interrupted brusquely. His features were grim. "We don't talk about Hannah, either. It upsets her."

My brows drew together and I bit my lower lip, recalling the rumor Connie had mentioned. My fingers fiddled with the stem of my wine glass. I waited for Gage to go on.

He dragged a hand through his hair and fixed his eyes to a spot somewhere over my left shoulder. Clearly he found this difficult to talk about. At last, he spoke. "Hannah disappeared over twenty years ago. She vanished without a trace and was never found."

I put a hand to my mouth. So it wasn't just a rumor. Hearing him blurt it out like that made the truth of it more shocking than I could have imagined. My heart swelled for my long lost friend and tears prickled the corners of my eyes. What pain her family must have endured. No wonder Maureen had nightmares.

Gage continued, clasping his left fist in his right hand. "Maureen blames herself. And worse than that, our parents blame her too. Mom had a nervous breakdown. My dad finally had to take her away from here. As soon as I finished high school, they moved to Florida. We hardly ever hear from them anymore." He took a deep breath and exhaled heavily.

"How could Maureen be to blame?" I asked. "She was just a girl. I mean..." Words failed me. That Maureen could have done something to her little sister was unthinkable.

"She was supposed to be babysitting while our parents went out for the day, but she snuck off to meet her boyfriend and left Hannah alone in the house. I was out riding my bike like a stupid jerk, completely unaware." His voice faded to a grating whisper. "Hannah was only eight years old."

I stood then and took a step toward him, feeling helpless, my earlier pique forgotten. "Oh, Gage. I am so sorry."

I tried to recall some of the words of condolence I had received after Jason's death, but couldn't think of anything that didn't sound trite.

Gage seemed to remember himself. He dragged his eyes back to my face and gave me a rueful half-smile. "Like I said, we don't talk about it." He straightened his shoulders and continued briskly. "Anyway, I told Maureen about you, and she claims that she does remember you and she'd love to see you. I'm supposed to ask you over for dinner tomorrow night," he glanced at Connie who had come back into the room and added, "both of you."

For a moment I didn't say anything. I felt torn. It had been twenty-five years and so much had happened. Running in to say hi was one thing, sitting down for a meal and engaging in a whole evening of conversation was another. Hannah had been my friend. How could I avoid talking about her?

Gage rubbed the back of his neck. "Look, I totally understand if you don't want to. Believe me, I wouldn't blame you. Dinner with us can be pretty depressing."

"Of course we'd love to come," I said, making a quick decision. "I think having a nice dinner party would be good for Maureen. What a horrible burden she's carried all these years. After all, she was just a kid, too, when all this happened. Fifteen or so, wasn't she? I feel sorry for her. We were friends once, a long time ago, and I'd like to be friends again."

His face relaxed. "You're very kind. But I should warn you, it doesn't take much to upset her."

I nodded. "I've had some experience with losing a loved one." I fought the catch in my throat. "But I've come to believe that a person is never really gone as long as someone remembers them."

"Thanks for understanding," he said. For the first time, the hint of a smile showed on his face. "It's really nice having you back, Brenna. And I think you're right—seeing you again will be good for Maureen. How does six o'clock sound?"

"We'll be there."

I closed the door behind him as he left, then turned to Connie. "You hear all that?"

She bobbed her head and gave a low whistle. "Wow," was all she said.

Chapter Three

I woke the next morning as the sun's first light tinted the sky outside my window. It took me a second to remember where I was. Then I yawned and stretched, and headed for the shower. I wanted to get an early start. It was Sunday, and some friends had agreed to meet me at the condo to help with the tedious task of moving. I had rented a heated storage unit downtown, and over the last few weeks had been packing cardboard boxes with books, sheets and towels, dishes, and other personal belongings.

As I nibbled on toast smeared with peanut butter and sipped a cup of hastily brewed coffee, Connie shuffled into the kitchen wrapped in a pink terry bathrobe. The flower shop she owned was closed on Sundays.

"You call that *breakfast?*" Her face puckered in disapproval. "At least let me fry you an egg or something."

"No, thanks. This is plenty. Besides, I've got to get going. Lots to do today. I have to get all the boxes out of the condo so my realtor can start showing it. She's pushing to have an open house next weekend."

"Would you like me to come along and help?"

I considered my cousin's doughy physique and shook my head. I loved Connie for her willingness, but questioned the extent of her stamina.

"Nope. I've got it covered. A couple of Jason's old friends are coming with handcarts. We'll be hauling stacks of boxes down to the cars to take to storage. At least we don't have to move the bigger pieces of furniture for now. The real estate agent said leaving a few tables and chairs would make the place look homier. Something about staging."

"Okay," Connie said, plopping into a chair. "Just don't forget we're having dinner next door tonight." She sucked air in through clenched teeth, piping, "*That* should be fun."

I gave her a reassuring look. "I'll be home in plenty of time. And don't worry, it'll be fine." Famous last words.

I left my car in the parking garage and took the elevator up to the eighth floor. Entering the condo and knowing it wasn't home anymore felt sad and surreal. Everything that had made this a warm, cozy home had been removed. The kitchen counters were smooth and bare, the glass-fronted cabinets empty. In the living room, the expansive built-in shelves running along one wall now stood empty, devoid of all the books, photos, and memorabilia Jason and I had collected over the years of our marriage.

We met at the University of Arizona. I was an English major, he a computer science wiz. At first, I was attracted by his good looks and fun-loving personality. People liked him, and he always seemed to have a crowd of friends around. As we grew closer, I found that he had a brilliant mind and a real instinct for all things tech. He loved to talk about his innovative ideas for the future. We married shortly after graduation and two years later moved to Seattle. Life had been idyllic.

Then one year short of our tenth anniversary, everything fell apart.

I stood in the entryway feeling numb—past thought, past tears—absently fingering the wedding band on my left hand. In the center of the modern open-concept floor plan were two stacks of cardboard boxes piled like building blocks, one labeled "donate," the other "storage."

My life reduced to so many boxes.

"So, you're really doing it," came a familiar voice behind me.

I turned to find my friend Tamara Munroe standing in the hall behind me, her warm brown face lined with concern. In three strides, she had me in a crushing bear hug.

"I knew it was coming," she whispered, "but I didn't think it would be so soon. I'm going to miss you so much."

The vivid gold and magenta tunic she wore over skin-tight orange leggings perfectly defined her vibrant personality. Tamara and her husband Curtis lived in the next unit down the hall. We had been friends since the day they moved in four years ago, discovering early that we shared similar interests in music, movies, and getting sweaty in the gym. The building had an exercise room on the first floor, and we often used to meet there in the evening to work out.

She let go and I stepped back, giving a quick remonstrative laugh.

"Hey, it's not like I'm moving to China," I said. "I told you—I'm renting a room with my cousin in my grandmother's old house. It's less than an hour away. I promise we'll stay in touch."

I was going to miss her too, but I knew that if I let myself think about it the waterworks would start up and this wasn't the time for it.

"What about your job?"

"I told you, my boss retired. Friday was my last day."

Tamara made a pouty face and put her hands on her hips. "You *were* planning to come down and say good-bye, weren't you?"

"No, I was hoping to sneak out without telling you. Of *course* I was. But right now, I'm waiting for some friends of Jason's—people he used to work with—who are coming to help me with these boxes. Once we get finished, I'll come straight down to see you."

She gave a petulant little humph.

"Besides," I said, "it's Sunday, and I didn't want to bother you too early." I cast her a sly look. "I know you and Curtis like to stay in *bed* on Sunday mornings."

She slapped unconvincingly at my arm, then broke into a grin. "You know who's *really* going to miss you, don't you?"

My eyebrows rose. "Who?"

"Todd." She folded her arms and nodded smugly, like

I was supposed to know who she was talking about.

"*Who?*" I wracked my brain. I couldn't place the name.

She laughed. "You know—Kelly's dog walker. Todd the *bod*."

Kelly Hopper, another neighbor on this floor, had an arrangement with a cute young college student to walk her pair of miniature poodles every day while she was at work.

I let out a sputtering gasp. "*What?* No! Oh, *god*. I thought he was *gay!*"

"What? A guy can't be gorgeous these days without being gay? I've seen the way he looks at your tush when you pass him in the hall." A scandalous smile spread over her face.

"Oh, *puleez*." I rolled my eyes. "Besides, isn't he only, like, twenty years old?"

Tamara grinned. "So, he's into cougars."

I wrinkled my nose. "I'm not old enough to be a cougar." Then I paused and tapped a finger against my lips. "But now that you mention it, I think I've seen him staring at Curtis, especially when he wears those tight little shorts down to the gym. You'd better keep an eye on that man of yours."

She let out a laugh, her bright obsidian eyes glistening with amusement.

Just then, boisterous voices in the hallway announced the arrival of my moving crew. Two strapping men and one robust young woman, friends of Jason's from the software company where he had worked, pushed through the door with eager smiles on their faces. The men each pulled a wheeled handcart behind them.

The woman, a twenty-something in ragged cut-offs and a Mariners baseball cap, rushed over to give me a hug. "We're so glad you called," she exclaimed. "We've been wanting to help out any way we could ever since Jason died. He was such a great guy. We all miss him so much."

The two men nodded their agreement.

I returned their smiles. These three were part of a cabal of role-playing game enthusiasts whom Jason and I used to hang out with all the time. It had been fun, but more Jason's thing than mine. Without him to encourage me, my taste for it had waned. In fact, I found it hard to get excited about anything these days and really didn't know what I wanted to do now.

To keep from falling headlong into a chasm of despair, I had sought a grief counselor for help. Following her recommendation, I had made an effort to "find myself." I visited a couple of art galleries and took a drawing class, I attended a music festival and attempted to learn the guitar, and I endeavored to spend more time outdoors. But all I found was that I couldn't draw, I had no musical talent, and my forays outdoors consisted mainly of meandering aimlessly around the zoo on random afternoons. In the end, I had wound up throwing myself into my job and working myself into oblivion every night.

Ultimately, it had been the support of people like Connie and Tamara and these friends that had saved me. When my boss retired, I could have moved laterally in the firm or used his contacts and references to find another stressful, high-paying job downtown, but my friends had convinced me that I needed to slow down and make some lifestyle changes. I would be forever grateful.

"Lori, thank you so much for coming," I said. "Kyle,

Trevor, I really appreciate all your help."

"No problem," said the woman in the Mariners cap, speaking for all three. "We've missed you, Brenna. You know we'd love to have you come hang out with us any time you want."

"I know—and thank you. I miss you guys too. We'll see." I gave a quick shrug. "It's been rough." I looked down at my fingers, absently fiddling with my ring again. Things just weren't the same without Jason.

"That's okay," Lori said. "You don't have to explain. We understand. You have to make a new life for yourself."

I smiled gratefully, then coughed to clear my throat, and swung my hand around toward the wide, desolate living room. "I have things pretty much packed up in these boxes. I just need them moved out of here. I've rented one of those storage units over on Vine Street."

Tamara broke in. "Brenna, why don't you come over when you get done? I'll boot Curtis out and we can talk. I've got cinnamon rolls, and I'll make some coffee."

"That'd be great," I said. "Shouldn't be more than a couple of hours." I watched as she disappeared down the hall, then with a sigh turned back to my helpers and rubbed my hands together. "Okay, shall we get started?"

I returned home just after four thirty and headed for the shower. It had been a long, tiring day, but satisfying. All the boxes had been delivered to their assigned destinations, and a quick phone call to the real estate agent had confirmed that the condo was ready to go on the market.

Connie and I left for the Morelands' just before six. Gage met us at the door and ushered us into the living room. This house was larger than ours, older and more upright, with a tall second story and wide veranda, plus dormer windows and gables more characteristic of a classic farm house. Where ours languished in a tired, mid-century funk, Maureen's had been stylishly remodeled, displaying modern features and furnishings. Hardwood floors ran throughout, and the walls were painted a cool gray, offset by splashes of vivid color in the window treatments and various fabric accents.

Maureen sat curled in an armchair next to a marble-tiled fireplace; a crackling fire burned low, adding a warm radiance to the room. She looked up as we entered, swiping at her bangs with delicate fingers. Wispy brown curls covered her head.

"Happy birthday!" Connie and I said in unison.

A timid smile answered on Maureen's face. I was alarmed at how pale and thin she looked. I wouldn't have recognized her. She was only six years older than me, but her frail appearance made her seem much older. *She desperately needs to get outside in the sunshine*, I thought.

"Maureen," Gage said in a measured voice, "this is Brenna Price. She used to come and visit when she was a kid, remember?"

Did he have to speak to her as though she were an invalid?

"Brenna's my cousin," Connie inserted. "She's going to be living with me for awhile."

"Brenna Price," Maureen repeated, studying my face. "I remember." Her voice was barely audible. "You used to play with Hannah."

Recalling what Gage had told me, I hesitated. How should I respond to that? The last thing I wanted to do was upset her. Indeed, I hoped my presence would arouse happy memories. I took a seat on one end of the sofa facing Maureen across a large coffee table set in the center of an oval rug on the floor between us. Connie sat at the other end, smoothing her hair, then placing her hands in her lap.

"It's Brenna Wickham now," I said, striving to keep my voice light. This was so awkward. All we had in common was our childhood. How was I supposed to carry on a conversation with Maureen and avoid mentioning her sister when Hannah and I had been inseparable friends, playing together all day, every day over the course of those long-ago summers?

"Arlene Price was Brenna's grandmother, same as Connie," Gage said. He sat in another armchair to Maureen's left, separated from her by a low end table. His dark brown eyes shone as they reflected the warm glow of the fire.

Maureen smiled. "Arlene was a lovely lady. She used to come over and visit with me. I was sorry when she moved out. I didn't like the renters."

"Grandma had a weak heart," Connie said, adjusting her glasses. "The house was just too much for her to keep up. She moved into assisted living to make her life easier at the end."

"I was sad when I heard she had died," Maureen said. She lowered her gaze and picked at a thread on the sleeve of her sweater.

"Do you remember when my mother and I used to

come here to visit?" I asked brightly. "Sometimes I'd spend the whole summer. It was always such fun."

I saw Gage's face stiffen. A faint line cut between his brows.

"Of course," Maureen said, rousing a little. "How is your mother? I always liked her. She was so pretty. I never thought she looked old enough to be a mom."

I laughed. "That's probably because she was only 19 when she had me. She and my father married right out of high school."

I often wondered if my mother ever thought about him. They had been so young and it had been a whirlwind courtship. She seldom spoke of him, and the only picture I'd ever seen was a blurry snapshot of a young man in uniform that my mom kept in her top dresser drawer. Both our marriages had ended in eerily similar tragedies, but I had had Jason for nine years and I knew I would never forget him.

Maureen nodded. "Your father joined the army and was shipped overseas before you were born, right? And he was killed in some sort of accident. That's why your mom took back her maiden name." She smiled when she saw my look of surprise. "I heard her tell my mother about it. Your mom and grandma used to come over here all the time. You don't remember because you were just a baby, but I used to sit and listen to them talk, pretend to be one of the grownups." She gave a soft, wistful sigh.

Gage cleared his throat and cast me an uneasy glance.

Jeesh, I thought, *is it really necessary to walk on eggshells like this all the time?* Maureen seemed a little subdued, but nothing to suggest she was anything close to psychotic.

"Mom remarried," I said. "She lives in Phoenix now

and works part-time in a book store. I also have two younger brothers now, Paul and Michael."

"And now you're living with Connie?" Maureen asked, tilting her head curiously.

"I'm renting the spare room. It's a lot cheaper than living downtown."

"I thought you were married."

Uh-oh. Another depressing topic. I'd put my foot right into it. Well, if we were going to be neighbors, she might as well know.

"Widowed," I said. "My husband was killed in an accident two years ago." I gave a quick shrug, twiddling the ring on my finger. "I'm living with Connie while I sell my condo downtown and figure out what to do next."

Gage broke in, his stern features softening as he leaned toward me. "I'm so sorry, Brenna. I had no idea. I thought maybe you were divorced or something."

Maureen smoothed the front of her sweater, keeping her eyes turned down. "I'm sorry for your loss," she said.

"Thank you," I said. "Things are getting easier—I just take it one day at a time." It felt strange talking about how I was dealing with Jason's death after two years when Maureen still wasn't coping with her sister's after twenty-five. *I hope she doesn't think I'm judging.*

Before things could get any more maudlin, Gage clapped his hands to his knees and said, "Why don't we go eat? Dinner's all ready. I've made my world-famous homemade vegetable soup, along with my equally famous store-bought dinner rolls." He stood and directed us toward the dining room.

I took a seat across the table from Maureen, and Connie sat next to me opposite Gage. The savory aroma of onions and garlic simmered with parsley and bay leaf set my mouth to watering. We dug in with hearty appetites. It was a perfect autumn night for hot soup; the chunky vegetables and tender bits of beef really hit the spot.

I looked at Gage in admiration. "You made this? It's really good."

He smiled crookedly and for a moment I caught a glimpse of the boy I remembered. He gave a little shrug. "It's the only thing I know how to make."

I noticed that Maureen played with her spoon, stirring the soup, but eating little.

Gage saw too. "Eat it, Maureen," he said, "it's good for you."

She could certainly use the calories, I thought.

Obediently, Maureen took a sip of the warm broth, then nibbled on a roll. Gage sighed and turned his attention back to Connie and me. Throughout dinner, we talked about the weather, the Seahawks, and our favorite movies—painstakingly avoiding potentially distressing subjects.

"So, Gage," I asked, "what do you do these days?"

He spooned up a chunk of carrot. "I'm an architect. I design custom homes."

"*Wow*, impressive." I don't know why I was surprised. Maybe because he'd been so rowdy as a boy, I had expected him to wind up selling used cars or something. Architecture was downright respectable. "I'd love to see one of the houses you've designed."

"That could probably be arranged." He smiled and I saw another glimmer of the old Gage: the tilt of his head, the glint in his eye, the way the corners of his mouth edged up. Clearly, he was pleased that I'd shown an interest in his work.

"What about you?" he asked. "What do you do?"

"Well, until last week I was a legal assistant in a law firm downtown." I took another roll and tore it in half.

"Sounds like interesting work."

I laughed. "Not as much as you'd think. We didn't do criminal law like on TV. We mostly did wills and contracts. Pretty boring stuff, really. But as of Friday, my boss retired and I joined the ranks of the unemployed. I need to find something less stressful—any place but downtown. That traffic is awful. Most days I could have walked home faster than driving."

Persistent rain, carpool lanes, one-way streets, steep hills, and toll roads regularly put Seattle on lists of cities with the worst traffic in the country. Add buses, bicyclists, and pedestrians to the mix and driving downtown in rush hour can be a real nightmare.

"I'm sure you can find something out here," Connie said. "We have lawyers in Shoreline too, believe it or not. Or maybe you'd like to try something completely different for a change."

I gave my shoulder a quick bounce. "I've been thinking about it. I don't really know what I want to do yet."

"*I* know," Connie said. "You can come work for me at the flower shop." Her mouth widened in a playful grin, her cheeks plumping like ripe peaches. "I can always use another person to help make deliveries."

I laughed. "I may just take you up on that. It would be a good excuse to get out of the house and learn my way around." Of course, I hardly knew a dandelion from a snapdragon, but working in a job surrounded by flowers had a certain appeal. And with GPS, how hard could it be?

When the last bite had been consumed, Gage stood up and began moving around the table, stacking dirty dishes, collecting silverware. He flatly refused my offer to help. Maureen remained in her seat, quietly rubbing at a spot on the table. She had spoken little throughout the meal, picking unobtrusively at her food as though hoping to escape notice.

"Shall we have the rest of the cake?" asked Connie with enthusiasm. "Brenna made it from scratch from an old family recipe." She gave Maureen a spirited wink. "We can do your birthday all over again. I even brought candles."

Maureen smiled. Connie's ebullience had finally evoked a positive response. It was nice to see.

Gage turned to me. "You really shouldn't have gone to all that trouble."

I laughed. "After that fiasco with Buster, it was the least I could do."

"What happened?" asked Maureen curiously.

I groaned and placed a hand flat to my cheek. "I was taking Buster—Connie's beagle—out for a walk..."

Connie had risen to retrieve the birthday candles. Suddenly, she frowned and frantically shook her head at me.

"...when he saw this little girl across the street, and..."

The smile slid from Maureen's face like melted wax sloughing off a candle. She rose halfway out of her chair. "What little girl?" she cried.

Gage spun to face his sister. "Maureen, *don't!*" He dropped the stack of plates he'd been carrying onto the table with a thud that made the silverware rattle.

She ignored him. Her eyes held mine. "Did she have pigtails? A pink jacket?" Her pale face was drawn, her voice pleading, wracked with emotion.

"Um, I think so," I said, bewildered at the outburst. I looked from her to Gage. His mouth was set in a hard line, a muscle twitched in his jaw.

"You *saw* her," whispered Maureen. She held her hands over her heart.

"She *didn't* see her," said Gage, enunciating through clenched teeth. "It *wasn't* Hannah. Can't you get that through your head? It was just some neighbor kid. That's all it was."

Tears rolled down Maureen's cheeks. With trembling hands, she grabbed a napkin off the table and pressed it to her eyes as she sobbed.

Hannah? The little sister who had disappeared twenty-five years ago?

Gage's face burned scarlet. "Can't we have just *one* nice evening without you going all to pieces?" He turned to Connie. "You see what I have to deal with? You guys might as well go home." He turned his back and stormed out of the room, leaving an awkward silence.

Stunned, I sat wordlessly and stared at Maureen. Her bony shoulders quaked as she wept, her long, thin fingers clutching the napkin to her face.

I glanced at Connie. She heaved a sigh. "Let's finish cleaning up, then we can go." She picked up the plates Gage had stacked and took them to the kitchen.

Looking at Maureen, I felt only pity. What had happened? Obviously, her mental state was far worse than I imagined. I went around the table and reached out a hand, hoping to offer solace, but she pulled away, lurched to her feet, and ran from the dining room. Moments later, her rapid footsteps could be heard pounding up the stairs.

I sought Connie in the kitchen. "We can't leave her like this," I said.

"She'll be all right," Connie said. "Gage knows how to take care of her. He's been doing it for years."

We returned home and settled on the couch in the living room. Connie gave her forehead a vigorous rub, then leaned toward me.

"I should have warned you," she said. "In fact, I started to. Remember when I said Maureen went almost catatonic after her last fit?"

My brows knit together. "Yeah. From a nightmare, wasn't it?"

"No—that's just it. I was going to say it *wasn't* a nightmare. She claimed she saw a little girl outside her front window."

"So?" I didn't like where this was going.

"She *insisted* it was Hannah's ghost come back to haunt her!"

Chapter Four

That night I could hardly sleep. I kept thinking about Maureen and her startling reaction to the mention of the little girl I'd seen on the street.

Gage said she blamed herself for what happened to Hannah. But what *had* happened? Apparently, nobody knew. The girl had simply disappeared. What unfathomable grief her family must have suffered. Hannah had been eight years old, and Maureen, the big sister, had been responsible for watching her. The fact that Maureen imagined herself haunted by Hannah's ghost after all these years attested to the burden of guilt she carried.

At dinner, Maureen had seemed withdrawn, almost restrained. Was it the memories my being there had dredged up? Or was it Gage? Was she intimidated by him? I frowned. Connie had implied that they didn't get along very well, and after last night it was clear Gage was frustrated.

I had to admit that when Connie first mentioned Gage and told me the Morelands still lived next door, I had felt a surge of excitement. The days and weeks spent here in my childhood had been among the best times of my life. Maureen, of course, had been the oldest. We younger girls had thought her so pretty and sophisticated, but she was also fun and creative. She had occasionally played dress-up with Hannah and me, joining us in acting out our favorite fairy tales, usually taking the role of wicked stepmother or evil witch. I wondered if this very imagination that had so endeared her to us, had now become her curse.

And Gage. How he had changed. From the mischievous, fun-loving boy whom I had loved to tease, to a stiff, irritable sourpuss who got angry and impatient with his mentally ill sister.

Perhaps Gage also blamed Maureen for Hannah's disappearance. I felt a flush of anger. It wasn't fair. Maureen had been a fifteen-year-old girl. Okay, she had done something dumb—sneaking off to meet her boyfriend—but kids did dumb things all the time. That tragedy had resulted in this case was heartbreaking, but surely Maureen wasn't all to blame. How could her parents have just left her, their teenage daughter, hanging out to dry, withdrawing their love and support when she needed it most?

Connie said that Gage came around to check on his sister every couple of weeks. What did she do in the meantime? How did she fill her time if she never went anywhere? I couldn't imagine never going outdoors.

Siblings and Secrets 45

How did she tend those flowers Connie had mentioned?

She must have a computer and a TV. And she must use the internet—everyone did, didn't they? At least that would help keep her connected to the outside world.

By the time I finally fell asleep, I had decided to pay another call on Maureen to see how she was faring. I thought she could use a friend.

The next morning was Monday and I woke early as I had for the past ten years. But as I swung my feet to the floor, it suddenly occurred to me that I had no place to be, no job to go to. For a moment, I felt lost.

Then I remembered a story a friend had told me several years ago about how her indoor cat had escaped out the front door one day. The cat had never set foot outdoors in its entire life. Now it suddenly found itself surrounded by an endless expanse of wide open space. The cat had halted and cowered in the grass, terrified of the vast unknown. Rather than relishing its new-found freedom, it had turned and slunk back inside to the security of the familiar closed-in environment.

I gave a quick snort of laughter. *Don't be that cat. Take a break while you have a chance, enjoy the freedom.*

I would need to find a new job, but not right this minute. I wasn't desperate enough yet to take Connie up on her offer. The generous severance package I'd received from the law firm would carry me through the next few months. And I could always sign up for unemployment. Meanwhile, this week I would indulge in a well-deserved vacation. With any luck, the condo would sell and my problems would all be over.

I pulled on my black knee-length leggings and a comfortable t-shirt, laced up my awesome purple running shoes, and grabbed my windbreaker out of the closet. No need to get flabby while I figured out what to do with myself.

There was no sign of Connie. Not an early riser apparently. I headed out the front door.

Since I wasn't familiar with the neighborhood I decided not to venture too far, maybe just around a couple of blocks. I did some stretches, then glanced about to get my bearings. To my surprise, the same little girl I'd seen yesterday stood once more across the street.

I smiled and waggled my fingers at her in a friendly gesture, amazed at how well she fit the description of Maureen's "ghost." Her blond hair hung in braids down the front of her pink jacket. I estimated her age at about eight or nine years old. I could certainly see how this girl might be mistaken for Hannah.

She's up early, I thought, taking a quick look at my watch: 7:10. The sky above the eastern horizon glowed in a rosy haze. The morning air was cool and crisp, typical of September. In another month there would be frost on the ground.

When I looked up again, the little girl was gone. I glanced up and down the street, but didn't see her. I shrugged and finished my stretches. Then I took off jogging, going north in the opposite direction from Morelands'. Two houses down, I ran past a middle-aged man in a bathrobe who had come out to pick up his paper. He flicked his hand in a quick salute, and I gave him an amiable nod as I cruised by.

The sun grew brighter and it promised to be a pleasant day. *I could get used to not working.*

When I returned to the house, Connie was at the stove.

"Hurry and change," she called as I headed for the bathroom. "I'm making breakfast. Buster's in the back yard."

I didn't usually eat much breakfast, but the smell of frying bacon wafting from the kitchen was enough to make me rethink. After a quick shower and change of clothes, I joined Connie at the kitchen table. She poured me a cup of coffee and dished up a plate of bacon and scrambled eggs with a piece of whole grain toast on the side.

"Connie," I said as I forked up a big bite of eggs, "I hope you don't think you have to get up and make me breakfast every day. This *isn't* a bed-and-breakfast, you know."

She waved a dismissive hand in the air. "Oh, I know, and believe me, I won't. I just wanted to get your first week off to a great start. Besides, I always go in late on Mondays. I have to wait for Andy to bring the groceries."

"Oh, that's right. It's Monday. Your weekly delivery. What time does he usually get here?"

"Any time after eight thirty—usually by nine. He should be here pretty soon. What do you think of the toast?" She pointed with her chin toward my plate. "I baked the bread myself."

As well as being a great cook, Connie had always loved to bake. She had taken bread baking and pastry classes at a nearby community college and often experimented with "designer" breads, even coming up with her own tasty recipes.

The toast was delicious and I nodded enthusiastically with my mouth full. "Kind of sweet and nutty," I mumbled between chews. "But then, you've never baked anything that wasn't to die for."

"*Ha*, that's because I've never let you taste any of my failures. I made this sprouted wheat bread once that tasted…" She stuck out her tongue and made a gagging noise in her throat.

I laughed aloud. "Oh, come on. It couldn't have been *that* bad."

She opened her mouth to reply, but at that moment the doorbell rang.

"Oops—there's Andy!" she said and hurried to answer the front door.

I followed, curious to meet this guy who was willing to deliver our groceries every week at no charge. Connie had implied that he might have feelings for Maureen. Or did he just feel sorry for her? Either way, it was kind of him. *That's the difference between a local, family-run grocery and a faceless national mega store,* I thought.

When Connie swung the door open, all I could make out was a mop of ginger-brown hair above a pair of wide greenish eyes peering over the tops of two grocery sacks. Large hairy hands grasped the bulging bags tightly around the middle.

I hurried forward to take one of the sacks. "No, thanks," boomed a sonorous voice as the figure strode past me and headed for the kitchen. "I've got 'em. Do this all the time."

He plopped the bags on the counter and turned to Connie. "We're having a sale on eggs so I brought you an extra dozen." Glancing at the remains of our breakfast on the table, he grinned and added, "By the looks of things, it's a good thing I did."

He reached out to shake my hand. "You must be

Connie's cousin. She said you were coming to stay for awhile. I'm Andy Brubaker. Pleased to meet you."

He was a brawny man of average height, barrel chested and thick limbed with a healthy growth of whiskers covering his face from ear to ear. Taking in the plaid shirt he wore, my mind immediately made the leap to Teutonic lumberjack. His eyes shone with enough wattage to light a small city.

"Brenna Wickham," I said, grasping his hand. My fingers disappeared within the folds of his beefy paw. I couldn't help smiling in response to his exuberant grin. "Connie tells me you also bring groceries to our neighbor, Maureen. That's very nice of you."

"Well, it's the least I can do." His face sobered. "I 'spect Connie's told you Maureen has problems going outside." He gave his beard a scratch. "We've been friends since we were kids. I like to think my bringing her groceries every week helps make her life a little easier."

Does he know Maureen thinks she's being haunted by her sister's ghost?

"Have you been over there yet this morning?" I asked.

"Nope. On my way there now."

"Do you mind if I tag along? I'd like to say hi, and…and just see how she's doing. We went over there last night and she got a little upset. I've been worried about her."

"No, that'd be fine," Andy said. "I'm sure she'd like to see you. She doesn't get many visitors."

Connie went and got her purse so she could settle up with Andy for the groceries. She pulled out a key chain with a dangling yellow smiley-face disk attached.

"Here, Brenna," she said. "I got you your own key so

you can come and go. Now, I've got to go change and get to the shop. Oh, and don't forget to bring Buster in when you get home. If he's left alone in the yard too long he gets bored and that's when he starts digging." She stacked the breakfast dishes in the sink, then headed for her room.

I followed Andy to his van where he collected a couple more large paper bags brimming with groceries. Once again, he insisted upon carrying the bags himself while I trailed behind. When he reached Maureen's house, the door swung open and Gage stepped outside onto the porch.

"Hi, Andy," he said, holding the door open. "Maureen's waiting for you in the kitchen. Brenna, can I talk to you for a minute?"

Wary, I nodded and reversed back down the steps to the front walk. He joined me, running a hand over his hair as he collected his thoughts. Finally, he looked at me, a grim expression on his face. "Look, I'm sorry about last night. That blow-up was inexcusable, but it's exactly the reason I didn't want you to come over. Sometimes Maureen...I don't know...she gets these crazy ideas in her head, and I just..." he threw his hands up, "...I just don't know what to do."

I frowned and crossed my arms over my chest. "Well, you could start by not yelling at her."

He exhaled deeply. "I know, I know. I just lost it. I wanted to have a nice dinner. I thought...maybe...if you and she hit it off, you might be willing..." his voice trailed off.

"What? I might be willing to be her friend?" I stared at him.

He shrugged. His dark hooded eyes looked away, and

his broad shoulders sagged as though under a heavy burden.

"Like Connie's *willing* to be her friend in exchange for having her groceries delivered?"

He spread his hands in a helpless gesture. "What am I supposed to do? I can't be here to babysit her every day." His mouth tightened. "Maureen sees ghosts, Brenna. *Ghosts.* She thinks Hannah is haunting her. How am I supposed to deal with that?"

"Patience?" I suggested. "Understanding?"

He made a noise like a growl and began pacing.

I narrowed my eyes. "Tell me something. Do *you* blame Maureen for Hannah's disappearance? I'm sure she can sense it. She probably thinks the whole world is against her."

He stopped, his gaze dropping to his hands. "I don't know. I've tried not to blame her. I have. But it's a *fact* that if Maureen hadn't left Hannah alone, none of this would have happened."

"Are you sure about that?" I gave him a piercing look. "Are you telling me that Hannah *never* went outdoors to play by herself? She was eight years old, not a baby. She and I used to play outside all the time without anyone watching us."

He grew thoughtful. "It seemed safer back then somehow. More young families, less crime. The street wasn't as busy."

"That's what I'm saying. It could have happened to any of us. There were lots of kids in the neighborhood, and we *all* ran around outside without much supervision. And by the way, has it occurred to you that if it was a kidnapper and Maureen *had* been home, *both* of your sisters might have gone missing?"

He said nothing, but his eyes drifted toward the undeveloped plot of land adjacent to his house. Tall fir, maple, and alder grew there amid a dense tangle of variegated underbrush.

I followed his gaze. "We *all* used to tramp around in those woods, remember? Do you think she might have wandered in there alone and...and got hurt?" I shuddered, imagining the little girl falling and breaking a leg, or impaling herself on a branch protruding from a fallen log. If no one had found her...the thought was too awful to contemplate.

High in a tree, a crow gave a loud squawk and launched itself into the air. A breeze sent a flurry of yellow leaves spiraling to the ground.

Gage shook his head. "The police searched the woods with dogs. They didn't find anything."

"What do *you* think happened to her?"

He rubbed the back of his neck. "I don't know. I don't like to think about it."

"A hundred years ago wasn't this whole neighborhood part of a large farm? Maybe there's an old well somewhere. If Hannah fell in…"

"I don't think so. The police combed the area thoroughly. Most of the neighbors came out to help. I'm sure they would have found her if she'd been anywhere within a five mile radius."

"What about the beach?" A popular park, Richmond Beach was only a few miles away. As kids we had hiked there more than once with Maureen. It wasn't inconceivable that Hannah might have tried to walk there by herself.

"Again, I don't know. They searched and never found anything." He let out a heavy sigh. "The point is, I've tried to move on, have a life, a career. Maureen can't seem to let it go. She insists on being miserable—and this whole *ghost* thing is insane."

For a moment we both stared at the ground. I had said my piece, he didn't need a lecture. Finally, I sighed and looked around. I should go inside and talk to Maureen. It was interesting that Andy hadn't come back out yet. I smiled to myself. Apparently, Maureen *did* have a friend. Maybe I shouldn't hurry.

I jerked in surprise when once again I noticed the little girl in the pink jacket and long braids. She stood looking at me from across the street. Shouldn't she be in school by now?

"What's the matter?" asked Gage.

"It's that little girl again." I swung around to catch Gage's eye. "She *does* look a lot like how I remember Hannah. It's no wonder Maureen gets hysterical when she sees her. Do you know who she is?"

He turned, searching the street in both directions. "I don't see her."

I looked again. She was gone. My forehead puckered in annoyance. "She was there a second ago."

"She must have gone in," Gage said.

"Or she's hiding, playing tricks." Any of the trees and shrubs along the road would have provided ample cover for an impish child. I scoured the surrounding gardens for a snippet of pink.

"Maybe Connie knows who she is," I said.

"Doesn't matter," Gage said with a shrug. "We ought to go inside and liberate Andy. He probably needs to get back to the store. And I should be going pretty soon too. I've been working up some sketches for a new house I'm designing. I told the client I'd have them finished by the end of the week."

When we went into the house, we found Maureen and Andy sitting comfortably on the couch in the living room deep in conversation. I caught a quick movement between them and realized he had been holding her hand. He coughed and sprang to his feet, hurriedly straightening his jacket.

"I'd better get back to the store," he said to Maureen. "Let me know if you'd like some of those apples—they're great for pies." He aimed a curt nod in Gage's direction, then pivoted and headed for the door.

Gage watched as the stalwart man lumbered away, then he turned to his sister with an accusing look. "Anything I should know?"

"No," snapped Maureen. "We were just talking."

What's Gage's problem? Connie told me that Andy Brubaker had had a crush on Maureen since school, and it appeared he still did. Wasn't that a *good* thing? I shot Gage a puzzled look, but he turned away, still frowning.

Maureen's eyes flicked to me then. "Hi, Brenna," she said. A slight flush colored her cheeks. "I'm sorry about last night. I know you must think I'm crazy."

I sat next to her on the couch and put a hand on her forearm.

"Not at all," I said. "I understand. It's okay to get upset. Hannah was a sweet little girl, and we all miss her. But it's been over twenty years—she wouldn't want you to keep blaming yourself. She loved you."

Maureen looked down at her hands and said nothing.

A brass clock on the mantel tick-tocked loudly. Outside the window, the bright autumn sun had set the green lawn ablaze with light.

Gage cleared his throat. "I have to collect some things from my room. I'll be back in a few minutes." He strode out.

Maureen turned her face up to mine and said in an agonized voice, "I was supposed to be watching her, but I left to go meet Andy." Her voice dropped to a whisper. "He was my boyfriend then. Hannah was all alone in the house. I shouldn't have left her."

"You were only fifteen," I soothed. "Practically a child yourself. And she was eight years old, not a baby."

"I *told* her to stay in the house," Maureen said. "I *told* her I'd be right back." Her body shook with a sudden tremor as tears welled in her eyes. "But she was watching TV and I don't think she heard me. Now she's *dead* and she *haunts* me."

I threw my arms around her and let her bury her face in my shoulder. I could feel the sharp edges of her shoulder blades beneath my fingers. I thought back to the days after Jason died. Everyone had tiptoed around me, fearful of mentioning his name in case it upset me. They couldn't understand that what I really wanted was to talk about him, to remember how he laughed, to recall the happy times and the funny things he did, to discuss the issues he cared about, the hobbies and sports he was into. I didn't want people to forget him.

"Maureen," I said when the crying subsided, "I know Hannah wouldn't want you to be sad. She was such a happy girl. Remember how she used to laugh? She had the silliest giggle. And remember how she used to cross her eyes and stick out her tongue? She liked to pretend she was Pippi Longstocking. That's why she always wore her hair in braids."

Maureen looked up, a tentative smile on her face.

Encouraged, I went on. "Remember when we used to play horses in the back yard?"

Maureen nodded. "You used to drag boards out of the garage to make jumps, and you tore switches off the forsythia to use as riding crops."

I grinned. "Do you remember that time I tried to jump over Gage's bike? He'd left it lying in the driveway and Hannah dared me to jump it. I tripped and tore up my knee."

Maureen gave a feeble laugh. "Hannah ran in and got a kitchen towel to wrap around it. Didn't you have to get stitches?"

"Yeah, and I still have the scar."

Gage's voice broke in behind us. "You never were a very smart kid."

I turned and saw him leaning against the door jamb leading from the hallway. I gave him a sarcastic grin. "At least my face didn't look like a donkey."

He winced. "Careful," he warned, "or I'll get my water pistol." He looked at Maureen. "I'm sorry I got mad. It was your birthday. I shouldn't have lost my temper."

Her expression was cool and detached as she murmured, "I'm sorry too. It's just that...I thought..."

Gage cut her off with a sigh. "Just *stop*, okay? It's getting late, I've got to get to the office. And I'll be going back to my place tonight, so you're on your own for a few days. Call me if you need me. Brenna, come over any time. Have Maureen show you some of the things she's made."

He turned abruptly and strode out. I heard the front door close behind him. I frowned as I realized I'd been doing a lot of staring at his back lately. Why did he have to be that way?

Chapter Five

"I don't know why he refuses to believe me," Maureen said. "Is it really so hard to accept that Hannah's spirit is still with us?"

A basic philosophical question. Do ghosts exist? Do they walk the earth among us? If I believed, would I see Jason again? My grandmother? How about the father I'd never known who had been killed in a freak army training exercise? If one believed in Heaven, did it follow that one must believe in spirits? A weighty question, and not one I felt qualified to tackle. But I wanted to give Maureen a thoughtful answer, to let her know I took her seriously and didn't dismiss her feelings out of hand.

I mustered an earnest look and shrugged. "Honestly, Maureen, I don't know. I won't say it's impossible, only that I've never personally seen a ghost. I guess I've never really thought about it."

She nodded, apparently satisfied. "But you *did* see a little girl outside the house who looked like Hannah."

"I did. I saw a little girl in blond pigtails wearing a pink jacket. But I'm not convinced she was a ghost." I hazarded a smile. "There must be other little girls in the neighborhood who wear braids and pink coats."

"I suppose." She sighed and went quiet.

Crisis averted. I knew she wasn't convinced, but at least she had regained her equanimity. I hoped we could set the subject aside. In truth, the notion that ghosts might exist made me uneasy.

I searched for something to say, to change the subject, then remembered what Gage had said on his way out.

"What did Gage mean when he left?" I asked, genuinely intrigued. "What things do you make?"

She smiled and came back to life. Twisting around, she pulled a quilted throw off the back of the couch behind her. "This," she said as she spread the small coverlet across her lap.

The vivid design was made from a patchwork of squares and triangles running at angles in a complex diamond pattern. Then I noticed two other multihued quilts folded over the backs of the armchairs, and a decorative rack in the corner displaying several more.

"What beautiful quilts," I said. "Did you make them all?"

Maureen nodded bashfully. "I love making them. Gives me something to do." She turned and pointed. "The one hanging in the hallway took months."

I ran to look. Suspended from a dowel sewn onto the back, a large intricately constructed quilt was displayed on the wall like museum art. Tiny squares of multi-colored fabric were arranged and stitched together to create an image of a sunrise over snowcapped mountains with green trees and a blue lake in the foreground. Two brown suede deer appliquéd on beside the water's edge completed the picture.

Maureen came up behind me and peered over my shoulder. I put my palms together and pressed them to my lips as I admired the detailed stitching.

"Incredible," I breathed. "This is *awesome*, Maureen. Really awesome. You have an amazing talent."

She gave a quick, embarrassed laugh. "And a great sewing machine. I've converted the attic into a sort of workroom. There's more if you want to see it."

Her face beamed with heightened color and her voice carried a lilt I hadn't heard in twenty-five years. I was anxious to foster her cheerful humor so I nodded enthusiastically and followed her back to the living room where she pointed to the oval rug beneath the coffee table. Its vibrant shades of blue, gray, and silver perfectly complemented the room's décor.

"I made that too," she said proudly.

"What?" I exclaimed. "No way." I fell to my knees to get a closer look, lifting the edge of the rug to examine the elaborate craftsmanship. It was ostensibly an old-fashioned braided rag rug, yet it was woven together so expertly that it appeared as chic as any designer piece available in a high-end department store.

"This is gorgeous," I said. "Where did you learn to do this?"

Maureen's soft laugh reminded me of a tinkling wind chime. "Actually, it was your grandmother who taught me. She used to come over and spend hours with me, teaching me to sew and embroider and make rugs. She was full of creative ideas."

I looked up and smiled. That was my grandmother all right—a generous soul, kindly and down-to-earth. I could well imagine her coming over and sharing her knowledge of these old, traditional crafts with her poor, lonely neighbor.

"That sounds just like her," I said. "I'm so glad you had each other. I didn't get to see her much after we moved to Arizona. I always sort of regretted that, but my parents were so busy all the time with work and the boys."

Grandma had come to visit every Christmas, but looking back it seemed like we never had any time, just the two of us, to pursue anything meaningful.

Maureen sighed and brushed her fingers through her hair. "Everyone's always so busy these days."

"Have you ever tried to sell these? Or the quilts?"

"Oh, no," she demurred, waving a hand in the air between us. "I just give them away. I'd love for you to take something—as a gift."

"Thank you, that's very generous, but I was actually thinking of the internet. I'll bet people would flock to buy the things you make. There are lots of options online for selling homemade crafts." My voice increased in tempo as I warmed to the possibilities. "You could start your own cottage industry, create your own website—make yourself some money. I assume you have a computer."

Her reaction was less than enthusiastic. "I have one. Gage set it up for me, but I don't use it that much. I've ordered a few things here and there since I don't leave the house to shop, but mostly I find it more frustrating than helpful." She grimaced and shook her head. "I don't know anything about computers. Creating a website sounds way too complicated. I'm forty years old—too old to start learning new tricks."

I knew that wasn't true, but I didn't want to overwhelm her and turn her off the idea altogether. With time and a little guidance, I hoped she might gain enough confidence to try it. But in the meantime...

I fingered my chin thoughtfully as a new possibility began to take shape. "I have another idea. Christmas is in three months. I think we should hold a bazaar! What do you think? It would be the perfect opportunity to show off your beautiful handiwork. I'm sure people would love to buy your handmade quilts and rugs. This kind of quality just isn't available in stores."

Maureen licked her lips, her face looking tremulous. "I don't know..."

"You wouldn't have to go outside if you don't want to," I assured her quickly. "I'll take care of everything. Just let me talk to Connie. I'll bet we can get the whole neighborhood involved."

I took both her hands and encouraged her with a big grin. "It'll be fun."

She looked doubtful, but didn't protest.

I stayed and had lunch with Maureen so we could discuss ideas for putting on a holiday bazaar. I was pleased to see her happily devour a tuna sandwich, a cup of vegetable soup, and a respectable handful of potato chips. I attributed this increase in appetite to the relaxed tenor of our conversation and her pleasure at having a friendly visitor who demanded nothing. Again, I couldn't help but wonder if Gage's proximity had caused her reticence the night before.

After we finished, she took me upstairs and showed me her sewing machine and the work area she'd set up in the large farmhouse attic. At one end of the space stood an old Ping-Pong table. Swatches of fabric were spread across its surface.

"It's perfect for laying out quilt blocks," she explained.

When I finally left at one thirty and approached the front steps of Connie's house—correction, *my house* (it was going to take some time getting used to calling it that)—I was dismayed to find Buster lying on the porch, busily gnawing on some unspeakable object he had dragged home. I had forgotten all about him.

"Buster!" I cried. "You little *Houdini*. How did you get out of the back yard?"

Judging by the dirt caked on his paws and forelegs, he'd been digging. The little escape artist had obviously dug his way out under the fence. Connie had warned me. I was going to have to be more diligent.

The beagle wagged his tail and looked up at me with bright, beady eyes, keeping his jaws firmly clenched on his slobbery prize.

"Don't worry," I said, wrinkling my nose. "I don't want your bone, or stick, or...what is that, anyway?"

I leaned closer to get a better look. A shoe? It was dirty and pretty well mangled, but definitely had the look of a small tennis shoe. I imagined him ingesting bits of rubber as he chewed which couldn't be good for him. I made a move to pry it away, but he made a low growling noise in his throat. The dog would not give up his plunder easily.

This was going to take some strategy. I pushed back my hair and straightened up. Perhaps a trade. I unlocked the front door and shoved it open, then reached down and grabbed Buster by the collar, pulling him in behind me. I went straight to the refrigerator and scanned the contents for a likely selection. I had heard somewhere that dogs like cheese, so the block of cheddar I found seemed just the thing.

Buster apparently agreed because as soon as I unwrapped the cheese, he dropped the disgusting article and began to bounce eagerly around my knees, mouth open, eyes wide and glistening as glass marbles. I cut off a chunk and tossed it across the room, then quickly seized the shoe between my thumb and forefinger, lifting it daintily to eye level for a closer look.

The shoe was definitely a child's sneaker, and judging by the blackish mildew and moldy stench permeating the rotted canvas, it had been left outdoors for a considerable length of time. Not something anyone would want returned.

Access to the garage was through the back of the kitchen, and I headed there now, dropping the shoe into the trash can. From there I grabbed a shovel and exited to the back yard through a door at the rear of the garage. I was intent on filling in the hole Buster had dug under the fence before Connie got home. If I could find a large rock to stuff in the hole, even better.

The lots on this side of the street were good sized, perhaps a quarter of an acre, harking back to a time when this area was more rural. A wooden fence surrounded the yard, separating it from the neighboring properties. Around the perimeter, late-blooming hydrangeas blossomed in blue profusion in contrast to the spent rhododendrons, while a pair of Japanese maples spread lacy canopies of brilliant burgundy-colored leaves.

The lawn itself was crisscrossed with paths worn in the grass by the little dog. Here and there, evidence of previous digs gave the yard a slightly pockmarked appearance. It didn't take long to find Buster's escape route. A telltale mound of fresh dirt beneath the bottom branches of an overgrown rhody pinpointed a shallow gap under the fence on the north side.

I thrust dirt in the hole and tamped it down, capping it with a couple of large rocks I'd found. I didn't know how long it would deter him, but resolved to keep a better eye on him in the future. *Can't have him getting in trouble on my watch.*

Finished, I straightened up and flexed my shoulders, leaning on the shovel and taking a moment to check the length of the fence line. There must be a better solution. Chicken wire buried along the bottom, maybe?

My gaze strayed back toward the house and I was startled to see the little girl in pigtails standing near the corner of the garage. The afternoon sun was in my eyes so I raised a hand to shield them, and in that instant she disappeared into the shadows around the side of the house.

"Hey, *wait!*" I called. Still gripping the shovel, I hurried after her. I was becoming more than a little curious to find out who this kid was. But by the time I rounded the garage, she had vanished. Frustrated, I kicked at a pebble on the driveway and went to put the shovel away.

As I washed up at the kitchen sink, a niggling thought kept nudging at the corner of my brain. There had been something off about the girl. Something I couldn't put my finger on. What was it? I concentrated hard, trying to remember every detail of the little girl's appearance: blond hair and braids, pink jacket, blue jeans, pink tennis shoes... I stopped. That was *it*. She had only been wearing *one shoe*. For a second, I was dumbstruck. The old shoe. What if...?

Wait, *what?* No. I laughed out loud. That was just absurd. My imagination was playing stupid tricks on me. *Maureen and her ghosts.* I blew sharply through my nose and massaged my temples with the tips of my fingers. *I've lived here for two days and already I'm losing it!*

Chapter Six

I put together a macaroni and cheese casserole for dinner to surprise Connie. It was one of the few recipes I was good at and I'd already discovered we had cheese in the refrigerator. Digging through the freezer, I found a bag of frozen peas and decided they would suit as a green vegetable to go along with the pasta.

Connie arrived home at six and was delighted to find I had cooked. "Hey," she said with a broad grin, "I think I'm going to like this arrangement."

"Well, it seemed like the least I could do. Go ahead and sit down. It's my turn to wait on you."

Connie filled water glasses, then took her seat while I got plates from the cupboard and placed the food in the center of the table. Buster sat close by and keenly tracked my every move, ready to spring into action should something happen to land on the floor.

"So, how was your day?" Connie asked as I sat down opposite her. "Did you watch TV and eat bonbons all day?"

I made a face. "Hardly. Actually, I spent most of the day over at Maureen's. Gage left early to go to his office. I see what you mean about their not getting along. There's definitely an odd tension between them."

Connie scooped up a plateful of the hot cheesy casserole. "I told you. I think Gage resents having to take care of her, and *she* resents him resenting her."

"Yeah, once Gage left, Maureen and I had a great visit. She was much more relaxed. Which reminds me, I wanted to ask you something. Have you seen the quilts she's made? They're gorgeous."

"Maureen *made* them?" She shoveled up a forkful of peas.

"The braided rugs too. Our grandmother taught her how. She said Grandma used to spend lots of time over there teaching her things like sewing and embroidery."

Connie smiled. "Doesn't surprise me. You know, it was Grandma who first got me interested in baking. I'll never forget the first time we decorated cookies. I think I was about four." She laughed. "I got more frosting on me than on the cookies."

I leaned forward, ready to deliver my pitch. "So, listen, after looking at all the things Maureen made, I got this brilliant idea. It's three months till Christmas, right? I think we should put together a holiday bazaar."

"You mean like a craft fair?"

"Exactly," I said. "A craft fair."

"Hmm…" She dallied with the peas on her plate. "I like it! I'll bet we could get everyone on the street to make something. Bill Prescott makes the most fabulous birdhouses, and I know Nancy Chumley makes candles."

"Perfect," I said. With Connie on board, maybe we could pull it off.

"I've always thought it would be fun to decorate Yule logs," she said.

"Yule logs? You mean like cakes?" I pictured flat little cakes rolled up like logs with white creamy frosting in the middle. I'd buy one.

"No. You're thinking of Swiss Rolls. I mean like real wooden logs with ribbons, holly, and pine cones glued on. They're very festive. You burn them in the fireplace for luck on Christmas Eve, or some people put candles on them and use them for centerpieces. I think it's an old Norse tradition. We sold a couple at the store last year."

Of course. Connie owned a floral and gift shop. Decorating Yule logs sounded exactly like the kind of project she'd be into. I hadn't even thought about making something myself.

"What I'm really hoping for," I said, "is to show off some of Maureen's handmade quilts and rugs. That's the whole point. If she can sell some of her things, I think it will boost her self-confidence."

Connie squinted an eye at me. "It's really nice of you to do this for her, but I hope you're not expecting too much. You're not going to cure her overnight by selling a couple of quilts."

"I know that. I'm not trying to cure her—just let her know she has friends, people who support her."

She looked doubtful, but acquiesced with a nod. "Okay...well, we should start getting organized as soon as possible. Have you thought about when and where?"

"We'll have to look at a calendar, but I'd say either the last Saturday in November or the first Saturday in December. That should give us enough time. As for where, I was hoping you might have an idea. You know the area better than I do."

"The grade school gym would probably work," Connie said, thrumming her fingers on the table, "but we might be getting ahead of ourselves. Maybe we should run it by the neighbors first and see what they think."

I nodded. "What if we set up a meeting, invite everyone? It would be nice to get as many people involved as possible."

"Great idea," Connie said. "I think they'll really get into it. And once we work out the details, we can start advertising."

"Let me call Maureen and see if she'll let us have the meeting over there. I want her to be involved. If we hold it at her house she'll be able to meet everybody and have a say in the planning without having to leave the house."

"Perfect," Connie said. "Do you have her number? Good. Then you can call her right after dinner. Now," she leaned back, "what's for dessert?"

"Dessert? Um…how about those cookies you mentioned yesterday?"

"We also have some ice cream in the freezer." Connie rose and gave Buster a sidelong glance as he leaped to his feet to follow her. "At least you managed to stay out of trouble today."

I stifled the laugh that threatened. I had already decided to keep Buster's little excursion to myself. However, this reminded me of something else.

I cleared my throat. "There's something I've been

meaning to ask you."

Connie plunked the package of cookies and a carton of chocolate caramel swirl on the table. "Help yourself," she said. "Now, what did you want to ask?"

I took one of the soft molasses cookies and savored a small bite. My favorite. I swallowed, then looked at my cousin. "I keep seeing that little girl, the one I told you about with the braids that started the whole disaster with the birthday cake."

"The one that Maureen thinks is a ghost?" She gave a throaty chuckle. "What about her?"

"I just wondered if you knew who she was, where she lived. I thought if I could give her a name—make her human so to speak—it would take away the mystique. Maureen would have to acknowledge that she's just a kid from the neighborhood, and not Hannah's ghost haunting her."

"Hmm...the only girls I know on this block are Nick Donato's two daughters, just across the street. They're about the right age. He's divorced, but he has full custody. Something about his ex-wife being an alcoholic. I remember once—"

I interrupted. "Do they have blond hair?"

She shook her head. "Nope. Dark brown. Both of them. And they don't wear braids."

"There must be other kids living around here."

"I'm sure there are," said Connie. "I just don't know them all. But the elementary school's just a few blocks south of here. You could go hang out on the street in the morning and watch all the kids walking to school. Maybe you'd spot her."

And get picked up for loitering. Somehow I didn't think

spying on little girls would go over well in the community. But there might be a way.

"I go jogging every morning," I said. "I don't suppose it would look too suspicious if I just happened to run in that direction."

"Not at all," Connie said. "That's a great idea."

"What time does school start?"

"How should I know? Sometime after nine, I guess. Maybe nine thirty?" She scratched her head. "Let's see, I usually leave here around seven thirty and there aren't any kids on the street. But on Mondays I leave later—any time between nine and, say, nine twenty. There's always loads of kids then."

One corner of my mouth quirked as a thought occurred to me. "Even if I *do* spot her, it won't help much. I can't very well accost her on the street."

"No," Connie agreed. "You'll have to catch her coming out of her house, or maybe you can follow her home in the afternoon and find out where she lives."

I picked cookie crumbs off the tabletop, then gave a feeble laugh. "I don't know, this is starting to sound slightly depraved. I don't want to be picked up for stalking."

Connie waved her hand in a throwaway gesture. "Just think of it as detecting. If she lives in this neighborhood, she has to go to that school." She paused, then added, "Unless she's home-schooled, or goes to the Catholic school a few miles from here." She tapped her lip. "I think they have a bus."

"You're not helping," I said.

"Just forget it then. What difference does it make? If Maureen wants to believe she's being haunted by her dead sister, then finding that girl isn't going to change her mind. She's a certifiable head case, and you're not going to fix her."

I let out a sigh. Maybe Connie was right. What could I do that an army of therapists couldn't? It just seemed sad that everyone had thrown Maureen over as a nut job and quit trying. Maybe what she needed was just someone to *care*. If nothing else, I could at least do that.

"I *do* like your craft fair idea, though," Connie continued. "That should help her as much as anything. It'll give her something else to think about."

"I hope so." I sat upright with new determination. "And if I'm going to call her, I should do it soon. What do you think? Thursday night? That'll give us time to invite some of the neighbors."

"Sure," Connie said. "Thursday's fine with me. I'll call a few people too. Let them know what we're up to."

"You won't have to do a thing," I assured Maureen when I had her on the phone. "We'll arrange the whole thing. Connie and I will even bring cookies. How does Thursday night sound, around seven?"

"I guess that's okay," Maureen said. "I can make coffee and tea."

"I'll make up a letter with details about the meeting," I said. "Then I'll hand-deliver copies around the neighborhood tomorrow. Whoever shows up gets to be on the planning committee."

"That's a good idea."

She sounded positive. I was encouraged.

"There's just one thing I need you to do," I said.

She hesitated. "What's that?"

"Teach me how to make one of those rugs. Otherwise, I won't have anything to sell. I can type 80 words a minute, but when it comes to crafts, I'm a total dud. I've never made anything crafty in my whole life."

She laughed—a relieved, carefree laugh. "I'd love to teach you to braid a rug," she said. "*That* is something I *can* do."

The next morning, I got up at seven and had a piece of toast with Connie before she left for the shop. Then I put on my running clothes and departed the house at ten after nine, heading south toward the elementary school. The grass was wet with dew, but the morning haze was clearing as the sun burned through. I kept my pace slow and casual, gazing around as I jogged in hopes of spotting the little girl with blond pigtails.

As Connie predicted, the path along the street was crowded with boys and girls walking to school, many accompanied by parents. At times, I had to slow and move aside to avoid clusters of children walking together. When I got within half a block of the school, I found a stone retaining wall where I could sit ostensibly to catch my breath and re-tie my shoes. A number of kids gave me curious stares as they passed.

At twenty-five after nine, the number of walkers had dwindled to only a few stragglers. I had seen no sign of the girl and was beginning to feel awkward sitting there. Apparently, my presence had also piqued another's curiosity, for I was suddenly approached by a crossing guard wearing an official-looking orange vest and badge. A whistle dangled from a cord around her neck and in her hand she carried what looked like a two-way radio.

"Are you waiting for someone?" she asked. She was an older middle-aged woman, possibly the grandmother of one of the younger students, but she carried herself with authority.

I laughed, putting on the most innocent, non-threatening face I could muster.

"Oh, no," I said. "I just moved into the neighborhood and was out jogging, enjoying this beautiful morning. I didn't realize there was a school here. All the kids swarming the sidewalk made it hard to run, so I decided to sit and wait for them to pass. I guess I'll be going now."

I stood and raised my arms straight over my head, twisting my torso, making a show of stretching. "You have a great day!" I said with a friendly smile, stepping around her and heading off at a trot.

"You too," called the crossing guard.

As I ran back in the direction of the house, I imagined her eyes like laser beams, boring holes in my back. Well, so much for *that* idea.

I spent the remainder of the morning composing a letter to the neighbors detailing our ideas for a holiday craft fair, and urging attendance at the planning meeting to be held at Maureen's on Thursday evening. I wasn't sure how many copies to make, so settled finally on two dozen. I figured if a quarter of the recipients showed up, we'd have a good meeting.

At noon, I made myself a sandwich and took Buster out for a romp in the backyard. I gave him ten minutes, which seemed like adequate time to get his business done, then brought him back inside. I wasn't going to chance a repeat of yesterday.

After that, I took the letters, steeled myself, and set out to meet the neighbors. I started by knocking at the first house next door on the north side. It was answered by a plump older woman in a faded pink t-shirt. Her hair was pulled back in a long ponytail liberally streaked with gray. She eyed me curiously.

"Yes?"

Here goes. I had rehearsed a sort of introductory speech so I fixed a smile to my face, and in my most genial voice, began: "Hi, I'm Brenna Wickham, your new neighbor. I just moved in next door with my cousin Connie Kestler. We..."

"You're Arlene's other granddaughter?" she interrupted, her jowly face suddenly splitting into a wide smile.

"Yes, that's right," I said. I took a step backward as the screen door opened wide and the woman's queen-sized frame filled the space.

"Connie called and said you might be stopping by. Lisa's your mother, isn't she?"

I nodded. "She used to bring me here every summer when I was a kid."

"My goodness, I remember those days. How you kids used to run all over the neighborhood. Things around here were a lot livelier back then." She clucked her tongue and gave her head a wistful shake. The fleshy wattle below her chin quivered.

"Uh-huh," I said, "and now..."

"I remember your mother. Such a pretty thing. You

look a lot like her. It was a real shame about your grandmother. She was such a lovely person."

I smiled. *If I could just get a word in edgewise.*

She continued, apparently without the need to stop for breath. "I'm Nancy Chumley. Connie and I are good friends. I'm sorry Oliver's not at home. He used to dote on you kids when you were little. He would have loved to see you." Suddenly, she seemed to remember herself, fluttering a hand and pressing it against her cheek. "Where are my manners? Won't you come in? I made scones this morning. What was your name again?"

"It's Brenna, and I'm sorry I can't stay. I just wanted to let you know about a holiday craft fair we're putting on."

I grabbed her hand and stuffed one of the letters into it. I proceeded to talk as fast as I could, hoping to stave off any more interruptions. "Here, this will tell you all about it. We're planning a meeting Thursday night to start getting organized. Hope you can make it."

I turned and trotted off the porch, leaving her to examine the crumpled sheet of paper in her hand. If I had to stop and make small talk with everyone on the block, this was going to take all afternoon.

Welcome to the neighborhood, I told myself with a short, sardonic laugh.

The next door was opened by an attractive middle-aged man with a neatly trimmed salt and pepper beard. He wore gray slacks and a navy blue sweater over a white polo shirt.

"Can I help you?" he asked.

I started my speech. "Hi, I'm Brenna Wickham, your new neighbor. I just moved in with my cousin Connie

Kestler, two doors down." I waved a hand in the direction of the house.

He studied my face. "You were jogging past the house yesterday morning when I went out to get the paper."

"Right," I said, keeping my smile firmly in place. "And I'm here now to tell you about a holiday craft fair Connie and I are planning. We're hoping to get the whole neighborhood involved. Here's some information." I held out the letter, which he took with scarcely a glance. "We're having a meeting at Maureen Moreland's house on Thursday night to start getting organized. Hope you can come."

Whew! I was relieved to make it all the way through my spiel, but disconcerted by the way he was looking at me.

His brows drew together. "You remind me of someone," he said. "Did you say you've moved into the Price house? And Connie is your cousin? So, that makes Arlene Price your grandmother."

Here we go again. "Yes. You might remember my mother, Lisa Price. She grew up here. People say I look like her." I had heard it all my life and had to admit it was true. We had the same long, wavy chestnut hair, same wide brown eyes. When I was in college, we had more than once been mistaken for sisters.

He nodded. "I'm Bill Prescott." Slowly, he reached out to shake my hand. "I'm very pleased to meet you."

I shook his hand, then cleared my throat and pulled away when he held on a bit longer than necessary.

Abruptly, the door opened wider and a female voice said, "Who is it, Bill?"

A short, sturdy woman with bleached hair crowded

into the doorway and peered at me through horn-rimmed glasses. Her blunt nose and fleshy cheeks made me think of a chipmunk.

Bill Prescott stepped aside. "This is my wife Sylvia," he said.

The woman offered no greeting, but simply stood staring, her lips constricted in a peevish frown.

I remembered Connie describing one of neighbors as "prickly." This must be the one. Nevertheless, I leaned toward her and made the effort. "Hi, I'm Brenna Wickham. I've just moved in with my cousin, Connie Kestler. You may remember my grandmother Arlene…"

Sylvia's face remained fixed. "I know who you are," she interrupted. "Connie called me. We're not interested." She turned sharply and retreated into the house.

"I'm sorry," Prescott said with a lame half shrug. He held up the letter I'd given him and added, "Don't mind her. I'll take a look at this later."

I coughed and scratched my nose self-consciously. "It's about the craft fair we're planning. The meeting's on Thursday." I took a step backward, anxious to be gone. "Hope you can make it." I pivoted and hurried off the porch, heading for the next house.

When I got to the street, I took a surreptitious glance over my shoulder. The man still stood there watching me.

Chapter Seven

By the time I returned home from delivering all twenty-four letters, I was completely worn out. Most of the responses had been positive. On hearing my name and connecting me with my much-loved grandmother, many of the neighbors had invited me to come in and visit for a few minutes. Along with my introductory speech, I had been forced to perfect a battery of polite refusals. At houses where no one answered, I left the letter either under the mat, behind the screen door, or beneath a flower pot in hopes it would be looked at before being tossed in the trash.

Buster greeted me with his usual big grin and lolling tongue. His frenetic dashes toward the back door left little doubt he needed to go out. I was feeling the same urge myself, so I let him into the back yard, closed the door, and hurried down the hall.

Siblings and Secrets

When I emerged from the bathroom, I was distracted by the sudden strident crow of a rooster—the text alert on my phone. Jason had thought it highly amusing to program in as obnoxious a signal as he could find after I'd slept through the old insipid chime and missed an urgent message. Thus, every text I received now was accompanied by an earsplitting *cock-a-doodle-doooo*. I didn't have the heart to change it back.

I looked around for my phone. It had been in the pocket of my jacket. Where was my jacket? I hurried to the living room and found it draped over the arm of the couch, right where I'd left it.

The text was from Tamara: *Hey Brenna. Miss me yet?*

I grinned as I punched back a reply: *Of course I do!*

I took a quick look at the time and added: *Home already? It's only four.*

Tamara worked in a chic women's boutique downtown.

She texted back: *No, on a break. Off tomorrow. Get together?*

It took me less than a second to decide: *Love to.*

Her response: *Lunch at McGruders?*

Sounds good, I replied. *Also need some things from storage. Going crazy without my laptop.*

Can't have that, Tamara texted. *Meet you at noon? Storage afterward.*

As we texted, I made my way back to the kitchen thinking I could keep an eye on Buster from the window. Now as I looked outside, I was surprised to see him playing in the back yard with the little girl in the pink jacket. She ran back and forth with Buster chasing happily at her heels. My phone crowed again.

You still there?

Sorry, I answered. *Got distracted. Neighbor kid in the yard playing with my cousin's dog.*

Awww. So we good for tomorrow? I gotta get back to work.

I dragged myself away from the window and gave Tamara my full attention: *Yes. McGruders at noon. See you tomorrow. Can't wait!*

I jammed the phone into my jeans pocket, then hurried into the garage and out the back door hoping to catch the little girl to find out her name and where she lived. But once again, by the time I burst into the back yard, the girl was gone. I stood staring around with my mouth open. There was no sign of her. A breeze ruffled the leaves of the Japanese maples and somewhere overhead a Steller's jay gave a raucous call. Buster was busily snuffling in the grass, apparently unconcerned about the disappearance of his erstwhile playmate.

How in the world had she managed to get across the yard and out the gate by the corner of the house before I could get from the kitchen to the back door? *Maybe she really is a ghost.* My thoughts flew to Maureen. She was so *sure* Hannah was haunting her. But *why?* What reason would Hannah have to haunt her older sister? Did she also hold Maureen responsible for her death?

I stopped and smacked myself in the forehead with the heel of my hand. *Listen to yourself. A ghost? Really? When did you start believing in ghosts?* I looked around the yard again with a puzzled frown. Under the circumstances, the concept was becoming more plausible by the minute. I massaged my temples, then drew in a large breath and blew it out again. More encounters like this one and I might be convinced.

I could think of nothing else to do, and besides, I was tired. It had been a long day. Connie would be home in a couple of hours. I should go in and search the fridge for something to start for dinner. While my cooking wasn't in the same league as Connie's, in a pinch I could open a jar of spaghetti sauce with the best of them.

I called Buster and pulled him back inside just as the phone in my pocket gave a loud jangling ring. My cousin.

"Hey, Connie," I said into the phone. "What's up?"

"I'm going to be late," she said. "I've got a minor disaster here. The cooler quit working, and I've got to wait for the HVAC tech. Hopefully, he can find the problem and get it fixed right away. I don't know how long the darn thing's been off. I went into the cooler a little while ago to get some carnations for an arrangement and suddenly realized it was way too warm in there."

That didn't sound good. I knew she kept large quantities of fresh flowers stored in a huge walk-in refrigerator at the back of the shop. Without a way to keep the flowers cold, they would soon wilt and Connie could lose hundreds of dollars in merchandise.

"Need me to come over and help?" I said.

"No, but thanks for the offer. At this point, there's nothing to do but wait. I don't know when I'll be home, so you should go ahead and eat without me."

I knew she was trying to stay calm, but I could hear the tension in her voice. She couldn't afford to have the cooler out of commission for very long, especially with the warm weather we'd been having lately.

"Want me to feed Buster?" I asked.

"I'm sure he'd appreciate it. Dog food's in the lower cupboard next to the fridge. One scoop."

"Okay, no problem. Don't worry. Hope everything works out."

"Me too. See you later."

Poor Connie. The florist shop was her pride and joy. I'd only been in there a couple of times, but I thought the place was amazing. The interior of the store was bright and welcoming with twinkling lights strung across the ceiling. The walls were covered with a whimsical silver wallpaper adorned with lacy trees that reflected the lights, creating an almost magical atmosphere. Fanciful gifts were featured on shelves around the room: scented candles, polished stones and crystals, beaded necklaces, and ceramic figurines, as well as stuffed animals, potted plants, and woven baskets of various shapes and sizes. Also for sale was an array of artsy earthenware bowls and glass vases. A refrigerated display case offered selections of ready-made bouquets and cut flowers appropriate for any occasion. And if you didn't see exactly what you were looking for, there were catalogs available to look through which offered made-to-order floral arrangements.

"Well, Buster," I said to the little beagle. "Looks like we're on our own for awhile. Are you ready to eat?"

The vigorous wag of his tail assured me that he was. I emptied a scoop of dry kibble into his bowl, refilled his water dish, then went to get my jacket and purse. I thought I'd walk up to Brubaker's and get something to eat from their deli. They always had delicious fried chicken, thick-cut fries, and two or three different cold salads made fresh every day. It was only a few blocks away.

The glass door was propped open when I got there, letting in the warm autumn air. As I entered, a man strode out, walking briskly with his eyes focused on the ground in front of him. Swerving to avoid a collision, I recognized Gage, his face a stern mask, his mind obviously elsewhere.

"We've got to stop meeting like this," I quipped.

He looked up, startled. "Brenna..."

"Connie got held up at the flower shop and won't be home for dinner, so I thought I'd just grab some chicken to take home."

He put a hand on my elbow and steered me back outside to the sidewalk. "I'm glad we ran into each other," he said. "There's something I need to tell you."

I laughed at his choice of words. "Actually, this time we *didn't* run into each other. I swerved just in time."

He gave a wry snort. "True, and you don't have Connie's dog with you."

I grinned. "What was it you wanted to tell me?"

Glancing around, he leaned toward me and said, "I just talked to Andy Brubaker. He won't be delivering groceries anymore. Connie will have to do her own shopping from now on, and I'll take care of Maureen."

"What? *Why?*" The smile slipped from my face. Buying groceries would pose no more than a slight inconvenience to Connie, but after seeing Andy and Maureen together, I knew Maureen would be devastated. Gage had seemed displeased yesterday when he'd caught them holding hands. Had he terminated the arrangement because of it? What a mean, petty thing to do.

"Is this because he was holding Maureen's hand yesterday? Was that really so awful?" I gave him a frosty glare.

Gage's jaw tightened. He took me once more by the arm and maneuvered us further away from the door. In a low voice, he said, "Brenna, Andy's married."

I jerked back. "*What?*"

"He's married. And he has two kids."

"Does Maureen know?" This changed everything.

He gave me a measured look. "You haven't had dinner, right? You like pizza? Let's go over to Frankie's and I'll tell you everything." He nodded toward a red brick building across the street where a flashy neon sign hung above the door advertising authentic Italian pizza.

Still reeling from the unexpected revelation, I followed Gage to the restaurant and took a seat opposite him at a secluded table in the corner. A waiter hurried to fill our water glasses. The place was mostly empty, but it was early on a Tuesday. *Probably not their busiest night*, I thought. A good spot for a private conversation. We ordered a large pizza with the works, and beers from their selection of local microbrews. While we waited, Gage began.

"Andy had a crush on Maureen all through school," he said. "Andy was shy at first, but by graduation they were definitely together. Everyone expected...I mean, if things had been different..." He stopped and exhaled deeply—a sigh that seemed to embody a world of pain. "You know that Hannah disappeared, but you can't possibly understand how catastrophically it affected us—our home, our family."

I reached across the table and touched his hand. His skin was warm, and it occurred to me that this was the first time in all the years I'd known him that I had deliberately reached out with feelings of compassion. As kids we had tussled like siblings, squabbling, teasing, and provoking each other as we played.

"My parents doted on Hannah," Gage said. "She was the baby, and my stepdad's only child."

"Your stepdad? He wasn't your father?"

He shook his head. "No. My real dad died when I was three years old and my mom remarried a year later. My stepfather adopted us, but we never really bonded. I guess I was an obstinate kid—and a worse teenager." He gave a humorless laugh. "When Hannah came along, he pretty much gave up on me. I spent most of my life butting heads with him. Maureen had it a little better, but that's because she was willing to be submissive." He shrugged. "I could never do that."

How sad. My thoughts jumped to my own stepfather, the kind, loving man I'd been lucky enough to call "dad" since I was ten years old.

The waiter appeared with our drinks and a moment later the pizza arrived. I suddenly realized how hungry I was. We both dug in, talking around mouthfuls of pepperoni, sausage, and hot gooey cheese.

"Were you jealous of Hannah?" I asked hesitantly.

Gage poked at a piece of black olive on his pizza slice. "Oh, maybe a little at first, as all siblings are, but no, not really. She was sweet. I loved her."

He took a big swallow of his beer and went on. "After Hannah disappeared, the police investigation went on for years. There was never a ransom demand and no solid leads, but we were all under scrutiny—our family, our neighbors, our friends. The media was everywhere. It was a circus. Trying to maintain anything resembling a normal life was impossible."

I looked at him with growing sympathy. "Oh, my god, Gage, I can't even imagine. It must have been awful."

He nodded, staring at the table. "My parents stuck it out for six years, holding onto hope that Hannah would be found. But my mother was a wreck. She became more and more withdrawn. By the time I graduated high school Maureen was twenty-one and my parents figured we were old enough to take care of ourselves. They gave the house to Maureen and moved as far away as they could."

As I studied his face, I realized I had misjudged him. He had stepped up and supported his older sister when their parents had abandoned them. It had to have been hard and frustrating at times, but how many other guys would have done that?

I wiped a dribble of grease off my chin. "So, what about Andy Brubaker?"

Gage picked up his beer glass and set it down again, gazing at the amber liquid as though it would help him find the words. "It wasn't long after our parents left that Maureen started to lose it. She began hallucinating. She imagined she saw Hannah everywhere, which led to panic attacks whenever she went out in public." He wiped the condensation from his glass with a finger. "The final straw came when Andy took her to the Space Needle for dinner. He never said so, but I always suspected he was planning to propose. It's just the sort of place you go for something like that. But he never got the chance. Maureen had a whopper of an attack—screaming, crying, making a spectacle of herself. She swore Hannah had followed her there."

"Oh, my god," I breathed.

"As you can imagine, Andy was appalled. The

restaurant had to call the police and paramedics to subdue her. She spent two nights in the psych ward at the hospital. After that, she never left the house again."

Poor Maureen. Poor Andy. His consternation must have been intense. Maureen would have been devastated by humiliation, and ultimately by disappointment at the abrupt end to what might have been the most important date of her life. I shook my head sadly. "I'm so sorry."

Gage managed a half smile. "I give Andy a lot of credit, though. He didn't just dump her. He kept coming around for awhile. I don't know if he thought she'd get better or what, but over time they both realized it wasn't going to happen and they broke up. It was mutual and amicable—at least that's how they made it look on the outside."

"But it had to be painful on the inside."

"Sure," Gage said. "When Andy got married a few years later, Maureen was despondent for weeks."

"So she does know," I murmured, reaching for another slice of pizza.

"Yeah, she knows. That's one of the things I like about Andy. He's forthright. He told her himself. He didn't want her finding out through some chance gossip."

"So, when did he start delivering her groceries?"

"About two years ago," Gage said. "I'd been trying to take care of her—do all the shopping, gardening, and maintenance on the house—but the stress of all that, plus working full time and keeping my own apartment finally started getting to me." He expelled a sharp breath that said he could hardly believe he had managed it for so long. "That's when I reached out to Andy. I know there are other places that deliver, but I knew he'd take special care to see that she always got the best deals and the freshest produce. I also hired a landscaping service to mow the lawn and weed the gardens."

"I don't blame you."

"Fortunately, I had a job that allowed me to do it. Through sheer pigheaded determination—and a small sum left to me by my real father—I somehow managed to claw my way through architectural college and land a position with a highly-regarded Seattle company. I kept living at home for awhile, but when I turned thirty I moved out and got a place of my own. I figured by then I was too old to be living with my big sister."

"I take it you've never married?" *Not that I care,* I told myself.

He gave a soft laugh and shook his head. "Never had time."

"I'm a little surprised Andy's wife didn't object to him going over to Maureen's every week, considering how close they'd been."

"Well, I'm sure she didn't love the idea," Gage said, "but I met with her and explained the situation. After the three of us talked it out, she agreed that Andy should help. She's a caring person and feels genuinely sorry for Maureen, plus she knows she can trust Andy."

"No wonder you were upset when you saw him holding Maureen's hand. I can see why you put an end to the arrangement."

"Huh-uh," Gage said, shaking his head. "It wasn't me who ended the deal. It was Andy. He told me Maureen was starting to push herself on him. It was making him uncomfortable."

My respect for Andy went up another notch. A man

with fewer scruples might have taken advantage of the situation.

"I had to respect his feelings," Gage continued, "so now I've got to find another way to get my sister's groceries delivered. One of those commercial services I guess, or I think there's a local chain that delivers." He wiped his fingers on a napkin, then folded it and set it aside. "I was hoping you'd break the news to Connie."

I laughed. "Don't worry about Connie. In fact, since I'm not working now, why don't you let me take over the shopping for both of them."

"Are you sure?" he asked, looking hopeful. "It's not your responsibility. I'd hate for it to become a burden."

"It's no burden," I assured him. "It'll give me something to do, at least until I get another job."

His whole demeanor relaxed, as though a weight had been lifted.

Then something occurred to me. "Do you mind if we hold off telling them for a few days?" I feared Maureen would be upset when she heard that Andy wouldn't be coming anymore, and I didn't want to jeopardize the success of our meeting Thursday night. After that, I would help her cope by diverting her energy into teaching me how to make a rag rug.

"No." He looked at me curiously. "Why?"

"Has Maureen told you about the craft fair we want to put on?"

His eyebrows rose. "Craft fair? She hasn't said a word about it."

"I'm not surprised. We only came up with the idea yesterday after Maureen showed me the quilts and rugs she's made. I told her they were way too beautiful to keep hidden and that I felt sure people would love to buy them. One thing led to another and we came up with the idea of getting the whole neighborhood involved in selling homemade crafts for the holidays."

He downed the last of his beer and canted an eyebrow, giving me a dubious smile. His dark eyes shone with a trace of the old impishness I remembered. "Good luck with that," he said.

"Well, Connie thought it was a good idea too. So we've decided to have a meeting at Maureen's house Thursday night to discuss it and start making plans. I handed out letters this morning to everyone in the neighborhood inviting them to attend."

"I see. Quite an undertaking." He tilted his head, baiting me with a grin. "And what are *you* planning to make for the fair?"

Before I could answer, the waiter appeared at the table. "Another beer?" He glanced at each of us in turn.

I shook my head.

Gage rubbed his chin thoughtfully. "No more beer," he said, "but what do you have in the way of dessert?"

"We have spumoni ice cream," said the waiter, "and an apple cobbler we make here." He smiled broadly. "It's very good."

"I don't need any dessert," I said. "I couldn't eat another bite."

"Bring us one cobbler and two spoons," Gage said.

When I started to protest, Gage put up a hand. "I'll eat the whole thing if you don't want any." He waved the waiter away, then leaned toward me. "You'll probably think this is stupid, but I'm not ready for the evening to end. I've enjoyed getting to know you again after all these years, and seriously, it has been ages since I've been out with anyone. I hope we can see more of each other."

Whether it was the shadows deepening as evening closed in, the lambent glow of candles placed about the room, or the soft music floating in the background, the mood in the restaurant subtly changed. Looking at Gage, I was surprised at how attractive he had become all of a sudden. Thick brown hair framed a well-formed face, accentuating his square jaw and firm cheek bones.

My pulse quickened and I felt a warm flush crawl up my neck. I took a hurried gulp of water, keeping my eyes on the table.

"Besides," he teased, "you haven't told me what you're making for the craft fair."

The waiter returned with a bowl of cobbler topped with vanilla ice cream. The aroma of warm apples and cinnamon filled my nose. In spite of myself, I grabbed a spoon and scooped up a generous portion, murmuring in bliss as I savored the decadent treat.

Gage laughed and attacked it with the other spoon.

It's nice to hear him laugh.

"Maureen's going to help me make a rug," I said between bites.

He nodded sagely, barely hiding a smile. "Of course she is. She's got boxes and boxes of fabric scraps. She spends hours making that stuff."

"I thought if the quilts and rugs go over well, she might like to start a home business and sell them online. It would give her something to do outside herself, a way to connect with other people."

He looked doubtful. "I hope you're right, but don't get your hopes up. The therapists have been trying to get her to do stuff like that for years. Nothing seems to work for very long."

I licked a smear of ice cream off my spoon. "Well, if nothing else, the craft fair should help get her mind off of Hannah for awhile and give her something to look forward to. Hopefully, it'll boost her confidence."

He smiled and his expression softened. "It's a great idea, Brenna. I really appreciate you trying to help her this way."

"It'll be fun," I said. "And besides, I'm eager to learn a new skill. I foresee homemade rugs for my entire family for Christmas this year."

Chapter Eight

After a moment, he sobered and tapped his fork lightly on the table as though searching for the right words. Finally, he looked up and said, "Did you mean it when you said you'd like to see one of the houses I designed? The latest one is under construction and nearing completion. I thought I might run over there on Friday to check on things. I wondered if you'd like to come."

A date? I thought with apprehension. I'm not ready for that. *No,* I told myself, not a date. Just two old friends getting reacquainted after a number of years. And I *had* said I'd like to see one of the houses he'd designed.

"I'd love to," I said. "Where is it?"

He looked pleased. "West side of Mercer Island, on a bluff overlooking the lake. It's a beautiful spot. I have to see a client first thing Friday morning, so how about if I pick you up around noon? We can grab lunch on the way."

"Sounds like fun."

"Give me your number and I'll text you when I'm on the way."

I gave him the number and he added it to his contacts, then stashed the phone back in his coat.

"Good," he said, "then when we get back Friday afternoon, I'll give Maureen the news about Andy." He grimaced. "I'm not looking forward to it, but I guess I always knew the arrangement couldn't last forever."

If Maureen had known all this time that Andy was married, she must also have known the arrangement wouldn't last. Had she hoped to convince Andy to have an affair with her? Sadly, it showed just how lonely Maureen was.

"You want me to be there?" I asked.

"That'd be great," he said. "She likes you. Maybe your presence will help soften the blow."

"I hope so," I said. I dabbed my mouth and laid my spoon on the table. "And now I think I'd better be getting back. I don't know what time Connie will be home, and I'm sure Buster must need to go out by now."

"Let me drive you," said Gage. "It's gotten dark outside."

Gratefully, I accepted his offer. I'd only brought a lightweight jacket and the evening was cool. I climbed into the front seat of Gage's sporty blue SUV and within minutes we had reached the house. Connie's small sedan was in the driveway so he angled his car into the wide margin along the street, tires crunching in the gravel. As he did so, the vehicle's headlights swept briefly over a small figure standing beside the fence.

I sat bolt upright and gasped. "There she is again!"

The little girl stood in the shadows, barely visible in the peripheral gleam of the headlights. I wanted to turn to see if Gage saw her too, but an irrational voice in my head warned that if I took my eyes off her, she would vanish. So I sat staring, afraid to move.

The little girl's body was backlit by the feeble shimmer of the porch light which created an eerie sort of corona around her. For a moment, I had the peculiar sense that I was looking through her. *A trick of the light*. The car halted and I heard the parking brake engage. The headlights switched off and we were plunged into sudden darkness. I scoured the shadows, but the girl was gone.

We sat for a moment in silence, darkness enveloping the car. Gage shifted in his seat. I turned to find his eyes fixed on my face.

"Not you too," he groaned.

I heaved a sigh. "I take it that means you didn't see her."

He rubbed his hands wearily over his face. "No."

"I *swear* I saw a little girl."

Shaking his head, Gage declared, "I do *not* believe in ghosts. She *has* to be a kid who lives somewhere in the neighborhood."

"Did I *say* she was a ghost?" He was already fed up with his sister's hallucinations. I didn't want him thinking *I* was unbalanced as well.

I don't know why I suddenly felt so defensive. I wanted to state categorically that I didn't believe in ghosts either, but I couldn't get the words out. I wasn't as convinced as I had been a week ago, although I wasn't about to tell him that. I just needed to do more investigating. There *had* to be a simple, logical explanation. I turned again to stare at the empty space where the girl had been standing a moment before.

Gage turned the dome light on in the car. He pulled out his wallet and began to dig through it. "I have an old school photo of Hannah in here somewhere," he muttered.

Finally, he pulled out a small, dog-eared picture and considered it for a moment before handing it to me. "Is this the girl you saw?" It sounded almost like a challenge.

I took the picture, and without thinking, let slip a little gasp. My free hand rose to cover my mouth. The resemblance was uncanny. The little girl was either a ghost or an amazing look-alike.

"Then answer me this," Gage said in a measured voice, "if it *is* Hannah's spirit, why doesn't she appear to *me*?"

I had no answer for that.

"Was that Gage who brought you home?" Connie asked as soon as I walked through the door. She sat in the living room in her favorite overstuffed chair, feet propped on a matching ottoman. Buster ran to greet me and I gave him a quick scratch behind the ears.

"I ran into him at Brubaker's. I was going to get some chicken to bring home, but he took me over to Frankie's instead. We had a long talk." I took off my jacket and tossed it over the arm of the couch as I sat down.

"About what?"

I gave her a narrow look. "Well, for starters, did you know Andy was married?"

She shrugged. "Yeah. So?"

"So?" I laughed sharply. "Gage told me that Andy and Maureen used to be a couple. They nearly got engaged. Under the circumstances, don't you think it's a little inappropriate, his going over there alone every week?"

Connie shrugged again, disavowing involvement in any potential impropriety. She patted her knee and Buster leaped onto her lap, panting happily as she stroked his head. "I knew they were good friends," she said. "I didn't know they'd almost been engaged. Anyway, it's none of my business. As far as I'm concerned, he's just doing a favor for a friend. Besides, where's the harm in a little flirtation?"

I gave her a disbelieving look. "Andy's wife must be a saint."

I was tempted to disclose then and there that Andy wouldn't be coming anymore, but knowing how Connie liked to gossip, and given the fact that we would be spending Thursday evening with Maureen, I held back. Better to wait till Friday as planned and give Gage a chance to break the news to Maureen first.

I leaned back in the couch cushions, flexing my shoulders. "So, how did things go at the shop?" I asked. "Did the HVAC guy figure out what was wrong with the cooler? Did he get it fixed?"

She straightened in her chair and her eyes fired up. Andy and Maureen were quickly forgotten. "Oh, my god, Brenna, you are *not* going to believe what he found." Her hands became animated as she plunged into the details of her harrowing experience. "It was a coolant leak—caused by a *mouse*, of all things. It somehow managed to crawl in behind the condenser coil and make a nest. Over time, a buildup of pee and droppings caused the line to corrode."

I made a face. "Ew, that's got to be a first."

"Yeah—and when it started to leak, the automatic safety valve shut the unit down." She groaned dramatically. "Who'd have thought a little thing like a mouse could do so much damage?"

"So, did he get it fixed?"

"Unfortunately, no. It needs a new condenser coil and he didn't have one with him. He said he had one back at his shop and he'll bring it by first thing in the morning. Thank goodness for insurance, that's all I can say."

I expressed my sympathy in little murmurs. Precisely the reason I never wanted to own my own business. Let someone else manage the headaches. Which reminded me, I ought to be thinking about looking for another job. I expelled a deep breath. Maybe next week…or the week after that. I closed my eyes, choosing to fall back on that time-honored rationalization: I didn't have time right now. I was helping to organize the holiday bazaar.

The next morning after a short run, I was sitting at the kitchen table with my usual piece of toast, sipping some coffee when the doorbell rang. Buster reacted with a burst of barks and howls as he raced to the door. I grabbed him by the collar as I cracked open the door and peered out.

It was Bill Prescott, the neighbor from two doors down. He had on a pair of faded jeans and a black bomber jacket over a casual green button-down shirt. His bearded face wore an affable smile.

"Hi," I said, surprised. "What can I do for you?"

"May I come in?" he asked. "I wanted to apologize for

my wife's behavior."

Pulling Buster aside, I swung the door wider. "Of course, come in. But there's no need to apologize."

He strolled in and pulled off his jacket. The short sleeves of his shirt revealed thick, sinewy arms covered in elaborate tatoos. He settled himself at one end of the living room couch, tossing the jacket on the seat beside him.

"Would you like some coffee?" I asked.

"No, thanks." He shook his head. "I can't stay long."

I took the armchair opposite, letting go of Buster's collar. The beagle approached the man and sniffed curiously at his shoe. Prescott patted the dog on the head, then looked up.

"There was no call for Sylvia to be so rude," he said. "You'll have to forgive her—she's just kind of shy and doesn't get on well with people she doesn't know. But since we're neighbors now, I expect we'll be seeing a lot more of each other. She'll come around."

I smiled. Shy wasn't the word I would have picked to describe his wife, but the offense had been trifling and I'd already forgotten it. "Don't worry about it." I folded my hands in my lap and leaned forward slightly. "Did you get a chance to look at the letter I gave you?"

"I did, and I think it's a great idea. You can count me in."

"Connie told me you make birdhouses."

"Yeah, and lots of other stuff. I have a woodworking shop in my garage. I like to build birdhouses, jewelry boxes, toy trains, and what have you." His dark brown eyes were alight with enthusiasm. "If it's made of wood, I can probably make it."

"Do you think Sylvia will want to participate?"

"I doubt it, but you never know. She likes to keep up with whatever's going on in the neighborhood." His smile broadened and he winked conspiratorially.

Is he *flirting* with me? *No, this guy's old enough to be my father.*

He rubbed a hand over his beard and glanced around. "Time sure flies, doesn't it? I remember when your mother lived here."

"You *have* lived in this town a long time." *Jeesh. Did that sound as dumb to him as it did to me?* It felt awkward making small talk with a middle-aged man I hardly knew.

He gave a little chuckle. "I guess you could say that. I remember when *you* were little too, when your mom used to bring you to visit your grandma." He paused for a moment. "Speaking of your mom, how is she? Married, I suppose. Still living in Arizona?"

And they say *women* gossip.

I nodded. "Married and happy, working in a book store."

He laid an arm casually along the back of the couch and brought his right leg up to rest on the opposite knee. "I heard you got married too."

Seeing my look of surprise, he laughed and added, "Your grandma showed me a picture once. She used to brag about her grandkids all the time. I think she carried pictures around everywhere she went."

I gave a quick laugh. "That doesn't surprise me. Anyway, yeah, I got married, but my husband was killed in a car accident two years ago." I averted my eyes, picking a stray bit of dog hair off my pant leg. "I'd rather not talk about it."

His smile evaporated and he looked genuinely grieved. "I'm so sorry to hear that, Brenna. I really am."

It was jolting hearing him call me by my first name in that soft, intimate tone, like we were old friends. *Too familiar, too soon*, I thought. I couldn't explain why—all he had done was express sympathy—but I was beginning to feel uncomfortable.

Anxious to change the subject, I focused my gaze on the elaborate ink emblazoning his arms, partially hidden beneath the short sleeves of his shirt.

"Those are pretty impressive tattoos."

He cranked his head around to look at the biceps he had thrown across the back of the couch. Pushing up his sleeve, he stared at the image of a flaming motorcycle like he'd never seen it there before. The other arm sported a wicked-looking eagle with wings and talons outstretched.

His expression sobered as he ran a hand over his jaw. "Relics of my misspent youth. You wouldn't know it to look at me now, but I was something of a hell raiser back in the day."

I smiled. "You were a biker, I take it." My mind conjured an image of a long-haired, leather-wearing badass straddling a huge Harley-Davidson, thundering down the highway with Steppenwolf singing *Born to be Wild* in the background.

He shrugged. "Yeah, but it's been awhile. I've put all that behind me now."

"Must have been exciting," I said. Hard to believe this was the same guy who went outside in his bathrobe to pick up the newspaper.

"Sometimes. But those days are best forgotten. I did some things I'm not proud of." He grabbed his jacket and swung his foot back to the floor. "I guess I ought to be gettin' back. Sylvia just ran up to the store. She'll be unhappy if she gets home and I'm not there."

Funny, he didn't strike me as the type to be cowed by his wife.

I walked him to the door and watched as he strode off the porch and headed for the street. I glanced at my watch and yelped when I saw the time. I had to take Buster out and get changed. I needed half an hour at least to drive downtown to the restaurant where I was meeting Tamara for lunch. If traffic was slow I'd never make it.

Chapter Nine

McGruder's Seafood Grill was situated on a hill overlooking the dazzling blue waters of Lake Union at the north end of downtown Seattle. Wraparound windows offered views of the city in all directions. Directly below sat a marina where yachts rested languorously in their slips, and a forest of tall-masted sailboats rocked idly in the gentle breeze. Jingling lines and rigging added to a dockside harmony of purring engines, lapping waves, and raucous seagulls. Here and there, kayakers plied the waters, and seaplanes took off and soared above the surface of the lake destined for any number of remote locations in the scenic San Juan Islands in the far northwestern corner of the state.

Tamara had already secured a table by the window. She flagged me down with a wave of her hand.

"So, how do you like unemployment so far?" she

asked, an expansive grin on her heart-shaped face. Dark eyes, black hair, and sepia-toned skin gave her an exotic look. Today she wore a multi-colored bohemian tunic, perfectly in keeping with her lively style. A circlet of turquoise beads around her neck matched an opulent pair of blue earrings that dangled nearly to her shoulders. I felt positively austere in my navy slacks and plain pink blouse.

"It's tough," I said, easing into my chair. "Nothing to do all day but lounge in front of the TV."

"Oh, you poor thing," Tamara drawled with a distinct lack of sympathy. "Maybe you'd like a nice bowl of gruel."

"You're just jealous," I said, returning tease for tease. "So, have you seen any activity over at my place? Anyone with wads of cash beating down the door to buy the place?"

"Huh-uh. I've seen the real estate lady a couple of times, but it looks to me like she's still prepping for the open house this weekend."

I let out an audible sigh.

"Relax," Tamara said. "It's only been a few days."

"I know, I know. Seems like longer. I just want to get it all behind me. Problem is, I still have to make the mortgage payments while it sits there empty, and with the HOA threatening to stick us with the cost of a new roof next spring..."

Jason had had the standard minimum life insurance policy supplied by the company where he worked, but funerary costs and two years of living expenses had chipped it away to almost nothing. If the condo didn't sell soon, I would have to get off my backside and start looking for a new job in earnest.

Just then the waitress arrived, setting a basket of delicious-smelling herb rolls and butter on the table between us. She held a pen poised over a small notepad. "Are you ready to order?"

We each requested a glass of white wine, and Tamara selected the crab cakes. After a moment of indecision, I settled on the grilled filet of sole.

If there's one thing I love about Seattle, it's the amazing seafood.

"So, tell me what you've been up to," Tamara said. "What's it like out there in the sticks? You dying of boredom yet?"

"Actually, it's more interesting than you'd think. Let's see…I've met a few of the neighbors. Mostly your standard crop of housewives, busybodies, and retirees. The guy two doors down is sort of flirty…"

Tamara's eyebrows rose.

"…but not in a good way." I grimaced. "He's old enough to be my father."

She laughed.

"Then there's the woman next door who never leaves her house. I just learned she's been trying to seduce the nice married man who delivers her groceries."

That prompted a grin. "Doesn't sound much different from downtown."

"*And* she sees ghosts. That is, a *particular* ghost. The ghost of her younger sister who died twenty-five years ago."

This time Tamara's eyebrows arched in surprise. "Okay, *that's* different."

I didn't mention that I thought I might also have seen the ghost.

"It's sad, really," I said. "I knew this neighbor a long time ago when I was a kid. We all used to play together when my mom and I would visit, especially me and the little sister."

"The one who's now a ghost."

"Yeah. And their brother. He's a couple years older than me."

"Does he live there too?"

"No, but he comes around every week or so to check on the older sister."

"The one who sees ghosts."

"Right."

"Is he cute?"

"What?"

"The brother. Is he cute?"

I gave a short laugh. "No. Well, sort of. Maybe. I don't know. I never thought of him that way. When we were kids, I always called him 'donkey face.'" Fearful that I might be blushing, I grabbed my glass of ice water and took a long sip.

She tilted her head and gave me a sidelong glance. "Has he asked you out?"

"No." I sputtered as I choked on the water. *What's wrong with me? Gage and I are just old friends. Why am I getting so flustered?* "We ran into each other at the store last night—just by coincidence—and then we went for pizza. Not a big deal. Then Friday I'm going with him to look at a house he designed. He's an architect."

Tamara's eyebrows rose again as she leaned forward on her elbows giving me her rapt attention.

"It's not a date," I insisted. "He has to go check on the builders and I'm just going along for the ride."

"Uh-huh."

Before I could frame a retort, the food arrived and we shelved the discussion to concentrate on eating. The fish was done to perfection and came with a side of lightly roasted vegetables. The waitress returned a moment later to refill our water glasses then left us alone to resume our tête-à-tête.

"It wouldn't be a crime to date him if you wanted to," Tamara said.

"I know." I kept my eyes fixed on my plate. My left thumb stroked the smooth contours of my wedding ring.

The movement didn't escape Tamara's notice. "You could get a nice gold chain to wear that on." She knew me well and knew I'd been lonely. "I'm sure Jason would want you to move on."

"I know," I said again. "I just don't think I'm ready to start dating."

Tamara twirled her fork in the air and laughed. "Hey, nobody's telling you to *marry* the guy. Just go out and have some fun. You're too young to be alone."

I thought about Gage—his dark, forbidding eyes, his grim expression. Yeah, he'd be a barrel of laughs. But he *had* been easy to talk to once he opened up. There was a rare sort of sympathy there, hidden under the surface.

I gave her an oblique smile. "I'll think about it."

When we'd finished eating, the waitress came back and we ordered dessert. I knew from experience that McGruder's served an awesome crème brûlée.

"You know," Tamara said slowly, "my grandmother always believed in ghosts."

"What?" I laughed at this odd statement out of the blue.

"She did, and she was no fool. She said there's a reason a spirit comes back, like there's something they have to do." She fiddled with the turquoise beads around her neck. "After my grandfather died, she swore he appeared to her and told her where he'd stashed some money he'd been putting away on the sly. Five thousand dollars. She'd had no idea it was there until his ghost came back and showed her where it was."

"Tamara," I said, "are you messing with me?"

"No," she said. "I was thinking about your neighbor. You said her little sister died twenty-five years ago."

"Yeah…" Where she was going with this?

"Was it under suspicious circumstances, by any chance?"

"Yeah, actually, it was. She disappeared without a trace when she was eight years old. Nobody knows what happened to her. By now I guess they presume she's dead."

"Well, *obviously*," Tamara said, "if her *ghost* has come back."

I laughed out loud. The couple at the next table glanced over. I leaned forward and lowered my voice. "Oh, come *on*. Didn't you tell me once that your grandmother was Creole and into all sorts of weird superstitions? Are you telling me you believe that stuff too?"

She shrugged. "I don't know. I guess I'm just not convinced that ghosts don't exist. Think about it. There must be a reason your neighbor says she sees her little sister after all these years."

"Yeah. She's mentally disturbed, plus there's a kid in the neighborhood who looks just like her. I've seen her."

But even as I asserted this, I was needled with doubt.

Tamara sensed my uncertainty. "So how do you know she's not a ghost? You said you and she used to play together. That means you have a connection."

"But why me and not her brother? He's never seen this girl."

"Who knows? Maybe they didn't get along. Maybe you're more receptive."

"More gullible, you mean."

She ignored this. "Maybe she wants your help."

"To do what?"

"I don't know. Find her killer maybe, or her body. You said she was never found, right? All I know is that if she's trying to tell you something, you should listen."

I sat back and massaged my forehead. The whole thing seemed so preposterous, but when it came right down to it, I couldn't honestly say I thought she was wrong.

To change the subject, I told Tamara about the holiday bazaar we were planning for the neighborhood, and how Maureen was going to teach me to make an old-fashioned rag rug.

"If you're not careful," Tamara said, "they're going to turn you into a real homebody. Next thing you know, you'll be canning peaches and darning socks." Her expression said she found the very idea abhorrent.

"No way. That'll never happen. I'm whatcha call a 'modern woman.'"

"Yeah? You started looking for a new job yet? Something pithy and high-tech out there in the suburbs?"

I winced. "Not yet, but I will. Any day now."

After we left the restaurant, Tamara followed me to the

storage unit where I'd stashed most of my belongings. I was eager to pick up my laptop. I couldn't believe I'd left it behind, but my mind had been in such turmoil when I'd packed, I had ultimately taken only two suitcases full of clothes.

I unlocked the door and turned on the light. Besides my computer, I wanted to gather a few personal items to take back with me to make my room feel more homey. Boxes were piled along the wall labeled in black felt pen. I set aside the box marked "desk," and began rummaging through the stack for the bedroom box. I knew I had packed my jewelry in it, as well as a digital clock radio my mother had given me for Christmas when I was in high school. It was a little old fashioned but it had sentimental value, much like the gold watch my parents had given me for my college graduation.

"Keep an eye out for my laptop," I said to Tamara.

She nodded, then cried, "Oh, here's something you can't live without." She dragged out a box with the word "shoes" written boldly on the side.

"Absolutely! Add it to the stack. Oh, and here's my books. I need those." I struggled to extricate the heavy box from a pile along the back wall.

"Uh-oh," Tamara said. "Here's something else you'd better take."

I looked and was chagrined to see a large, decidedly wilted philodendron in a tall wrought iron tripod stand.

"Oh, no," I said, caressing a large yellowed leaf. "Poor baby. You were supposed to stay in the condo. Somebody got over-zealous with the moving."

"It'll probably come back if you give it some water and get it back in the sun," Tamara said.

I picked up the plant and set it near the door. "I'll give it a try. I've had this thing for years. I'd hate for it to die."

"What about this?" Tamara asked.

She pointed to a large framed oil painting leaning against the wall. Jason's aunt and uncle in San Diego had given it to us as a wedding present. We'd hung it in our living room, but I'd never been overly fond of it; I thought it looked like someone had smeared wet paint all over a sheepdog, then stood him in front of a canvas and waited for him to shake. Blobs and splatters covered the surface in riotous color.

I made a face. "I don't know. It would certainly brighten up my room, but truthfully, I've never actually liked it."

"*Really?*" She looked astonished. "I *love* it!"

Why wasn't I surprised?

"Then it's yours," I declared. "A gift. Hang it over your bed with my blessing."

"Are you sure?" Her eyes danced. "It looks expensive."

"I'm positive. I want you to have it—unless it turns out to be worth a fortune, then I get half."

She grinned. "Deal." She grabbed the frame and headed for her car.

As I waded through the boxes, I came upon a heavy cardboard mailing tube over two feet long and three inches wide. I felt my chest tighten as I picked up the tube. My castle posters.

Twelve years ago, when Jason first proposed, he made the extravagant promise to bring me the sun, the moon, and the stars. I laughed at his effusive boast and, giggling, suggested he get me a more modest token instead, such as a castle in Europe. A few days later, he presented me with a poster of the Neuschwanstein castle in the Bavarian Alps.

After that, on every anniversary, he gave me a new poster of some splendid castle somewhere, claiming that one day he would take me to see them all in person. It had become a private joke between us, and our unspoken bucket list.

Fighting down a lump in my throat, I replaced the tube on the stack of boxes where I had found it. Someday I would have to decide what to do with the posters, but not today.

I finally unearthed my laptop case from a tight space between two boxes and added it to the pile set aside to take with me. I was aching to spend some time searching online for old news articles about Hannah's disappearance twenty-five years ago. My phone was okay for looking up certain things, but I found the small screen exasperating for extensive investigations. After working for years in a sophisticated law office, I'd become spoiled by the ease of using a real keyboard and reading off a large screen.

I wasn't quite ready to concede that the little girl I'd seen was a ghost, but I had to admit I couldn't say for certain she wasn't, either. I could hardly believe I was actually giving the thought credence, but Tamara's comment about listening to the ghost had hit a chord.

Chapter Ten

The first thing I did when I got home was leash up Buster and allow him to drag me out the front door and down the porch steps. The afternoon was waning and the poor dog hadn't been out since morning. A quick walk around the block would be good for him.

Without thinking, I turned left at the end of the driveway and started past the Chumleys'. Too late, I realized Nancy Chumley was in her front yard watering the roses along her fence.

"Lovely day," I remarked with a casual nod, intending to walk on without stopping.

She waved and hurried over, a wide, jovial grin spread across her face. Courtesy demanded I stop and chat for a moment. Buster pulled impatiently on his leash as he endeavored to sniff at a tuft of grass just out of reach.

"Brenna, how nice to see you," Nancy exclaimed. She

wore a baggy pair of dirt-stained sweat pants and a shapeless, over-sized t-shirt. Her head was covered by a wide straw hat knotted firmly under her chin with a length of cord. She turned and called over her shoulder. "Oliver, come here and meet Brenna."

I hadn't noticed him on the other side of the yard, but now Nancy's husband shuffled obediently over to join us. This was my first acquaintance with Mr. Chumley. Thin and balding, slightly stooped, with wire-rimmed spectacles perched on a hook nose, he reminded me of a cartoon caricature of a buzzard. A plain brown cardigan hung loosely from his shoulders. He looked several years older than his wife.

"You remember I told you about Brenna," Nancy said to her husband. "She's Lisa Price's daughter—Arlene's youngest granddaughter. They used to come and visit every the summer when she was a child."

Oliver nodded. His face was genial if somewhat placid. "I remember when you were little."

I wondered if he really remembered or was simply responding to the cues fed to him by his wife.

"We're so excited about the craft fair," gushed Nancy. "Aren't we Oliver? It's a wonderful idea. I've got plans for some new candles I want to make with melted crayons. I got the idea from a picture I saw once in a magazine."

Oliver added nothing, but smiled agreeably.

"That's great," I said. "We'll see you at the meeting tomorrow night then. We have a lot to do to get this thing organized."

"I'm looking forward to it," she said. "I wasn't a high school teacher for forty years without learning something about being organized."

Buster kept tugging against the leash. "Well, I'd better get going before Buster yanks my arm off." I gave the beagle his head and allowed him to pull me away. "See you tomorrow."

To my annoyance, we only made it a few steps before we were stopped again—this time by Bill Prescott at the next house. The way he was loitering near the fence, I could tell he had been waiting for us.

He greeted me with a friendly grin. "Taking the pooch for a walk, eh?" He leaned over the top rail and gave Buster a pat on the head.

"Yeah, I thought he could use some exercise since he's been cooped up inside all day."

"He's your cousin's dog, isn't he? I see him running around the neighborhood from time to time."

I winced. "Sorry. He's usually in the house, but sometimes we put him out in the back yard. Trouble is, he likes to dig under the fence when he gets bored. I hope he hasn't bothered you."

"Oh, no, he's a nice little dog. I just wouldn't want him to get hurt is all. There's a fair amount of traffic on some of these streets."

"I know," I said, giving a resigned little shrug. "That's why I'm taking him for a walk. If I can tire him out maybe he won't want to go exploring."

He seemed not to hear. Instead, he murmured, "I just can't get over how much you look like your mother." His voice carried a soft, almost sensual tone that I found disturbing.

I gave Buster's leash a little tug and took a couple of steps backward, eager to end the conversation. "Well, I need to keep walking. Hope to see you at the meeting tomorrow night."

As I turned away and continued down the well-beaten path along the street, Sylvia Prescott's shrill voice cut through the air: "Bill, what are you doing out here? Come inside. I need your help with something, *now*."

In a bent of wicked humor, my mind supplied the inevitable next words: *"yes, dear."*

I returned to the house thirty minutes later and unpacked my car, arranging my room with the things I'd brought back from storage. It was amazing how a few knickknacks, books, and pictures could transform a place, making it feel like home.

I set the wilted philodendron next to the window and gave it a good soaking. "There you go, little plant," I crooned. "The rest is up to you."

Eagerly, I put my computer on the desk and connected it to the internet, settling down to hunt for articles on Hannah's disappearance. I wasn't sure I'd find anything after all these years, but I was determined to try.

During my years as a legal assistant, I had become adept at searching the Seattle Public Library for news articles. I went to the site now and clicked on the library collections, which led me to newspapers, and finally to the Seattle Times Historical Archives. Inputting the name "Hannah Moreland" awarded me several articles pertaining to the little girl's mysterious disappearance and the police department's intense search and investigation. Many of the articles were accompanied by pictures, including the same school photo of Hannah that Gage carried in his wallet.

I read that the parents, John and Gail Moreland, had been eliminated as suspects as they had been golfing all day with a group of friends at a local country club. A wide search had been conducted. The police had interviewed numerous neighbors and persons of interest, but no real evidence had ever been uncovered. Kidnapping wasn't ruled out, although no ransom demand was ever received. The newspaper was also quick to reiterate the harsh fact that the missing girl's older sister had sneaked out to meet her boyfriend and left the eight-year-old alone to fend for herself. Over time, the case had grown cold and the media's attention had shifted elsewhere.

I dropped my hands from the keyboard and turned my gaze to the window where the late afternoon sun was just touching the tops of the trees on the western horizon. I ran my palms over my face and rubbed my tired eyes.

Poor Maureen. To have this kind of damning publicity following her around everywhere she went, especially as a teenager and young woman. Had she been shunned at school? Vilified by her classmates? No wonder she had panic attacks. One could hardly blame her for not wanting to leave her house.

If only I could...if only I could *what?* I gave a soft, self-deprecating laugh. If only I could solve a twenty-five year old mystery? Find out what happened? Something a whole contingent of police detectives and FBI agents could not? Sure. I expelled my breath in a rush, defeated before I even started. Then Tamara's words came back to me: *if she's trying to tell you something, you should listen.*

But how?

Just then, I heard a rattling of keys at the front door

and Connie came in. I looked at my watch and realized I had let the time get away from me. I hurried to greet her and nearly ran her over in the hallway.

"Hey, cuz," I said. "How'd it go at the shop? Did the HVAC guy show up this morning with the new whatchamacallit for the cooler? Everything back in working order?"

"Yep. He replaced the condenser coil and swept away the remnants of the mouse nest—yuck—and we're back up and running. How was your lunch downtown?"

"Great, and I managed to bring back a few treasures from storage to liven up my room. Now, go get changed and I'll start something for dinner. Any suggestions?"

Buster bounced happily at her feet as Connie removed her coat. "Hey, buddy," she crooned to the dog. Then she looked at me and pursed her lips. "Let's see. There's one of those boxes of easy pasta dinners in the cupboard and a pound of hamburger in the fridge to go with it."

Didn't sound too complicated. "I'm on it," I said.

Half an hour later as we sat down to eat, I asked Connie, "What do you know about Bill Prescott?"

She shrugged and adjusted her glasses. "Not much. He runs the appliance store in Lynnwood started by his father-in-law fifty years ago: Lynnwood Grand Appliance, 'We'll make you a steal of a deal.' Remember those commercials?"

I shook my head.

"They used to run on TV all the time. Annoying as hell—but pretty successful. They made a ton of money for Sylvia's father, Big Mike Quigley. He used to be quite the local celebrity."

"For selling appliances?"

"For the commercials. He put masks on animals, dressed them up like burglars—monkeys, dogs, goats, llamas, even a bear once—and made it look like they were robbing the store. Then he'd jump in and say, 'There's no need, *We'll make you a steal of a deal.*'" Connie shook her head, remembering. "Some worked better than others, but they were always flamboyant. Bill took over the store when Big Mike retired ten years ago, but he doesn't do the commercials. Why do you ask?"

"I'm not sure. There's just something about him. He keeps telling me how much I look like my mother."

Connie laughed. "Well, you *do*."

"Yeah, but it's the way he says it, and the way he looks at me. It seems sort of…I don't know…inappropriate."

Her eyebrows pulled together in a look of concern. "Has he done anything?"

"No, nothing like that. It's just weird, that's all."

"Well, have you seen his wife?" She snickered. "It's no wonder he's got a roving eye."

"I thought you liked Sylvia. You said she was nice when you got to know her."

Connie flicked a hand in the air. "I was being charitable. Really, she's kind of a shrew."

I recalled my two brief encounters with the petulant Mrs. Prescott. "I'll say. And a nag. Poor old Bill seems awfully henpecked. Do they have kids? Maybe they stay together for the children."

Connie shook her head. "I'm pretty sure they never had kids. I don't know why they stay together. They must have one of those love/hate relationships."

I shrugged. "Guess it works for them."

After lunch the next day, I headed over to help Maureen get ready for the meeting. The craft fair had been my idea and I was determined to pull it off. I took along a spiral notebook and a pen for taking notes.

Maureen met me at the door.

"I'm having second thoughts," she said, her voice raised to a high, cracked pitch. "What if nobody shows up tonight? What if they all think it's a stupid idea?"

I threw my palms outward in the universal sign for *stop*.

"It'll be fine," I said. "It doesn't matter how many come tonight. I don't expect *everyone* to come. We really only need a few people to get this thing organized. And if no one else comes, it'll be you, me, and Connie. That will be enough. You'll see."

She looked doubtful.

"Come on," I said, "let's sit down and write up an agenda."

At the dining room table, pen poised over paper, I asked, "Okay, what's first?"

"I suppose we should decide on a date."

"Absolutely." I wrote that as item number one.

"We'll need a place to hold it," she said. "Someplace with lots of room."

"Right." I made a note, pleased as her confidence gained momentum. "Connie suggested the grade school gym. Nancy Chumley used to be a teacher. She might be able to look into that for us. What else?"

She tapped her nails on the tabletop. "Um…well, how about advertising? We'll need signs and maybe an ad in the local paper."

"Sure," I said eagerly, "and social media, and maybe even the radio."

She frowned. "How much do you think all this is going to cost? I suppose we'll have to charge a fee to cover expenses."

I rubbed my chin thoughtfully and drummed the pen on the paper. "Which means we'll need a treasurer." I made another notation.

"There's something else," Maureen said, her voice halting, her breath becoming rapid and shallow. "I won't be able to help at the sale itself. You know I don't leave the house." Her face flushed. "I can't bear crowds…"

"I know," I said, hastening to ease her fears. "It's okay. Really. You don't have to. I'll handle a table for both of us." I gave her a conspiratorial smile and added, "I'll bet I can even get Gage to help."

A vertical crease cut into her forehead. "You like Gage, don't you?"

"Sure. He can be nice if he wants to."

She chewed her lip as though searching for words.

Something was bothering her—something beyond her fear of going outside.

"What is it?" I asked.

"It's just that…he's…I mean…there's something…" Her voice trailed off.

"What? What are you trying to say?"

She rubbed a hand over her face. "Never mind. I shouldn't have said anything. Just…be careful. I wouldn't want you to get hurt."

She had my full attention now. What was she intimating?

"I'm going with him tomorrow," I said, "to look at a house he designed on Lake Washington. If there's something I should know, you'd better spill it."

"I'm sorry." She shook her head in a panicky way, giving the impression of a cornered animal. "I didn't mean to say you were in *danger*. Nothing like that. It's just that…he has a past. Something you wouldn't like."

"Like what? Dealing drugs? Human trafficking? Hit man for the mob?" I gave a jittery laugh. "It *can't* be *that* bad."

She waved her hands in the air as though trying to erase what had been said.

"Never mind," she pleaded. "Just forget it. It was…a long time ago."

"Okay." I pressed the pen to the paper again, sketching doodles in the margin. How was I supposed to forget it? Was she actually trying to warn me of something? Should I be concerned? Or was this simply an extension of her illness? Not only did she see her sister's ghost, but she also imagined her brother to be involved in some nefarious activity?

Maureen coughed. "Is there anything else we need to cover at the meeting?"

I looked up and tried to get my brain back on track. "Um, I suppose we'll need tables."

"Maybe the school can supply them," she suggested. "Or we can ask everyone to bring their own."

We made a few more notes, then Maureen stood up and paced in front of the window as though the movement helped to dispel her nerves.

"Shall we go ahead and move these chairs to the living room?" she asked finally. She gripped the back of one of the wooden dining room chairs. "How many do you think we'll need?"

"Let's just move a couple for now," I said. "You have the couch and two chairs in there already. I think, psychologically, it would be better to have to bring in more chairs if we get a crowd than to have a room full of empty chairs if only a few people show up."

She nodded. "Good idea."

"I'd also love to bring that quilt rack into the center of the room, make it a conversation piece. We want to get everyone talking about their projects and ideas. I also want to be sure and point out the beautiful rug you made."

Her face lit up. "I have another smaller rug in the bathroom I can bring out to show."

Her enthusiasm was returning.

"That would be perfect," I said.

"I'll set up the coffee here in the dining room. People can help themselves. You said you'd bring cookies, right?"

"Yep. I'll run up to Brubaker's and get some as soon as we're finished here."

"I'll make some brownies too," said Maureen. "I want to have plenty."

"Sounds good. When Connie gets home, we'll have a quick bite and be here by six forty-five."

Chapter Eleven

Nancy and Oliver Chumley were the first to arrive. Seven o'clock on the dot. Maureen and I met them at the door.

Taking a deep breath, I pasted a welcoming grin on my face. "Come in, come in."

"We wouldn't have missed this," Nancy said. She seemed to embody the very essence of kinetic energy. "We think this craft fair is a wonderful idea. What a great way to see all our neighbors and get everyone involved in the holidays."

"We're so glad you could come," Maureen said.

"Connie's waiting for you in the living room," I said. I had given Connie a copy of the notes Maureen and I had made hoping that between Connie's business acumen and Nancy's enthusiasm, along with their combined knowledge of the area, they'd be able to come up with some great ideas.

Maureen pointed out the refreshments, then directed them to the couch.

Mr. Chumley smiled pleasantly, but let his wife do all the talking. Watching their interaction, I decided this must be their normal *modus operandi*. He appeared to be the complete opposite of his wife. Where she was plump, he was thin; where she exuded fervor, he was reserved; where she had a mass of dark gray-streaked hair, his was pure white and noticeably thin. He shuffled slightly when he walked, whereas Nancy seemed to bustle wherever she went.

Next to arrive were the Prescotts, Bill's enthusiasm and outgoing manner making up for his wife's taciturn petulance.

"Welcome," I said, swinging the door wide.

Bill strode inside with a broad grin on his face. He gave Maureen a friendly nod and called a greeting to Connie and the Chumleys sitting in the living room.

"Nice to see you, Brenna," he said. "You too, Maureen. It's been a while. You look great."

Sylvia turned her shoulder to me and faced Maureen. "Thank you for inviting us," she said politely. Then she minced her way into the other room and took a seat in one of the wooden chairs.

What's her problem? I thought. I barely knew the woman, yet she acted like I had stomped on her flowers and kicked her puppy. Was she actually jealous of her husband's attentions to me? How could she possibly think I had any interest in him? The idea was ludicrous, *unless he's shown a predilection for younger women in the past*. I would have to be careful in my dealings with him. I certainly didn't want him getting any ideas.

Three more neighbors arrived in quick succession, middle-aged women whom I had not met, but who were obviously known to the others. I hurried to fetch more chairs from the dining room.

When the doorbell rang again, I had my hands full moving chairs so Maureen ran to answer it. I turned in time to see her welcome a lean, dark-haired man with two little girls in tow.

"Hi. I'm Nick Donato," he announced as he shook Maureen's hand. "I live in the yellow house across the street. Hope you don't mind, I had to bring the girls."

I felt a twinge of concern upon seeing the two children, afraid their presence might trigger one of Maureen's paranoid episodes, but she welcomed them warmly and seemed perfectly at ease.

"That's quite all right," Maureen said with a beaming smile. "They're lovely girls. I've seen them from my window playing in your yard. I'm Maureen. Please, come in." She turned to the sisters. "Are you interested in the craft fair?"

The girls looked up shyly. They both had short, dark, curly hair, and bore no resemblance to Hannah whatsoever. The way Maureen gave them her attention, it was obvious she was taken with them.

"They are," Nick said, gazing proudly at his daughters. "This is Carly and this is Gina. They're in the Girl Scouts, and they've been learning to make all sorts of crafts. They brought a few things to show you." He held up a large paper bag.

"Wonderful," Maureen said, clapping her hands together. "I can't wait to see what you've made."

I strolled over to join them and said, "Maureen, why don't you and Nick go find seats in the living room while the girls and I go check out the cookies. You and Connie can get things started."

The girls grinned and looked expectantly at their father.

"Okay," said Nick. He gave them each a pointed look. "Just one." Then he went with Maureen into the living room where he was met with a salvo of noisy greetings. He seemed to be a neighborhood favorite. He took a chair next to Maureen near the fireplace.

I motioned Carly and Gina to follow me into the dining room. I couldn't pass up this opportunity to ask if they knew a girl in the neighborhood who wore blond pigtails. Gina appeared to be about the same age. If Hannah had a look-alike living nearby, these girls would surely know her.

The boisterous voices in the living room created the perfect cover for my questions. I leaned toward the younger girl as she scrutinized the plates of cookies. "Hey, Gina, I've been seeing a little girl around here about your age. She has blond hair and wears it in two braids. I was wondering if you knew who she was?"

Gina looked up and gave her head a shake.

"Could be Lexie Nash," said Carly. "She lives a couple streets over in the cul-de-sac."

"No," Gina said. "Lexie's in my class. Her hair is *red* and she wears two ponytails, not braids." She giggled. "They stick out from her head like dog ears."

"Emily Locke has blond hair," said Carly. "But she only wears one braid down her back, and she doesn't live in this neighborhood."

Suddenly, Connie hollered, "Hey, Brenna, let's get started. We don't want to be here all night."

"Coming," I called back. Turning to the girls, I said, "Oh well, thanks anyway. Now grab a cookie and let's go join the meeting."

Carly and Gina delighted everyone with the colorful Christmas tree ornaments they had made with flour and salt dough, cookie cutters, and bright acrylic paints. I knew they would be a huge success at the holiday craft fair. Once customers got a look at these girls' happy, eager faces, they'd never be able to resist.

Everyone wanted to talk about their own creations. One of the women brought beaded jewelry she had made, laying the necklaces out on the coffee table where the strings of crystals and semi-precious stones reflected the light like tiny shimmering rainbows, prompting an admiring chorus of *oohs* and *ahhs*. Another boasted her skills as a seamstress, announcing her intention to make aprons and pot holders to sell. Nancy Chumley talked up her candles, and Bill Prescott described his plans to build birdhouses, rocking horses, and various other wooden toys.

"Well, I can't sew or paint," said Connie. "But I can bake. I'm going to make a mountain of gingerbread cookies and maybe some small loaves of pumpkin and banana bread."

Bill turned to me then, his dark eyes brimming with eager curiosity. "Brenna, what are you planning to make?"

I ignored the needles shooting from his wife's eyes as I took the opportunity to brag about Maureen's artistic talents. "I've never been very crafty, so Maureen's going to help me. Take a look at the quilt laid over the back of the couch. She made it, and all these other quilts." I gestured at the rack that stood to one side of the coffee table. "Aren't they gorgeous?"

Connie stood and grabbed one off the rack and began to unfold it. Nancy joined her and between them they held it up for all to see.

Nick Donato turned to Maureen with genuine admiration. "Wow. Those are beautiful. You're really talented. My grandmother used to make quilts, but they were never this nice."

Maureen blushed, and demurred modestly. She had been sewing these stunning creations for years without acknowledgement, and now she was almost overcome by the fervent praise.

"And check out the rug," I continued. "Braided from strips of cloth. She made it too. I just love how the colors blend so well. Maureen's going to show me how to do it, and hopefully, I'll have a couple of small ones done in time for the fair."

Carly and Gina, who had been sitting on the rug, immediately bent to examine it closer. "Are they hard to make?" Carly asked.

Maureen smiled. "No, it's really just braiding. Once you get the hang of it, it's pretty easy. I think you girls could learn how to do this. Here's one I made for the bathroom." She held up a small mat plaited with strips of cloth in various shades of blue, green, and cream.

The girls' father tilted his head and gave Maureen a thoughtful gaze. "Do you think you could teach them? I know they'd love to learn how."

Both girls turned their eager faces to Maureen and nodded vigorously, bouncing on their knees. "Please,

please, please," they begged in unison.

There's no turning down that kind of entreaty, I thought.

"I think that can be arranged," said Maureen. Her smile implied that she would love to. "But now, I think we'd better get on with the meeting. Brenna and I made up a sort of agenda. There are lots of things we need to discuss if we're going to get this thing off the ground."

"School night," said Nick. The sternness in his voice was tempered with a wink to his daughters which sent them into a paroxysm of giggles.

Those girls are so lucky to have a father like Nick, I thought wistfully. If only I could have known my own. Over the years, I had fashioned in my head a sort of inflated image of my father resembling something akin to a cross between Superman and Gandhi.

Connie was already in the kitchen the next morning by the time I made an appearance. I was dressed in my shorts and running shoes as usual, ready to go out and work up a sweat. Buster lay on his rug by the back door. His tail thumped solidly on the floor when I entered the room.

"Good morning," Connie said. "Would you like some toast? There's yogurt, blueberries, and granola on the table. Help yourself. I also made coffee."

"I shouldn't," I said. "I must have put away half a dozen cookies at the meeting last night."

Connie lifted an eyebrow as she studied my running outfit. "Well, don't you need carbs to give you energy for all that jogging you do?"

I grimaced. "Ordinarily, yes. But I ate more than

enough carbs last night to keep me going for a week."

"Well, you need protein too. Have some yogurt."

"Yes, mother." I took a piece of toast and sat down, then spooned some yogurt into a bowl and topped it with a sprinkle of granola and blueberries. I had to admit, it tasted pretty good. "Now I'll have to run an extra mile."

She flapped a hand at me. "Oh, quit complaining."

"By the way," I said, changing the subject, "I don't remember if I told you. I'm going with Gage this afternoon to look at a house he designed over on Mercer Island somewhere."

She swallowed a mouthful of toast and looked up, her eyes bright with interest. "No, this is the first I've heard of it. When did this happen?"

"The other night when I ran into him at Brubaker's. The night the cooler quit working at the flower shop. I told you, we went over to Frankie's and had pizza."

"And now you're spending the day with him? That was quick."

She sounds just like Tamara. Why is everyone so eager to see me dating?

I frowned. "It's not a *date*. I told him I was interested in seeing one of the houses he designed. He was going there anyway and asked if I'd like to tag along. It just seemed like a good way to pass the time."

"Whatever," she said, licking yogurt off her spoon. "You don't have to explain. You can do anything you want."

"I just wanted you to know where I was…" My voice faltered. Unbidden, Maureen's veiled warning rose in the back of my mind: *I wouldn't want you to get hurt…he has a past…something you wouldn't like.* I cleared my throat and finished, "You know, in case we get back late, so you don't worry."

Connie looked at me curiously. "I assume you'll have your phone with you."

I laughed, feeling foolish. "Of course. I can always text you."

Gulping the last of her coffee, Connie stood and carried her dishes to the sink. She rinsed them and put them in the dishwasher. "I'd better get going," she said. "Have fun today, and don't worry if it gets late. Just let me know."

When I stood, Buster took it as his signal to leap up and check around my chair for fallen food. His super-adept hound's nose made loud snuffling noises.

"Buster," I said, giving him a lopsided frown, "you could give a person a complex. Am I really that big a slob?"

Connie laughed. "Don't take it personally. He's got you confused with Nancy Chumley. Every time she visits, she leaves a real mess on the floor around her chair. I love the woman but she talks with her mouth full, and when she stands up food practically cascades off her lap."

I grimaced as I watched the little beagle sniff around under the table, licking up the occasional stray crumb. "I guess with Buster on clean-up duty, you don't have to mop the floor as often."

"Now, if only I could get him to wash windows."

"By the way," I said, "will he be okay in the house if I'm gone all day? I'm not sure exactly when Gage is coming, but he said some time before lunch. That leaves Buster here alone all afternoon."

"Put him in the back yard when you leave. He'll be

fine. It's a beautiful day."

I hesitated, remembering a few days ago when he had dug out under the fence. I hadn't told Connie about that.

"What if he gets out of the yard?"

She gave her glasses a little adjustment on her nose as she considered. "Usually, he's fine. I leave him out there all the time. He only starts digging when he gets really bored, or if something attracts him on the other side of the fence."

"I'd hate for him to get lost or hit by a car."

Connie pondered for a moment, then her face lit up. "Why don't you take him jogging with you? The fresh air and exercise will get him so worn out he'll probably sleep all afternoon."

I nodded. "Good idea—and it's always nice to have a running partner. Right, Buster?"

Hearing his name, the dog trotted over for a quick ear rub. I attached the leash to his collar, secured my house keys and phone in my running belt, then headed for the front door. Connie grabbed her car keys and followed us out.

I plugged in my earbuds and started my favorite mix of running tunes, a compilation of lyric alternative rock, infused with a bit of Celtic flavor. Setting off down the street, I passed the Chumley house and gave a quick wave to Bill Prescott who had come out to pick up his paper. This time I didn't stop. I did not want to establish a pattern of halting every morning to chat. The last thing I wanted was to encourage him, especially since his wife already seemed to dislike me.

In the eastern sky, the sun was dazzling, promising another glorious autumn day. Fat little birds and lissome gray squirrels stirred in the tree branches overhead. Crowds of leaves whispered among themselves, quivering agitatedly when disturbed by passing breezes. I could hardly believe I had once been content to live surrounded by pavement, breathing air polluted by smog and diesel fumes with concrete edifices rising like soulless barricades between me and all things green and living.

Buster kept pace beside me. He seemed to enjoy the run. His eyes were alert, his mouth parted, showing just the tip of his pink tongue flicking in and out rhythmically as he breathed.

I settled into a comfortable pace. Distractions faded and my mind drifted to the previous night's meeting. Not counting Sylvia Prescott's snooty attitude, I thought it had been a great success. Everyone had seemed eager to help.

By the time we adjourned, the consensus had been to hold the craft fair on the first Saturday in December. Connie had been voted chairperson and Maureen treasurer. I had consented to handle advertising, and Nancy Chumley had agreed to be in charge of reserving a venue. After all her years working for the school district, she felt certain she could secure the gym at the elementary school down the street.

I ran four blocks and turned left intending to run at least another four blocks in that direction, but I noticed that Buster was beginning to lag and his tongue now lolled out the side of his mouth. Instead I turned left again after one block and headed back. By the time we turned onto our street, he was noticeably panting and had dropped back to the end of his leash.

Slowing to a walk, I smiled sympathetically at the chubby canine. "You are sadly out of shape Buster ol' pal.

It wouldn't hurt you to knock off a pound or two."

He barely had the energy to wag his tail.

"But it looks like mission accomplished. You should be too worn out to go gallivanting around the neighborhood now."

The expression in his deep brown eyes was inscrutable.

When we got to the house, I put him on the back porch with a full bowl of fresh water, then hurried to shower and change. I put on a pair of slim blue jeans and my favorite pink blouse, then brushed my hair till it was smooth and glossy, letting it fall in loose curls around my shoulders.

Gage would be here any minute. I felt my pulse quicken and was immediately consumed by a wave of guilt. *How could you? What about Jason? Have you forgotten him already?*

But Gage is just an old friend. Nothing more. There's nothing wrong with spending time with an old friend.

I picked up the small framed picture I kept on my nightstand and gazed at Jason's familiar, smiling face.

"It's been two years, my love," I whispered, caressing his features with my finger. I was young and had many years ahead. I inhaled deeply and exhaled. I knew in my heart that he would want me to move on, to have a life. *Like Mom,* I reminded myself. *She remarried and couldn't be happier.*

I fingered my wedding ring. Tamara had suggested I wear it on a chain around my neck like a pendant. It sounded like a good idea; the ring would hang close to my heart. Maybe someday I would, but not yet. I wasn't ready. I needed just a little more time.

Chapter Twelve

Gage texted at eleven thirty to say he'd be here in five minutes. The day was warm but I grabbed my jacket just in case. In Seattle one never knew when the weather might change, and this morning I had seen some dark clouds hovering on the western horizon. I went to the back door and did one more precautionary check on the beagle lying recumbent on the porch. The sleek patch of black fur covering his rib cage moved ever so slightly up and down as he slept. Occasionally, a back foot twitched and I imagined him chasing rabbits in his dreams.

Good. He should be out for the rest of the afternoon.

Moments later, I heard Gage's SUV pull up in front of the house. I hurried to head him off at the front porch, afraid the doorbell might rouse the sleeping dog.

"Ready to go?" he said. He led the way and opened the front passenger door for me.

His relaxed, upbeat expression made me glad I had agreed to come along. It was nice to see him without the frown and deep brooding lines that often marred his features. Today, in fact, his mood seemed exceptionally agreeable, while his tall frame and square shoulders filled out his blue shirt and gray sports jacket in a way that made me catch my breath.

He headed the car east, making his way to the freeway, then south through Seattle to the bridge across Lake Washington and onto Mercer Island. Situated in the southern half of the lake, Mercer Island is home to many old, well-to-do families, as well as a number of CEOs, sports celebrities, and nouveaux riches who have sprung from the hotbed of Seattle's flourishing software industry.

"Are you hungry?" Gage asked. "I know a place that makes killer sandwiches and homemade soup."

My stomach growled in answer. It seemed like ages since my toast and yogurt that morning.

"I could eat," I said, trying not to sound too eager.

He pulled off on Island Crest Way and after a series of turns, pulled into a strip of small businesses, parking in front of a hole-in-the-wall café called *Nosh This*. The interior smelled of warm bread and fresh herbs. My mouth began to water, and for a moment I wondered if it would be rude to ask for one of the enormous chocolate chip cookies displayed under the glass counter.

A hostess handed us menus and told us to sit anywhere. She wore a yellow t-shirt with the name of the restaurant silk-screened on the front. I noticed a pile of similar t-shirts for sale on the counter by the cash register. A clever advertising ploy.

The café was overtly funky, decorated with an eclectic

assortment of posters, neon lights, and mismatched odds and ends that could only have been salvaged from a flea market. The pulsing beat of Jamaican reggae playing in the background created an atmosphere of vital energy. Overall, the café had a trendy vibe, and judging by the crowd, was a favorite local hangout.

We took a table by the wall underneath a winged gargoyle that eyed us from a perch inside an old Victorian birdcage. I ordered the house specialty: grilled cheese on sourdough with a bowl of homemade tomato basil soup. Gage chose the barbequed pulled pork with coleslaw.

"How did you ever find this place?" I asked.

"A friend recommended it. When he heard I was working on Mercer Island, he said I had to try it."

I gazed around, taking in the other customers attired mostly in t-shirts, jeans, and baseball caps. "Somehow, I wouldn't have pictured you in a place like this."

He coughed and primly straightened his cuffs, but the corners of his mouth betrayed a hint of amusement. "Why's that?"

"Oh, I don't know." I looked at the way his perfect hair was meticulously combed in a fashionable sweep above his brow and his gray herringbone sport coat, tailored blue shirt, and crisply pressed slacks conveyed an air of urbanity. "Somehow, a posh gentleman such as yourself seems out of place in an artsy dive like this."

His eyebrows lifted slightly. "Are you calling me *stodgy?*"

I smothered a giggle. "No, not stodgy. Let's say...sophisticated."

"*Stuffy?*"

I was barely able to contain my laughter. "How about

conservative?"

"So," he said with an affected look of affront, "what you're saying is that I'm not quirky enough to patronize a cool, happening establishment like this."

"Well, look at you." I leaned over and gestured with my open palm in front of him like a game show hostess. "All coifed and buttoned-up. Now look around. What's wrong with this picture?"

He huffed and gave his coat a tug. "I'll have you know, I can be quirky if I want to. Why, I once wore a purple paisley tie with a tangerine-colored shirt."

"Scandalous."

"It was a birthday gift from Maureen. I think it may have been her first attempt at online shopping. Her taste is questionable."

I tapped the table thoughtfully with one finger. "Still…it *was* a tie, purple paisley or not, so I'm not sure it counts."

He fingered the collar of his shirt. "I'm not wearing a tie today. I must get points for that."

I gave him another once-over. "Quirky or not, you look great…for a donkey face."

His mouth pulled sideways and he let out a short, fractious grunt.

The waitress arrived with our sandwiches and we dug in with relish. As expected, the food was delicious and we tabled our debate in favor of chowing down.

Half an hour later, we were back in the car heading south. Gage followed a bluff along the island's west side overlooking the water. The usual fir, cedar, and big-leaf maple mingled with madronas, dogwoods, and rhododendrons to give the area a shady, forested look.

Interspersed were driveways leading to expansive homes on the hill above the lake.

Gage turned into one of these and parked the SUV in front of a luxurious, contemporary house clad in cedar and natural stone. Rather than lawn, the grounds resembled a naturalized park full of native plants, with granite boulders situated artfully among clumps of fern, huckleberry, flowering currant, and salal. I loved how the building seemed to merge with its environment.

"Wow," I breathed, gaping at the sprawling structure. "You designed this?"

"Yeah. Come on, I'll give you a tour." He jumped out of the vehicle and came around to my side.

As I slid out of the seat, I suddenly froze and put a finger to my lips. "Look," I whispered, pointing. Two black-tailed deer had emerged from the woods and stepped into a sunlit clearing near the corner of the house. Their tawny coats were perfectly accentuated by the contrasting hues and textures of the wild flora around them. I had seen deer on camping trips, but never so close; there was something spellbinding in the graceful way they moved.

Holding my breath, I reached slowly into my pocket for my phone, easing it out so as not to startle the deer. The larger of the two, a buck with a striking set of forked antlers, paused and stared in our direction; his ears swiveled back and forth like radar antennae. Quickly, I centered them in the frame and snapped a photo, then another as they sprang away and disappeared into a thick copse of vine maple at the edge of the property.

Gage looked over my shoulder at the pictures and gave a murmur of approval. "Nice," he said. "You have a good eye."

As he leaned in, I caught a whiff of his cologne. My senses heightened and I became acutely aware of the closeness of his body. Giving a little cough, I stepped away.

"Could you send those to me?" he said. "I'd like to add the pictures to my website, plus I've been keeping a separate online journal of this project."

He's proud of this house, I thought. From what I'd seen so far, he had every right to be.

"Sure." Then I raised my phone again, hoping to capture the aesthetic features of the building and the picturesque way it blended with the surroundings. "Stand over there," I said, "so I can get a picture of you in front of the house."

"What, and break your phone?"

I made a face. "Just do it. It'll look good on your website."

"You know, if you wanted a pin-up, all you had to do was ask."

Same old donkey face, I thought, cuffing him on the shoulder. Hope he didn't bring his water pistol.

He grinned but complied without further argument. Once I'd taken the picture and returned the phone to my pocket, he produced his own.

"My turn," he said.

I was going to object, but thought again. If I didn't pose for a picture now, he would undoubtedly sneak up on me and snap a candid shot when I wasn't ready. I could just envision him capturing me with one eye closed and my mouth all wonky, looking half drunk. So I leaned against the car and gave him a cheesy smile.

Pictures out of the way, he turned and led me up a curving path laid with stone pavers past a mossy fountain created to resemble a mountain stream burbling over layers of rough-cut basalt. One step up led to a wide aggregate concrete porch and a double front door inlaid with beveled glass.

Inside, a flagstone foyer joined a spacious great room which was cantilevered over the edge of a steeply plunging bank. Floor-to-ceiling windows running the full length of the wall offered a dizzying view of the Seattle skyline above the shimmering lake. To the left rose a staircase with near-invisible glass risers and balustrades, obviously devised so as not to interfere with the view.

To the right and up a step stretched an airy galley-style kitchen, sleek and modern, with natural stone countertops polished to a high gloss. No wall impeded the view from the kitchen; instead, the work space was separated from the great room by a lengthy island, the raised floor serving to enhance the feeling of panorama. Cherry cabinets and stainless steel appliances completed the elegant layout.

For a moment, I just stood with my mouth open taking it all in. The house even had that indefinable *new* smell, like fresh paint and varnish. I wondered which Seattle millionaire had contracted to have this home built. It occurred to me that Gage must have been responsible for the stylish remodel of the old farmhouse where he grew up and where his sister still lived.

I was so engrossed in gazing around at the house's stately architecture that I jumped when Gage called out.

"Hey, Bert," he said. "How's it going? Almost finished?"

I turned and noticed a man in white coveralls

approaching from a hallway that led off to the right beyond the kitchen.

"Yep," replied the man. "Just finished up the tile in the master bath. Once I hang the mirror and towel bars, it'll be finished. Deb's upstairs painting the bedrooms."

"Excellent," said Gage. He turned to me. "Come on, Brenna. Let me show you the rest of the house."

The hallway to the right of the great room led to a master suite that could only be described as palatial. The vaulted ceiling and generous use of glass expanded the feeling of limitless space. A semi-circular sitting room extended beyond the rocky cliff and gave the illusion of being suspended in mid-air. At the window, I experienced a moment of giddiness as I gazed out over the steep drop.

An engineering feat of steel beams and concrete, I thought, marveling at the ingenuity behind the design.

The massive closet was as big as my whole bedroom at Connie's and included a built-in dressing table and a wall of cubbies for shoes. *A woman's closet.* And I used to think my condo was chic.

I couldn't wait to see the bathroom.

Not surprisingly, it was enormous and resembled something you might find in a European resort spa with heated marble floors, Olympic-size soaking tub, double sinks, and a walk-in shower large enough to park a Cessna.

"Impressive," I said, raising an eyebrow in Gage's direction.

He didn't reply, but the turned up corners of his mouth told me he was pleased. I returned the smile. It was nice seeing him like this, in his element, confident and relaxed. He swept his hand around to indicate an archway leading to a passage beyond the bedroom.

"Through there are an exercise room and a study," he said.

Of course there are.

After ogling the rest of the master suite, I followed Gage back to the main part of the house where we ascended the glass stairs to a mezzanine overlooking the great room. Each step up the see-through staircase gave me the weirdest feeling of climbing on air. Yet I had to smile: despite its awesomeness, all I could think of was what a pain it would be to keep clean.

The second floor extended over a three-car garage and contained a media center and two more bedrooms with full en suite bathrooms. My admiration for Gage's talent increased incrementally with each room.

"This house is amazing," I said as we descended once more to the main level. "I can't believe you designed it."

"Not bad for a donkey face," he said with a modest chuckle.

I grinned. "Not bad at all. Your parents must be very proud."

His expression sobered as he gave a derisive snort. "You'd think, wouldn't you?" He turned his face toward the window, tightening his jaw.

I regretted the somber turn in his mood. I had meant to give him a compliment. Instead, I had hit a sore spot.

"They live so far away," I said, hoping to correct my misstep. "They probably just don't realize…" My words petered out as he shook his head.

He turned again to face me. "Oh, they know all right. I've sent letters and pictures, and a link to my website showing details of all my projects. But no, they've never thought of me as anything but a screw-up. Once a screw-up, always a screw-up. My stepdad and I have butted heads for as far back as I can remember. Hannah was his child and the only one he gave a damn about. I can go hang for all he cares."

"But what about your mother? She must—"

He made a scoffing sound. "She always takes his side. But thinking back, I know I wasn't the easiest kid to handle. And after Hannah…I didn't make things any easier."

"Yeah, but still…"

He shrugged and ran a hand briskly through his hair. "Look, I'm sorry. I don't usually dump on my friends like this." He narrowed his eyes and cracked a smile. "There's just something about you…"

I tilted my head and peered at him through my lashes. "It's my irresistible charm."

With a quick laugh, he changed the subject. "Why don't you head on outside and admire the view while I have a few words with the contractors. I'll join you in a minute."

I stepped onto the porch and took a moment to text the pictures I'd taken to Gage. Just as I finished, the phone erupted with the sound of a crowing rooster.

It was Connie: *Buster is sick. I'm at the vet.*

I glanced at the time: 2:57

I texted back: *Poor puppy. Anything I can do?*

Make dinner? I may be late.

No problem.

That's when I remembered I'd left Buster outside in the back yard. Had he dug out under the fence again and gotten into something he shouldn't have? I thought of the fertilizer and pesticides Nancy Chumley put on her roses and Nick Donato's garage full of paint cans, motor oil, and anti-freeze. I knew he often left his garage door open.

I held my lower lip in my teeth as I texted again: *What's wrong with him?*

Gage appeared beside me on the porch. "All set," he said. "Come on, let me show you the view of the lake."

I didn't answer. I was staring at Connie's next words.

Gage closed his fingers over mine, steadying my trembling hand. "What's wrong?" he asked.

"I have to get home. Connie says her dog was poisoned."

Chapter Thirteen

"Strychnine," Connie ranted. "Rat poison. Who would do that to a sweet, innocent little dog?" She had been sitting on the edge of the couch. Now she stood and began to pace. "Thank God I came home early and found him in time. The vet said if I had been any later, it would probably have been too late."

"Why *did* you come home early?" I asked. It wasn't like Connie to leave her shop two hours early on a Friday afternoon, normally her busiest time.

She stopped pacing and stared straight ahead, mouth open, as though working to recall some detail just out of reach. The creases deepened in her forehead.

"It's the strangest thing," she said. "I don't know. I don't remember why. It just—for some reason—seemed really important that I get home. It was like I *knew* Buster needed me." She scrunched up her face. "I know that sounds crazy."

I shook my head. "Not at all. You raised Buster from a tiny pup. You have a...a psychic connection. It's not strange at all that you knew he was in trouble."

Inwardly, I grimaced. *No stranger than seeing a ghost.* In that moment, I was startled to realize I had finally come to terms with accepting the ghost. In a way, it was a relief.

Connie blew out a heated breath. "But who gave him the poison in the first place?"

"How do you know someone gave it to him?" I asked. "You found him on the front porch, right? That means he got out of the back yard again. Someone might have put rat poison under their porch or in their garage where he could easily have found it. It was probably nothing more than a tragic accident."

She shook her head fiercely. "No. Someone gave it to him in a piece of meat. When I found him he was stiff and trembling, on the verge of convulsions. Then he coughed up a piece of raw meat—looked like liver. You *know* all I ever feed him is dry dog food and occasional table scraps. I *never* give him raw meat, *especially* liver. I hate the stuff. I'd never have it in the house. When I called the vet, she said to bring it in so she could test it." Connie clenched her fists, her eyes filling with tears. "It was full of poison."

I pulled her into a hug. I knew Connie loved Buster, but I realized suddenly that the little beagle was more than simply a pet. He was her family, her child. The thought that someone, possibly a neighbor she knew, had purposely tried to kill him was inconceivable.

After a moment, she sniffed and pulled away, removing her glasses to wipe her eyes on her sleeve. "I'm okay," she said. "The vet thinks I got him there in time.

They pumped his stomach and gave him activated charcoal to neutralize the poison. She said there's still a risk of kidney failure so they're going to keep him for a few days to watch him."

"Why don't you go rest while I make dinner," I said. "You look like you're done in."

"Thanks. I need to check in with Jerry. I sort of left him in the lurch. He's my sometimes delivery guy. He doesn't usually handle the counter, but I didn't have any other choice. I'm just glad he was there. Then I think I'll take a quick shower."

She disappeared down the hall and I set about cutting up veggies for a dinner salad. I topped it with cheese, hard-boiled egg, and slices of cold chicken. The evening was sultry—too warm to heat up the stove.

After a dinner made glum by the absence of the perky beagle underfoot, Connie took a book and retired to her room. She claimed she wouldn't be fit company.

I took advantage of the solitude and strolled out onto the front porch to think. It was still an hour before sunset but the sky was dark with the threat of rain. I ran my hands along the top of the railing, feeling the smooth, hard surface of the wood. Despite the warmth of the evening, I shivered and wrapped my arms tightly around myself, wondering if we might have a thunderstorm.

Up and down the street, the neighborhood was ominously still. Lights winked through windows in dwellings snug behind bulwarks of shrubs and fences. It was as though they hunkered down for a long dismal night.

A movement caught my eye and I turned my head with trepidation, bracing myself against the sturdy porch railing. The little girl stood motionless in the yard, gazing at me in her perpetual pink jacket and long braids. I took a deep gulp of air to steady the sudden quaking of my heart.

"Hannah," I murmured. My knuckles turned white as I tightened my grip on the railing. I fought to control the cold knot twisting in my stomach.

The ghost's arms hung at her sides as her eyes caught and held mine. She didn't speak but I understood her question.

I swallowed, then managed to croak, "Buster's okay. Connie found him in time. He's at the vet's, but it looks like he'll pull through."

A glimmer of a smile lit Hannah's face.

"It was you, wasn't it?" I said. "You somehow put it into Connie's head that Buster was in trouble and she needed to come home."

Hannah just looked at me but her consciousness nudged the edges of my mind, and her feelings, intangible as smoke, came across without words.

"You saved his life," I said.

I wanted to say more, to ask questions—*was I actually conversing with a ghost?*—but a sudden scream, followed by angry voices, erupted from the Moreland house next door. I looked over and saw Gage's SUV parked in the driveway. After dropping me off, he must have stayed to have dinner with his sister.

Oh, my god, I thought. *It's Friday night.* Gage was going to tell Maureen that Andy Brubaker wouldn't be coming anymore. Gage must have decided to go ahead without me. Sounded like Maureen had taken it pretty hard.

Not surprisingly, the commotion caused Hannah's

ghost to vanish. *Probably doesn't like the sound of her siblings fighting.*

A moment later, Gage burst out the front door and headed for his car. Raindrops had begun to splatter on the dusty ground.

"Gage!" I called. I wasn't sure what to say. I just didn't think he should leave Maureen alone in that state.

He glanced up and saw me. Leaning his elbows against the hood of the SUV, he dropped his head in his hands. He stood that way, unmoving, for the space of a breath, as though willing his body to relax while the rain picked up around him. Finally, he raised his head.

"Brenna," he called in a voice wrung with tension, "would you mind coming over and talking to Maureen for a few minutes? I just can't deal with her right now. Tell her I'll be back in the morning."

"I'll be right over." I stuck my head inside the door and hollered at Connie: "I'm going next door for a minute."

I heard her mumble something in answer, then I closed the door again and trotted down the steps, ignoring the pelting rain.

Gage was still standing by his car when I reached him in the driveway. He made a sort of apologetic grimace, running a hand over his hair to brush away the droplets that were fast accumulating. "How's the dog?" he asked. "Is he okay?"

"So far," I said. The shower was increasing and I regretted not taking a moment to grab my coat. "The vet pumped his stomach and they're keeping him for observation, but there's a good chance he'll recover."

"Good. Glad to hear it." He fumbled in his pocket for

his car keys. "Thanks for coming over. You needn't stay long. Just till Maureen calms down."

"I'll talk to her. She'll be fine. I'd better get inside before I get drenched."

A sudden flash against the dark clouds punctuated my statement. It was followed shortly by a resounding boom.

"Looks like we're in for a storm." Gage jerked open the car door and jumped inside. "Thanks again," he yelled. "I'll make it up to you."

I turned and ran for Maureen's front porch, anxious to get out of the driving downpour. Maureen answered the door the instant I knocked and I wondered if she'd been watching from the window.

"Yikes! What a change in the weather," I exclaimed, pushing damp tendrils of hair away from my face. My shoes were wet, so I kicked them off just inside the door.

Maureen stood with her fingers clenched. Her thin face was pale and wracked with anxiety. "I saw her just now, Brenna. I *swear* I did. Gage refuses to believe me. But it was Hannah. I *know* it was. Right in front of your house. Did you see her?" Her tortured face was pleading. "You *must* have seen her."

Nothing about Andy. This was not what I expected. I took hold of her hands, I could feel them shaking.

"I did," I said in a soft voice. "I saw her too."

Maureen stared, eyes wide.

"I talked to her," I continued. "She's real."

Her hands flew to cover her mouth and for a moment I feared she might collapse. I took her by the elbow and supported her to the living room where we settled side by side on the couch. Her breath came in quavering gulps.

"You're not just humoring me, are you?" she managed

to whisper at last. "Please be honest. I couldn't stand it if you were coddling me." Her eyes flashed anger for a brief instant. "I know Gage sent you in here to calm me down."

I shook my head. "I'm not coddling you. I really did see Hannah. In fact, I've seen her several times. It's kind of unnerving." An understatement.

Maureen reached over and put a hand on my arm. "I *know*. Sometimes I'll just be gazing out at the back yard and thinking how she liked to pick dandelions, and the next thing I know she's standing out there staring at me." She shivered.

"But she wasn't threatening," I hurried to reassure her. "All I felt was compassion. She just wanted to know how Connie's dog was doing."

Maureen's manner shifted immediately to concern. "Gage told me he was sick."

"The vet thinks he was poisoned."

She gasped. "*Poisoned?* That's terrible."

"Luckily, Connie found him in time and got him to the vet. It looks like he's going to be okay—thanks to Hannah."

"What? Thanks to *Hannah?* How?" A sharp crease etched between her brows.

"I don't know exactly," I said. "But I think, somehow, Hannah put the thought into Connie's head—like a *compulsion*—that she had to come home early from work, that Buster needed her."

Maureen smiled wistfully and pressed her hands together. "Hannah always loved animals. She could never stand to see one hurt."

"I actually saw her playing once with Buster in the back yard. She's so sweet. Just like I remember." I hesitated. "You know, she's never acted menacing. I'm sure you don't have anything to fear from her."

She dropped her gaze, picking nervously at a fingernail. "Gage thinks I'm crazy. So does Andy Brubaker. And so do all the hordes of doctors and therapists Gage has sicced on me. They can't see her. You're the only one besides me who believes she's real."

"Well," I said, "it seems sort of reasonable, doesn't it, that we can see her and they can't? I mean, you're her big sister and I was her best friend. She has a connection to both of us...a bond of love."

Maureen nodded, her face taking on a tight, resentful look. "They almost had me convinced I was insane."

"What I *don't* get," I continued, "is why Gage can't see her. He ought to have a connection with her too. I know he loved her."

Maureen pulled in a ragged breath and blew it out again.

"I *know* why," she stated in a low, flat voice. She turned away and stared into the cold fireplace. Outside, the rain could be heard pelting the shrubs and asphalted driveway.

I waited for her to go on, fully expecting her to say something about Gage's pragmatic attitude, his unwillingness to succumb to what he undoubtedly considered paranormal hogwash born of his sister's hysterical psychoses. All things considered, it made perfect sense. He didn't believe in ghosts—*wouldn't* believe. With such a mental blockade in place, it was no wonder Hannah's ethereal essence couldn't get through.

Guess this shows how open-minded I am. I found this curiously pleasing.

Siblings and Secrets

When Maureen didn't speak after several seconds, I urged her to continue. "Go on. Why do you think he can't see her?"

Raising her head, she gave me a searching look. "If I tell you, you have to *promise* me you won't tell anyone. No matter what. Swear it."

How bad could it be? "I promise."

"No matter what I tell you," she persisted, "you must *promise* not to repeat it to *anyone*."

I frowned. "I promise I won't tell anyone."

She held me in her gaze for a moment, obviously torn. Finally, she took a deep breath and whispered, "Gage can't see Hannah because he's the one who killed her."

I reared back. "*What?*"

She looked down at her lap again. "He killed her. I saw him bury her in the woods. When I confronted him, he admitted it."

I couldn't breathe. Invisible hands encircled my throat threatening to strangle me. Blood rushed in my ears like the roar of a locomotive.

"No," I finally managed to croak. There had to be a mistake.

"I haven't told another soul in twenty-five years," Maureen murmured.

I shook my head, unable to wrap my mind around this staggering revelation. My heart hammered wildly. All I could do was stammer like an idiot. "That...that...*can't* be true. Are you...are you *sure?* I mean...*how?* He...he *wouldn't*..."

"Do you think I would make up something like this?" she snapped.

"No, no, of course not, but..."

"And that's why Hannah haunts me," she said bitterly, "because I never told and she's still lying out there in an unmarked grave, cold and alone, grown over with brambles." She smothered her face in her hands; her shoulders gave a great shudder as she began to sob.

I sat stone still, feeling helpless. Now that I knew the truth, I could never *un*know it. How would I ever be able to look at Gage again?

I took a deep breath. What should I say? How could I comfort her?

She raised her head, wiping the tears away. Her eyes were red and swollen. In a barely audible whisper, she said, "Hannah will never have peace, never have justice."

My brain felt like it might explode. I sat there dumbly twisting my fingers as I tried to come up with the right words to say. Finally, I asked, "So, what happened? Was it an accident?"

She nodded. "Gage said he hit her with a motorcycle. He was going too fast and couldn't stop in time."

My eyes widened. "*Oh, my god.*"

She continued. "One of his friends had gotten a dirt bike for his birthday and was showing it off. All the boys were taking turns riding it. Gage said Hannah just came out of the woods and stopped in the middle of the road."

The mental image made my stomach lurch. "Right here on the street in front of your house?"

She sniffed loudly and wiped at her eyes. "No, no—a couple of streets over, on the other side of the woods. The road was closed for construction and no one else was around. There's an apartment building there now, but at the time there was just an old boarded up house and a hill where all the boys used to ride their bikes."

I pushed back a strand of hair. "What was Hannah doing there?"

"I don't *know*," Maureen cried. "She was *supposed* to stay in the house until I got back. She was watching TV when I left. I guess she got bored. It's all my fault. I left her *alone*."

"Maureen," I said firmly. "Stay with me. What happened after Gage hit her with the motorbike? You said you saw him bury her in the woods. Are you talking about the lot next to your house?"

She nodded, sniffing again. "I had met Andy—he was my boyfriend then—at the Burger Shack and was on my way back. There's a shortcut through the woods. That's when I saw Gage digging a hole. I hid behind a tree and watched. When he finished digging, I saw him drag a body into the hole. It was wrapped in a blanket but I saw a patch of blond hair sticking out the top."

I narrowed my eyes. "Did you confront him then? Did you see Hannah's body?"

She clasped her hands and pressed them against her chest, then shook her head. "I was stunned. I couldn't understand what he was doing—didn't want to believe what I was seeing. So I followed him back to our yard. I didn't know it was Hannah at that point. All I saw was a body wrapped in a blanket."

"Go on."

"I yelled at him, '*What did you do?*' He whirled around and said, '*It was an accident, she came out of nowhere! I couldn't stop in time.*'"

"He said '*she*.' You're sure?"

Maureen nodded. "Then he told me about the motorbike and *begged* me not to tell our parents. We both knew our dad—our *stepdad*—would *kill* him. They'd never gotten along, and lately Dad had been threatening to send Gage away to some military school."

"But, if it was an accident..."

"You weren't there," Maureen insisted, her voice rising. "You don't know what things were like. Dad sometimes hit Gage just for being in his way. Gage was terrified. You should have seen his face. He knew Dad would see to it he went to prison." She looked at her hands. "I knew it too. And I knew I had to protect him. He was my brother. We'd always been allies."

I frowned as a vile image of abuse began to take shape. Unconsciously, I clenched my fists. "Maureen, did your stepfather hit you too?"

She hesitated a moment, her eyes still downcast as she fiddled timidly with her fingers. "Sometimes, but only when I deserved it. Mostly, I just stayed out of his way."

I could feel angry heat coloring my cheeks, but forced myself to ignore it. It would do Maureen no good to dwell on that ugliness now. Instead, I asked, "When did you know it was Hannah?"

She shrugged and began picking again at her fingernail. "I guess I knew as soon as I went into the house and realized she wasn't there. I searched everywhere, but she was gone."

"What did Gage do?"

"He made himself scarce. He'd left his bike at his friend's house and had to go back and get it. I think he wound up staying there most of the afternoon. He told everyone he'd been with his friends the whole time and they backed him up."

"That was handy. But they *must* have witnessed what

happened. Didn't the police question them? I can't believe none of them said anything."

She gave another little shrug. "I don't know. I was dealing with my own problems at the time. My mother was hysterical and my dad was in a rage. We were all questioned by the police, and I had to tell them I'd been at the Burger Shack with my boyfriend. I couldn't tell them what I'd seen without turning Gage in. You know what happened after that. I was blamed for leaving Hannah alone and I've had to live with it ever since."

So Gage walked away free while Maureen took all the heat. How could he live with that?

There was a sudden flash outside the window. The lights flickered and thunder rolled over the house like a low-flying jet. Rain blasted against the glass with each gust of wind.

Maureen looked around. "Sounds pretty nasty out there. You should be getting back. Connie's probably wondering what happened to you."

"I don't know," I said, hesitating. "Maybe I should stay for awhile. I hate leaving you like this."

She put a hand on my arm. "Thanks, but I'm okay, really. It's actually a huge relief to get all this off my chest. Just remember, you promised to keep it to yourself. If anyone finds out, Gage could spend the rest of his life in prison. I probably shouldn't have told you, but I guess I thought that maybe—because you have a connection with Hannah too—that maybe we could share the secret together."

What could I say? After all these years, after all she had suffered, she was still determined to protect her brother. But I hadn't worked for nine years in a law office without learning something about the law. Just knowing the truth made me an accessory after the fact.

But how could I betray her trust? Her face looked so hopeful, so pleading.

"Besides," she went on, "I thought...the way you...that is, you and Gage...I know you like him..." She took a deep breath, then rushed on. "I thought you should know."

Me and Gage. I gave a soft, bitter laugh under my breath. No. That ended now. Any man who could let his sister take the fall for his own stupid actions was no man at all. Sure, it had been an accident and he'd been a kid at the time. I got that. But to knowingly let Maureen take the blame and carry the burden all these years. That was cowardly. I wanted nothing more to do with Gage.

I took her hands. "I've got to think about this, but I promise to keep it to myself."

Silently I added, *for now*.

Chapter Fourteen

From where I stood in the front foyer of Maureen's house, I was able to see through the dining room window to the woods next door. The sun had gone down, leaving behind a steel gray twilight. Lightning flashed again. The sudden brilliance illuminated the tree tops thrashing in the blustery wind. This brought to mind an uncomfortable thought.

"Maureen," I said slowly. "What if someone decides to build on that lot next door? I'm actually kind of amazed it hasn't happened already. Property values in this area have skyrocketed in the last decade. There must be almost an acre of prime real estate over there."

She shook her head. "It will never happen."

I gave her a questioning look. "You know this *how?*"

"I own it," she said matter-of-factly.

Another stunning revelation.

"You *own* it?"

"Part of my grandfather's estate," she said. "He bought this house and the wooded property next to it when it was part of an old chicken farm. The rest was sold to developers. When he died, he left it to my father—my *real* father—who moved into the house when he and my mother were married forty-two years ago. Sadly, my father died when I was six. My mother got the house, but the vacant property was willed to me as the oldest child and put in a trust till I turned twenty-one. Now I own the property free and clear."

"What about Gage?"

"He got a lump sum of cash which he used to pay off his college loan."

I gave a short, incredulous snort. "Lucky Gage."

Did Maureen see the irony here? Her father gave her a piece of property that had most likely tripled in value over the last forty years, but she would never see a penny of it as long as Hannah's body was interred on it. In essence, her father's legacy was a secret burial plot for the child of his successor.

Could this get any more twisted?

"Does Gage know you own that property?" I asked.

She shrugged in an offhanded way. "Yeah. Why do you think he keeps hanging around?"

Of course. As long as Maureen owns the property, Gage's heinous secret stays buried. And as long as she stays silent, he handles all her needs, probably pays her property tax. *What a weird symbiotic relationship they have. It's not love, it's extortion.*

But Maureen seemed to have accepted the situation and come to terms with it. She read my expression and held up a hand. "It's okay. I don't want to talk about it anymore."

Before I could object, she changed the subject. "Brenna, before you leave, let me get you my shopping list. Gage said you were going to be bringing the groceries next week since Andy won't be coming anymore. That's awfully nice of you."

I looked at her in surprise. "Gage told you about Andy?"

"Yes, but I already knew. Andy told me himself."

Another bombshell. I wasn't sure I could take many more of these.

"I thought you'd be more upset," I said.

She shrugged. "I was at first. But I understand. Andy said he's needed full time at the store these days. His father isn't getting any younger. It takes up a lot of his time, hunting down my shopping list, packing it all up and delivering it personally. Connie's too. It's not fair to expect him to spend so much of his time making a special delivery just for us, and they can't afford to take on another employee. It's such a small store."

She hurried to the kitchen for her list while I waited by the front door puzzling over her statement. Did Maureen really not grasp the reason Andy wasn't coming anymore? Or was she deliberately fooling herself? *It doesn't matter*, I told myself. The explanation was plausible, no one got hurt and everybody saved face.

She returned a moment later and I stuffed the note into my jeans pocket. I opened the door and was hit with a blast of cold wet air. Once more I regretted leaving my jacket at home. Then I remembered what Gage had said in the driveway as he was leaving. I turned back to Maureen.

"I almost forgot, Gage said to tell you he'd be back in the morning."

Connie greeted me at the door. "You were next door for over an hour. What happened?" She smirked. "Did Maureen see another ghost?"

"Yeah," I managed to mutter. I didn't find this funny anymore. In fact, after my conversation with Maureen, my whole mood was pretty sour. I felt like I'd been kicked in the gut. All I really wanted to do now was crawl into bed, pull the covers over my head, and pretend it hadn't happened.

"I should have called you," I said, "but I forgot my phone. It's in the pocket of my jacket."

"Which you also forgot." She handed me a towel. The rain had been coming down in sheets and I was soaked to the skin. My hair was dripping all over the floor.

I gave her a wry look. "Careful—you sound just like your mother."

Her face contorted. "Bite your tongue. So what *did* happen?"

She just wouldn't let it go.

"Maureen and Gage sort of got into it and he had to leave. So I went over and talked to her till she calmed down. Everything's okay now."

"Poor Gage," she said with a sad shake of her head. "What he has to put up with."

"Yeah, poor Gage." I tried to keep the sarcasm out of my voice, but wasn't entirely successful. Before Connie could start questioning me again, I changed the subject.

"By the way," I said, "I'll be doing the grocery shopping for you and Maureen for the next few weeks until I get a job. Maureen said Andy's getting too busy at the store to make personal deliveries anymore."

"Ha! You mean his wife finally put her foot down. I'm not surprised. It was only a matter of time. I'll bet *that's* why Gage and Maureen were fighting. But there's no reason you should have to do *her* shopping. It's not *your* job."

"I don't mind as long as I'm not working. It's easier for me to do it than for Gage to have to come all the way out here every week."

"But it *does* give him an excuse to come." She waggled her eyebrows.

When I only shrugged, she looked at me curiously. "I was under the impression you kind of liked him."

I blew my breath out with a sharp huff and shook my head. Not after what I'd just learned.

She frowned, but thankfully did not pursue it.

I trudged off to my room and changed into my comfy flannel pajamas, then padded back out to the kitchen to make a peanut butter sandwich. The rest of the evening I spent bingeing on old Star Trek episodes hoping the power wouldn't go out as the storm raged around us.

In my dream, I was lost in an endless black forest. Hulking trees with coarse bark and jagged limbs towered above me, silhouetted against a gray sky. Evil-looking crows and owls stared at me with glowing eyes as I crept fearfully along a narrow path. Sibilant whispers like the drone of a million mosquito wings filled the air sending shivers of terror up my spine. I turned this way and that, probing the shadows, searching for someone to take my hand. But I was alone. A great sob welled in my throat.

As I opened my mouth to cry out, I suddenly woke, still engulfed in that pervasive feeling of dread. I looked around, drawing in several deep breaths to still my pounding heart. All was quiet. The clock on my nightstand read 2:47 A.M. I closed my eyes and tried to go back to sleep, but it was no use. I was wide awake. Finally, I got out of bed and went to the window, pushing the curtains aside to view the back yard.

The storm had worn itself out and now the moon peered through parted clouds, shedding patches of dim light over the ground and revealing a windblown slew of fallen tree limbs. To the far left, beyond Maureen Moreland's house, lay the woods—a dark patch of unkempt trees and tangled underbrush. I remembered years ago how the neighborhood kids had played hide-and-seek there, building forts, and playing big game hunter.

But there was something inherently frightening about a deep, tenebrous wood. All the scariest fairy tales had one: Hansel and Gretel, Little Red Riding Hood, Snow White.

Hannah and I had only ever ventured into the clear, sunny areas within sight of the house to play Bambi and wild horses. We had stayed out of the thicker forested parts. Not only did we not want to run into any marauding older boys, but at eight or nine years old we were certain that bears and monsters lurked among the trees.

My mind drifted back to my dream and the lonely,

terrified feeling it had evoked. This stirred up a puzzling question: *Had Hannah followed Gage through the woods to where he and his friends were riding the motorcycle?* Gage had told Maureen that Hannah came out of the woods unexpectedly. Had she been looking for him? I bit my lower lip. That meant she had walked through the forest by herself. I just couldn't see her doing that. It didn't make sense.

I gazed across the yard. Everything appeared in muted shades of black and gray, all color washed out in the murkiness of night.

Suddenly Hannah was there. She seemed to glow with a faint inner light. Even now, after everything that had happened, her appearance shook me—an innate human reaction—and my breath did a sharp intake.

She looked up at me, then turned and skipped toward the fence on Chumleys' side, moving nimbly over the rain-soaked grass. I blinked and she was gone.

I spent the rest of the night with the covers drawn up tight around my head in a futile effort to block out all the disturbing things I had learned the day before. I finally achieved deep sleep some time around dawn and didn't wake again until nearly nine o'clock. I stumbled blurry-eyed into the kitchen and found Connie in a similar state huddled over a cup of coffee at the kitchen table.

"I couldn't sleep," she said. "All I could think about was poor little Buster, sick and alone at the vet's, probably scared to death." She removed her glasses and rubbed at her puffy eyes. "You're on your own for breakfast. I just don't feel like cooking this morning."

A true testament to how morose she was feeling. I had never known Connie not to want to cook. She gave her coffee an idle stir and dropped her chin lethargically into her hand.

I had to admit the house did seem forlorn without the plucky little beagle underfoot.

"Maybe you can go visit him," I suggested. From a cupboard next to the stove, I extracted the non-stick skillet, then opened the refrigerator and took out a carton of eggs, breaking four of them into a bowl.

Connie shook her head. "The vet said Buster had to be kept completely quiet and isolated for a couple of days. Any excitement can trigger muscle spasms which can lead to convulsions."

"Poor puppy," I commiserated as I put two pieces of bread into the toaster. "I'm sure they're taking good care of him."

"I know. But he's my baby and I can't help worrying."

"They have your number though, right?"

She gave a great sniff and rubbed at her nose. "Yeah, the vet said they'd let me know if there were any changes."

I melted a pat of butter in the pan and poured in the eggs. "So, I take it you're not going in to the shop today? You're not usually closed on Saturdays, are you?"

Connie shook her head, the effort seeming to require an inordinate amount of energy. "I've got a part-time assistant, Tracy, who usually works mornings and Saturdays, plus Jerry the delivery guy. I told them what happened to Buster and they both insisted I stay home today. They said they'd take care of things."

"That's nice of them," I said, giving the eggs a stir. "So, what do you want to do today? You need something to take your mind off Buster. We could go shoe shopping or see a matinée. When's the last time you saw a movie in the middle of the day?"

She smiled. "Thanks, but I was thinking I really ought to go in to the shop, just for a bit. Just to check on things. I left there yesterday in such a hurry, I don't know if the till got closed out or even if the front door was locked."

"I thought you said Jerry was there."

Connie made a dismissive gesture. "I'm sure everything's fine—he's very capable—it's just that he's never closed up before and I would just feel better if I checked things out for myself. Anyway, I shouldn't be long. What about you?"

I shrugged. "Don't know yet. Maybe I'll do the grocery shopping. Now then, do you want some more coffee? Scrambled eggs are just about ready."

Chapter Fifteen

Connie departed shortly before ten. Broken clouds obscured the sun but it looked like the day ahead would be mostly clear and warm. Peering out the front window, I noticed several people in their yards cleaning up debris strewn everywhere in the aftermath of the storm. With no pressing tasks before me, I decided to do the same.

A glance toward the Moreland house told me that Gage had not arrived yet this morning. Maybe he had changed his mind about coming. I hoped so. I didn't want to see him. I was still processing Maureen's shocking secret.

I found a pair of gloves in the garage and began to pick up fallen branches, tossing them into a heap by the side of the road. A layer of pine needles coated my poor old car parked by the fence in front of the house. *It could really use a good washing.*

After collecting all the larger limbs, I went back into the garage and found a rake. I worked my way around the front lawn, gathering soggy leaves and twigs into neat piles to be discarded in the yard waste bin I had discovered stowed beneath the eaves alongside the house.

Oliver Chumley emerged from his garage and made a slow circuit of his yard with a wheelbarrow, picking up fallen branches. He raised his head, peering through the spectacles perched on his nose, and acknowledged me with a flaccid wave as he shuffled toward the street dragging a large fir bough. I wondered briefly what his occupation had been. His languid nature seemed unsuited to the workaday stresses imposed on most businessmen. Perhaps a professor of dead languages at the university? I smiled at the thought. Mom always said it was the quiet ones you had to look out for.

Shafts of sunlight parted the clouds as I worked the rake and inhaled the sweet fragrance of the damp outdoors. Fresh leaves and grass mingled with the heady aroma of moldering loam. Here and there, water droplets clung to the leafy undersides of arching branches and hung sparkling in the sun like crystals. Fascinated, I watched as wisps of steam rolled off the asphalt-shingled roof of the house as it warmed.

Downtown was never like this.

My reverie was broken by a shrill voice calling my name. I turned to see Nancy Chumley bustling toward the fence separating our two yards. Her husband was nowhere in sight. He'd either moved around to the back of the house or gone inside.

"Brenna. *Oh, Brenna.* Do you have a minute?"

I sighed and strolled to the fence to meet her. "Sure," I

said. "What's up?"

She looked at me over the top of her rose bushes, taking in the rake and gloves. "That was quite a storm, wasn't it? *Goodness*. But that's Seattle for you." She threw back her head and laughed. "We're never more than a few days away from a good soaking."

I added my chuckle to hers, sharing a wink and a nudge for the joke perpetuated by Seattle natives that it rains here virtually non-stop all year round. In keeping with the jocular spirit, I refrained from reminding her that it had been weeks since the area had measured any appreciable rainfall. The downpour had actually come as a welcome respite after a long, dry summer.

Clapping her hands together, she got down to the reason she had called me over. "We had a good turnout at the meeting the other night, don't you think?"

"Better than I expected, actually. I wasn't sure the Prescotts would show up. I got the feeling Mrs. Prescott wasn't all that interested." It wouldn't hurt to feel Nancy out, to see what she had to say about her long-time neighbors.

She frowned and clucked her tongue. "I *know*. Now that you mention it, I wonder she even bothered to come. She's never had much interest in making things, as far as I know. She probably just came to keep an eye on Bill."

"Does he *need* keeping an eye on?" Maybe my apprehensions were closer to the truth than I thought.

"Oh, well, after all these years, I wouldn't think so." She brushed at a fly that had settled on her arm.

My eyebrows lifted. "What does *that* mean?"

She glanced around, then stepped closer, putting her hand up beside her mouth like a shield, as though guarding to ensure her words weren't overheard by some unsuspecting passerby. She lowered her voice to just above a whisper. "I probably shouldn't tell you this (which I knew meant, *I'm about to tell you everything*), but he's an ex-con. He spent time in prison."

She took my look of astonishment as a cue to continue: "He was convicted first of burglary—although he always swore he didn't do it, but that's what they always say, isn't it?—and then for manslaughter. He knocked a man down in a bar fight. The man hit his head when he fell and later died."

"Oh, my god," I murmured. I remembered Bill's own description of himself as a hell raiser, and recalled the wicked-looking tattoos on his arms. "He told me he'd done things he wasn't proud of, but I never imagined anything like this."

She leaned in, eyes wide as she warmed to her subject. "You wouldn't know it to look at him now, but he used to be quite the bad boy, cocky and brash, always in trouble."

"Nancy, how do you know all this?" I asked.

She flipped a chubby hand carelessly in the air. "I've lived in this neighborhood for forty-three years. I know everything that goes on here." She turned sentimental eyes toward her house. "Oliver and I bought this place the year after we were married—I was twenty-five years old. Seems like a hundred years ago. This was a quiet street then, ideal for raising kids."

It must have been. My mom and Aunt Peggy always spoke fondly of their childhoods growing up here.

"Not long after we moved in," Nancy went on, "Bill's parents bought the house next door. They were a nice older couple, but they didn't have a clue about raising a headstrong boy."

"What do you mean?" I asked. My two half-brothers were in their early twenties now and I adored them, but all through my teen years they had been holy terrors—throwing tantrums, making messes, getting into things. At the time, I couldn't imagine what had possessed my parents to have more children when they already had me.

Nancy raised her chin and assumed a disapproving air. "He was a teenager then, one of those kids who always gets in trouble at school. You know the type. He ran with a tough crowd—boys with tattoos, torn jeans, and long hair. We used to see them hanging around, smoking and drinking when Bill's parents weren't home. I can tell you none of the neighbors was very happy about it."

Frowning, she continued. "Bill was good looking too. Girls were constantly throwing themselves at him. I swear, every schoolgirl in town had a crush on him. Of course, this was before he and Sylvia were married, but she used to follow him around like a lovesick puppy, hanging all over him, desperate for him to notice her."

No wonder Sylvia is so prickly, I thought. She must have lived in a habitual state of jealousy. It's amazing they even got married, let alone stayed married all these years.

"Anyway," Nancy continued, "after high school his parents tried sending him to college, but he dropped out after less than a year and moved back home. Then he started riding a motorcycle—one of those great big noisy ones with the long handlebars. I'm sure he must have been in some sort of gang."

"Nancy," I said sharply, "*lots* of people ride motorcycles. That *doesn't* mean they belong to a gang, and it certainly doesn't make them criminals." I didn't say so, but my own father had ridden a motorcycle. My mother used to tell me how handsome he'd looked, seated on his classy black and chrome Harley-Davidson. I always wished she'd had a picture.

"Oh, I know, I know," she said with an indifferent wag of her hand. "But it was about this time that he and his friends were accused of breaking into a liquor store. Bill always claimed he wasn't involved, but since he was known to hang out with those guys and apparently didn't have an alibi, it sort of came down to 'guilt by association.' He did a year in jail, and his mother told me they had to pay a huge fine."

She shook her head, squinting a little as the sun broke out again from behind a drifting cloud. "The whole thing was really hard on her, as you can imagine. I wish I could have helped her out more but by that time I had a son of my own, Roger." She puffed out her chest proudly. "He's married now and lives in LA. My daughter Maribeth is a nurse at the University Hospital."

I smiled. "They must have been some of the kids I remember playing with as a child."

Nancy's broad face lit up. "Yes, there were quite a lot of kids in the neighborhood in those days."

I shifted my weight, adjusting my grip on the rake. I was still curious about our incongruous neighbor. The picture Nancy painted of him as a young man just didn't jibe with the older version I was acquainted with. "So, Bill must have gotten his act together after his stint in jail."

"Huh-uh," Nancy said with a resolute shake of her head. "If anything, it just made him worse, more rebellious. His parents were at a loss, but he was in his twenties by then and out of control. There was nothing they could do. He started hanging out in bars, drinking, playing pool, and just generally carousing. I told you he killed a man. It was in a bar. There was a quarrel and everybody got hot-tempered. This guy gave Bill a shove, and Bill pushed back. He didn't mean to kill the man, of course, but he was drunk and not thinking straight. He hit the guy and knocked him backwards. He fell and hit his head on the edge of the bar and later died in the hospital. There was quite a to-do about it in the local papers. Bill was convicted of second degree manslaughter and sent back to prison."

"My god," I said, pressing my fingers to my mouth. It occurred to me that my mother must have known him. Her house was only two doors down from Prescotts'. They'd been neighbors.

That's how he knew I looked like my mother.

Nancy straightened and scratched a spot behind her ear. "But that was a long time ago. After serving his sentence, Bill settled down and managed to turn his life around."

"So, what changed? Was he scared straight? Washington has a three strikes law. Another felony and it's life in prison."

"It was Sylvia," Nancy said. "She never got over her infatuation—some might say *obsession*. She was determined to have him. She convinced her father, Big Mike Quigley, to use his money and influence to get Bill's sentence commuted. Big Mike offered to pay the hefty fine, and promised the court he'd ride herd on Bill and see that he held down a full time job selling appliances. So Bill only served six months in exchange for agreeing to counselling and keeping his nose clean." Here Nancy paused and inserted a smirk. "Apparently, Sylvia was part of the deal because shortly afterward they were married."

My mouth crooked in a wry smile. "So you're telling me that Bill Prescott, rebel biker, traded his wild ways for a mundane life married to Sylvia, selling appliances in her father's store?" I shook my head. "The universe has a strange sense of humor."

"Well, in those days Big Mike was a man you didn't trifle with. Bill and Sylvia lived with the Quigleys for several years before eventually moving back here to Bill's parents' house after they moved to California." Nancy picked a stray twig off one of the rose bushes. "I think he was happy enough. He took up woodworking and seems to have a real talent for it. Wait till you see some of the things he's made."

Somewhere in a bush nearby, the melodious warble of a songbird burst on the air and I turned to look, envious of that fleeting note of cheeriness.

Nancy noticed my attention drifting so she cleared her throat and lifted her voice. "*Anyway*, I wanted to tell you I spoke with Shirley Dewitt—she's president of the school board—about getting the gym on the first Saturday of December for our holiday craft fair. It will have to be voted on by the board, of course, but she doesn't think there will be any problem. They meet Monday night and she's already added it to the agenda. I'll go to the meeting to present our plan."

"Oh, that's great, Nancy," I said, refocusing on her face. "Thank you for all your effort. As soon as we know for sure, we can really get started. I've already got some ideas for advertising."

"And I've been talking to lots of people around the

neighborhood who are dying to get involved. I just know it's going to be a huge success."

I smiled and nodded, grateful, but ready to wind up this conversation. I had a feeling she'd go on talking for another hour if I let her.

"That's wonderful," I said, taking a step backward, repositioning the rake in my hands. "Now, I guess I should get back to work. I'd like to get this finished before lunchtime and I haven't even started on the back yard."

"Absolutely. Don't let me keep you." She glanced around at her own lawn. Sunlight through the trees had cast a dappled pattern on the grass. "I guess I'd better go help Oliver or it'll take him all week. He's a good man, but he'll never be accused of moving too fast." She brushed a stray hair off her face. "*Goodness*, that was some storm. I keep forgetting it's September already."

With that, she turned and scuttled back the way she'd come. I headed for the garage and swapped the rake for a broom. I swept the driveway, then headed for the front porch, sweeping the walk as I went. I was nearing the steps when I heard a car pull up in front of Maureen's house. I swung my head, and with a sinking feeling, saw Gage jump from his SUV and amble toward me.

I took a deep breath and steeled myself. I had to break things off. Now that I knew the truth, I'd never be able to look at him the same way again.

"Hey, Brenna. Why don't you knock off and I'll take you to lunch." His smile was warm, and for a change he wore comfortable-looking jeans and a casual twill shirt with long sleeves folded up at the wrists. A shock of dark hair fell jauntily across his forehead. He had never looked more sexy.

With a regretful sigh, I fixed my gaze firmly on the sidewalk as I resumed sweeping. "Sorry. I'm busy."

He laughed. "It can wait, can't it? After lunch, I'll give you a hand."

"No, thank you, I prefer to do it myself."

"Well, why don't I go grab a broom and we'll get it done in half the time."

"Or how about if *I* take care of *my* yard, and *you* take care of *yours?*"

His smile dissolved and he gave me a searching look. "Is something wrong?"

I raised my eyes to his. "Look, I'm sorry if you thought there was something going on between us. There's not, okay? I came here to get my life sorted out, and I'm not ready for any kind of...relationship."

I turned my back and made my way to the front porch, sweeping briskly as I mounted the steps. Out of the corner of my eye, I saw him shuffle back toward his sister's house looking dejected. It was all I could do to stop myself running after him.

I reminded myself of what Maureen had told me yesterday: the horrible accident that had taken Hannah's life, and the way Gage had concealed her body in the woods and allowed his older sister to take the blame all these years. I thought of how this had destroyed Maureen's life, both physically and emotionally. My jaw tightened as I clenched my teeth in anger. No, Gage would get no sympathy from me.

Sweeping the porch, I was reminded of poor little Buster languishing at the vet's. It was appalling to think a person had come along and tossed him a piece of poisoned meat. I couldn't believe a neighbor would be so heartless.

I blew out a breath. Had the wayward hound gotten into someone's garbage? Dug up their flowers? Chased their cat? Had someone been so annoyed with the wandering beagle that they'd actually wanted to kill him? Connie seemed to think so. Perhaps there had been complaints she hadn't told me about.

I shook my head. I still thought it more likely that Buster had eaten a piece of bait set out by someone targeting vermin on their property. In a suburban area like Shoreline, rats weren't the only wildlife considered pests. Raccoons, opossums, and skunks, displaced by the encroachment of houses, were typically regarded as nuisances, although putting out poison in a populated area seemed irresponsible to me. Either way, we would have to be more proactive in keeping the dog at home.

I yanked at a leafy branch that had managed to get stuck between the bottom of the railing and the floorboards of the porch. It took a couple of good tugs to get it loose, and that's when I noticed the odd piece of debris wedged underneath it. I reached for the object, intending to toss it into the garbage, when my hand halted in midair.

For a moment I just stared, trying to make sense of it. Shoved nearly out of sight under the bottom rail, overlooked in the previous day's chaos, were the remains of another small tennis shoe, filthy, rotted, and stinking of mildew. Buster must have brought it home with him after his last ill-fated foray.

Then I recalled last night, watching Hannah from my bedroom window as she skipped across the grass in the moonlight. Her feet had been bare, slick and wet after the heavy rain. I had been too tired to take notice, but now it set off an alarm in my head like a siren.

My mouth went dry. Gingerly, I picked up the mangled shoe, a match to the first one, and I knew—*these are Hannah's shoes.*

But that meant Buster had gone into the woods and dug them up.

Chapter Sixteen

I jumped when my phone rang. I grabbed it out of the pocket of my jacket and frowned when I saw the number. It was Maureen. That is, I hoped it was Maureen and not Gage using his sister's phone in an underhanded strategy to get me to talk to him. I made a split-second decision and answered it.

"Hello?" I said tentatively.

"Brenna? It's Maureen. Glad I caught you. I just talked to Nick Donato. He's going to bring the girls over this afternoon for their first rug braiding lesson. I wondered if you'd like to join us? We'll make it sort of a group session. What do you say? You can all learn at the same time. It'll be fun."

She sounded breathy, excited. This was exactly the kind of social interaction she needed. I could hardly say no. I would deal with Gage when and if the need arose.

"What time?"

"Around two?"

"Perfect." That would give me time to finish picking up the yard, eat lunch, and get cleaned up. "Can I bring anything?"

"Nope. I've got everything we'll need. See you then."

I hung up the phone and stuffed it back into my pocket. I still gripped the half-rotted shoe between the thumb and forefinger of my left hand, debating what to do with it. Finally, I took it into the kitchen and wrapped it in a sheet of newspaper from the recycling bin, then stashed it in an empty shoe box in the back of my closet.

I'm not sure why I wanted to save it. Perhaps a shred of DNA still clung to it. As if I had a way of getting the shoe tested for DNA. *I've been watching too many crime shows*. Besides, even if I *did* have a way of getting the shoe analyzed, it would mean turning it over to the police which would result in a whole slew of questions which, due to my promise to Maureen, I wasn't in a position to answer.

I blew out a deep breath, then hurried to the back yard to pick up fallen branches blown down in the wind storm. I was also determined to scout out Buster's most recent escape route under the fence. The quickest way to the woods was through Maureen's back yard which bordered on the undeveloped lot. With no fence between her yard and the woods, it would have been easily accessible to the inquisitive beagle.

If I can find his trail, it should lead me directly to where Hannah is buried.

I moved around the yard, picking up twigs and broken limbs, keeping my eyes fixed on the ground along the base of the fence between our back yard and Morelands'. The grass was damp, but drying quickly as the sun rose higher. Finally, I straightened and stood with my hands on my hips, staring around. I could find no sign of digging, nor was the soil disturbed beneath any of the shrubs on that side.

I swiped a glove across my forehead. Hannah's ghost had appeared to me last night. I had seen her in the yard from my window, skipping over the wet grass toward the fence on Chumleys' side. I swung my gaze in that direction—to the same place where Buster had dug before.

Sure enough, peering beneath the rhododendron, I found evidence of a fresh dig. The stones I had placed there had been shoved aside like no more than a minor inconvenience. Clearly Buster had wormed his way into Chumleys' yard, which meant he had not made a beeline for the woods, but had taken a more circuitous route.

Before I could think any further, I was interrupted by the one voice I did not want to hear.

"Brenna," Gage called from his back yard. "Can we talk?"

I kept my face averted as I took a deep breath.

"Can't," I answered. "I've got to go inside and get cleaned up. I've got plans."

I turned and stalked into the house, closing the back door solidly behind me. Inside, I collapsed onto a kitchen chair and pulled off my gloves. I leaned my elbows on the table and dropped my head into my hands.

Why did I feel so torn up inside? I knew Gage's dark secret and it disgusted me. Yet in spite of that, there was something about him that still attracted me. I had seen his good side. He could be caring, responsible, and hardworking. The house he'd designed showed his remarkable creative ability. He could also be funny. Bantering with him these last few days had brought back memories of how we had teased each other as children and how I had harbored a little girl crush.

But none of that made up for the hurt he'd caused his older sister.

I couldn't avoid Gage forever. Sooner or later we'd have to talk. What would I say? *Sorry, man, you're just not my type.* I couldn't tell him the real reason. I didn't know how he'd react to hearing Maureen had spilled the truth to me about Hannah's disappearance. Would he be angry? Fearful? After all, if the authorities found out, he could still go to prison. I didn't want that.

I let out a sigh. Despite my better judgment, I would keep the secret for now.

Today was the open house at my condo. I wondered how it was going. With luck it would sell quickly and I'd have enough for a down payment on a new place. Once I moved out of this neighborhood and no longer lived next door to Maureen, I wouldn't be running into Gage all the time. Maybe then I could move on with my life.

Maybe I should move back to Phoenix. I made a wry face. My mother would love that. I thought about the wide, golden stretches of desert, the saguaro cactus, and the hills covered in spring with blankets of wild flowers. I remembered hiking Camelback Mountain with Jason, paddleboarding on Bartlett Lake, and rooting for the Diamondbacks at Chase Field. But the memories were bittersweet. I knew I could never live there again. Summers in Arizona were blistering hot, and baseball had been Jason's game.

For the past nine years I had lived in Seattle and come to love how green it was all year round. Like other northwest denizens, I had developed a fervor for tall trees, snow-topped mountains, and enormous bodies of azure water. Thanks to breezes off the Pacific Ocean, the region never got too hot or too cold. Plus by now, I had thrown my lot in with the rest of the impassioned throngs of Seahawks fans.

My spirits needed a boost. I wondered if Tamara was free for lunch. I needed her indomitable personality to bolster me up. She worked on Saturdays, but I knew she had an hour for lunch. If I left right away, I could get downtown by twelve. I grabbed my phone and sent her a text: *Free for lunch today?*

It took only a moment to receive her reply: *Love to. Café on the corner?*

Great. See you at 12.

The café was located a block from the boutique where Tamara worked. The place was busy as usual, but we were seated quickly. I ordered a cobb salad and Tamara got the fish and chips.

"So, what's going on?" Tamara asked, leaning toward me over the table with a concerned expression on her face.

I gave her a look. "What makes you think something's going on?"

"Well, three days ago you seemed pretty upbeat. Now, all of a sudden, you need me to drop everything and have lunch with you. Is this about your date yesterday? How'd it go?"

"*Date?*"

"You said you were going with your neighbor's brother to look at a house he built or something." The corners of her mouth curved up. "The neighbor who sees *ghosts*."

"Oh, *that*." I expelled a deep breath. Had it only been yesterday that I'd gone to Mercer Island with Gage to look at a house? "I don't even know where to start. Turns out he's a total jerk and we are completely incompatible."

Her eyebrows sprang up. "Really? What happened?"

I was all set to vent when it occurred to me that I couldn't tell Tamara the truth without revealing the secret I had promised to keep.

"Let's just say I found out something about him, something his sister told me. I can't talk about it without breaking a confidence, but it's definitely a deal breaker."

"I'm sorry to hear that," Tamara said. "I got the feeling you kind of liked him."

"And that's just the tip of the iceberg," I said. "When I moved in with my cousin she warned me she had weird neighbors, but I had no idea." I picked up my fork, studied it for a second and put it down again. "For instance, yesterday someone poisoned her dog. He's currently at the vet's fighting for his life."

Tamara's eyes widened. She mumbled an expletive under her breath.

"And then," I continued, "I found out that the flirty neighbor two doors down is an ex-con. He apparently killed someone in a bar fight thirty years ago."

Tamara expelled a humorless laugh. "*Wow.* There's more drama in that neighborhood than your average soap opera."

"I feel like I'm surrounded by crooks and liars." I shook my head. "I need to find my own place, as far away from there as possible."

We were interrupted at that moment by the waitress bringing our lunch. We put our conversation on hold as we dug in.

After a few minutes, Tamara swallowed a mouthful of fish and said, "Okay, Brenna, out with it. I have a feeling you didn't ask me to lunch just to rant about the wackos in your neighborhood. This is really all about the cute brother being a jerk, right? You were starting to like him and he let you down."

I worried idly at a bit of avocado on my plate, then sighed and looked up. "Yeah, and I don't want to see him anymore. I've tried giving him the cold shoulder and the 'I'm not ready for a new relationship' speech, but he's not getting the message. How am I supposed to avoid him as long as he keeps coming around to see his sister? Who I *do* like, by the way."

"So your solution is to move away? Huh-uh. Just tell him how you feel. Tell him to bug off." She gave her fist a little pump. "Whatever it takes."

It seemed so easy when she said it. I set my shoulders and gave her a grim smile. "You're right. Why should I let Gage drive me away? That's my grandmother's house, the house where my mom grew up. I *like* it there and I have a *right* to be there." Tamara's energy was rubbing off on me.

She grinned and nodded, her dark eyes shining. "Now you're talking."

"I've rejected slimeballs before," I said, my voice rising with my new resolve, "and I can do it again." For emphasis, I speared a chunk of lettuce and stuffed it into my mouth.

Then Tamara leaned toward me once more. "Okay, now that that's settled, what about the ghost? Have you seen it?"

If she had been anyone else, I would have laughed at the absurdity of the question. But Tamara was the one person in the world I knew who took ghost sightings seriously.

I peered at her over the rim of my water glass, then shifted my gaze left and right to see if anyone was listening. "Several times."

"So now you believe she's real."

"Oh yeah, she's real. And I've been trying to listen to her, like you said."

Intrigued, Tamara put down her fork. She put her elbows on the table and settled her chin in her hands, giving me her full attention. "So, what has she told you?"

I gave a quick laugh and shrugged. "I don't know. Nothing I can understand. She doesn't actually speak. Although she *does* seem able to convey mental suggestions, like feelings or images. She somehow managed to get Connie to come home early from work yesterday to find her dog and get him to the vet in time to save his life."

"Well, that's something. You know she likes dogs. What else?"

Should I tell her about my dream? Had it come from Hannah or had it simply been an outgrowth of stress and my imagination? How much could I say without revealing too much? I was dying to tell Tamara everything, but I had promised Maureen I would keep the secret. Eventually, I knew the matter would have to be dealt with legally, but not just yet. I needed time to sort things out in my head.

I shrugged again. "There really isn't any more. I'm taking this one day at a time. I just needed to blow off some steam. Thanks for putting up with me."

"No problem." She gave me a sideways look like she knew I wasn't telling her everything, but thankfully she didn't push it.

I glanced at the time. Maureen had invited me over to learn how to braid a rug and I was determined to go. If Gage was there I wouldn't hesitate to tell him to get lost. I waved at the waitress, signaling her to bring the check.

"Got to go," I said to Tamara with a grin. "It's time for my first rug braiding lesson."

My friend's face contorted in distaste.

"Okay," said Maureen with a lively smile, "we're about to get up to our elbows in rags."

Nick Donato gave a loud hoot, while his two daughters broke out in giggles.

"They should be good at that," Nick said, throwing a wink at the girls. He had the handsome, ruddy complexion and thick black curls distinctive of his Italian heritage. His wiry, muscular frame suggested a penchant for physical pursuits. *Like chopping wood or hefting large boulders with his bare hands,* I thought.

I kept my admiration concealed when it became clear that Maureen was attracted to him. She smiled and blushed whenever he looked her way, and peered coquettishly at him through her lashes when she spoke. I noted that she had fixed her hair and applied a touch of makeup.

I smiled to myself. *Move over, Andy.*

Nick sat on a folding chair in Maureen's attic, while the rest of us sat on pillows on the floor facing a large box overflowing with heaps of cotton fabric in a kaleidoscope of colors.

"These used to be t-shirts," Maureen said, her face beaming with enthusiasm. "I've already cut them up for you." She reached into the box and pulled out a handful of long narrow strips, one inch wide. "I want each of you to pick out four strips to start. Any color you like. Then I'll show you how to get started. While you're working, I'll make some more. I have lots of shirts for cutting up."

Nick leaned forward and eyed the box of flamboyant cloth ribbons. "Where on earth did you get all the t-shirts?"

Maureen laughed. "Thrift stores and garage sales mostly. Gage keeps an eye out for me and picks them up whenever he sees them. Occasionally, I find some online. I once bought a bundle of twenty-five old t-shirts for five dollars. The seller described them as rags, but they were perfect for rug making."

"Do you always use t-shirts?" I asked, fingering the smooth material. "Can you use other kinds of fabric too?"

"I've tried others," Maureen said. "I made a rug once using old bed sheets. But for this kind of braiding, I've found that t-shirt material is the easiest to work with. It's really soft and pliable."

The girls and I dug into the box for our four starter strips. Carly rummaged clear to the bottom and came up with some periwinkle strips to go with her other choices of bubblegum pink, eggshell, and magenta. Gina went bold with fire engine red, pine forest green, royal blue, and sunflower yellow. I settled on orange, pale yellow, moss green, and mink brown—warm, earthy colors.

"Come on, Daddy, you have to make one too," Carly said.

Nick laughed. "I don't know, I'm afraid I'll just make a mess." But he gave in and pulled four random strips out of the box. "If the guys at the shop could see me now..."

"Good," said Maureen. "Now that you've picked out your four strips, I want you to put three of them together, in any order, and bring them over to the sewing machine. I'll just put a few stitches in the top to hold them so you can start braiding."

Once this was accomplished, we all began plaiting our first three strands. When we each had completed a braid about twelve inches long, Maureen demonstrated the technique for adding in the fourth strip.

"This is almost a lost art," she said, smiling at the two girls. "And now I'm passing it on to you. Someday, you'll be able to show *your* children how to do it and then they can teach *their* children."

Carly and Gina screamed and giggled. As with all kids their age, the idea of children and grandchildren was so far in the future they couldn't even imagine the possibility.

But I could. Without warning, tears welled in my eyes and my throat constricted. My grandmother had taught Maureen this age-old skill. It should have been me. I should have had children to pass the knowledge on to. Now I wondered if I would ever have children.

I sniffed and wiped my eyes with the end of the rag I was holding. Maureen didn't notice. She was bent over

Carly helping her navigate a tricky move as the contour of her rug began to curve to form an oval shape. Nick's attention was fixed on Maureen.

But in glancing around, I abruptly locked eyes with Gage who was leaning against the wall beside the stairs, watching. My lips pulled into a hard, thin line as I redoubled my efforts to wield the strips of fabric into something resembling a rug. A minute passed and it took all my will power to keep from peeking over my shoulder to see if he was still there. *Damn* him. Where did he get off staring at me while I worked? He was totally messing with my head and disrupting my concentration.

Five minutes later, my cell phone crowed, alerting me to a text. I looked around. Thankfully, Gage had gone. I stretched my back and stood, grateful for the break, then went to retrieve the phone from my jacket which I had laid across the Ping-Pong/sewing table.

Reading the text from Connie, I smiled and murmured my relief.

"Good news?" Maureen asked.

I looked up. "Connie says she's talked to the vet and Buster's doing great. Better than expected. They're going to keep him for the rest of the weekend, but they think he can come home on Monday."

"What a relief," she said.

"Buster?" Gina asked. "The little beagle? Is he sick?"

"Yes," I said, "but it looks like he's going to be okay. He got out of the back yard yesterday and ate something he shouldn't have. Connie thinks someone might have come by and fed him something that gave him a tummy ache. Probably in the afternoon right after lunch. I don't suppose either of you saw anything?"

Both girls shook their heads.

"They would have been in school till three thirty," Nick reminded me.

I nodded. "Oh, right. I forgot."

"I came home for about an hour at lunch time," Nick said. "I'm a mechanic at the Chevy dealership on Aurora. The only people I saw were the mailman and one of the old neighbor ladies out for an afternoon stroll. Nothing unusual."

"That's okay." I shrugged. "Personally, I think he went wandering and stuck his nose in someplace it didn't belong. Connie and I need to spend some time stapling chicken wire to the bottom of the fence so he can't dig out anymore."

"Probably a good idea," Nick said.

After another hour, I noticed him glancing at his phone. Finally, he cleared his throat. "Well, girls, I think we should be heading home. It's almost dinner time."

In typical childish fashion, Carly and Gina immediately set up a protest. "*Please*, can't we stay just a *little* bit longer? *Please*, I just need to finish this row."

"Come on, now," he said. "It's getting late and we don't want to tire Miss Moreland out." He slapped his knees and stood up, exchanging a brief, playful look with Maureen. "Or she might not let you come back."

The girls gave up their remonstrations and scrabbled to their feet. Clutching their half-finished rag rugs, they turned to Maureen and asked, "Can we take them home?"

"I think it would be better to leave them here for now," she said with an affectionate smile. "I haven't shown you what to do when you get to the end. But maybe your father will bring you over again tomorrow." She tipped her head and hit him with the full wattage of her smile, to which the two girls added their enthusiastic entreaties. Under this onslaught, he had no choice but to agree.

As Maureen led the way downstairs, I heard her ask Nick if he and the girls would like to stay for dinner tomorrow after their braiding session. I lagged behind to give them a moment. If feelings were percolating between them, I didn't want to get in the way.

When I reached the bottom of the stairs I did a quick look around. With luck, I thought I could slip out the back door without running into Gage.

Chapter Seventeen

When Maureen's old farmhouse was remodeled, a sliding glass door was installed in place of the old back door leading onto an outdoor patio. Not surprisingly, the curtains were pulled to block the view of the garden. *In case Hannah makes a surprise appearance?*

Pushing aside the curtains, I opened the slider and stepped outside into the late afternoon sunshine. The lawn was clear of storm-tossed branches which I presumed meant that while we'd been inside braiding rugs, Gage had been out here cleaning up.

I strolled around, gazing at the pair of gnarled apple trees growing at the far end of the yard, all that remained of a bygone orchard. I thought back to the old days when we had played here, climbing the trees, laughing and yelling, tearing around in the grass, innocently oblivious to the world's iniquities.

I turned to stare at the tangle of trees growing on the wooded parcel next door, transfixed by the stillness that lay deep within the shaded forest. As kids, our childish imaginations had turned that overgrown acre into everything from an untamed African jungle filled with man-eating beasts to an enchanted kingdom ensorcelled by a wicked witch.

I recalled my nightmare. What could have made eight-year-old Hannah cut through those woods by herself?

"Brenna!" I jumped when I heard Gage call my name. He was coming toward me from the direction of the house.

I gulped and strode away, making for the gate between our two properties. It had been a mistake to come out here. The last thing I wanted was a confrontation.

"Brenna, *stop*," Gage demanded. "Tell me what's wrong."

I halted, feeling my shoulders stiffen. I rotated around to face him.

"Nothing's wrong," I lied.

"Something *is* wrong. I can tell you're upset." He looked bewildered. "I thought we were getting along. I was hoping we might see more of each other. If I did or said something, don't I at least deserve a chance to defend myself?"

I looked at the ground, flexing my fingers. I couldn't meet his eyes. How could there be a defense for what he had done? He had killed his little sister and concealed her body in the woods, refusing to come clean even though it had obviously been an accident. Then he had sworn his older sister to secrecy so that he could escape punishment, and in doing so had subjected her to a life of mental anguish. I felt betrayed. I had thought he was someone I could fall for, but instead he was a coward.

"Brenna, talk to me."

There was no escape. We were going to have to deal with this now. I glanced around to make sure there was no one within earshot, then I crossed my arms over my chest and pinned him with an angry glare.

"Okay," I said. "You want to talk, let's talk. The truth is, I know about the motorbike and the accident you had twenty-five years ago."

Gage took a step backward, his eyes wide.

"Maureen told me." I uncrossed my arms and jabbed a finger into his chest, pressing on without mercy. "She told me how she saw you bury the body in the woods."

"I was *twelve years old*," he sputtered, clearly perplexed. "I admit it was *stupid*, but really…after all these years…I think I deserve a break." He spread his hands out in front of him in a helpless gesture. "I can't believe Maureen has held it against me all this time."

"A *break?*" It was my turn to be shocked. "She was your *sister!*"

"*What?*" His agitation was almost palpable. His mouth dropped open and his eyebrows rammed together.

"Like a coward, you let Maureen take the blame." I looked around again to make sure no one could hear, then lowered my voice and hissed, "And poor little Hannah has lain buried in the woods all these years."

"Oh, my god," he said. He spun on his heel, then clenched his fists and pressed them to his forehead.

"Think of your mother," I continued relentlessly.

Fuming, he whirled to face me, a vein pulsing in his neck. "I can't believe this," he growled.

Grabbing me by the hand, he tugged me behind him as

he marched toward the house.

I tried to wrench free, but he held my hand fast. What was he going to do? My heart began to race. Until this moment, I hadn't considered him dangerous, but now it occurred to me that the looming threat of prison might cause him to become desperate.

"Come on," he said. "We have to go talk to Maureen and get this straightened out. After all these years…" He shook his head. "*Oh, my god*, I can *not* believe this."

He went back through the sliding glass door into the kitchen, pulling me with him through the dining room and into the living room where Maureen was just closing the front door after the Donatos.

She turned around and smiled when she saw me. "Oh, Brenna…" she started to say, but was interrupted by Gage.

"Maureen, Brenna, sit down." His expression was somber and his tone brooked no argument. "I have to explain something to you. There has obviously been a grave misunderstanding."

I took a seat on the couch next to Maureen and folded my arms. Maureen stared blankly at her brother, perplexed by this unexpected confrontation.

Gage took a deep breath and began to stride back and forth as he spoke. "Twenty-five years ago, as you know, I had an accident while I was riding my friend's motorcycle."

Maureen gasped and covered her mouth with her hand.

Gage combed a hand through his hair. "I was a stupid kid and I was showing off, riding too fast down the hill…"

I turned my face away, my stomach turning as he recounted the details of that horrific day.

"...and I hit a *dog*."

The statement hung in the air like an unexploded bomb. Each tick of the mantel clock seemed amplified, resounding in the void like the echo of a bass drum. For the space of two full breaths, nobody spoke.

At last, Maureen stirred. "But..." she stammered, "I saw you...in the woods." Her eyes were wild, filled with confusion. "You said you *hit* her. I thought...I mean...when we got home and Hannah was gone..."

Gage worked his hands, flexing his fingers to relieve the tension. "You assumed the worst," he said through gritted teeth, "like everyone else."

Maureen looked stricken, her face drained of color.

"I *did* say I hit her," Gage went on, "but I never said it was *Hannah*. You just thought that when Hannah went missing. But it was Mrs. Johnson's old golden retriever Bonnie that I hit."

"Bonnie," I repeated in a daze. "I remember. We used to play with her all the time. She had a red collar."

The friendly dog had lived on the next block but had often come to hang out with us kids when her owner was away at work. We used to throw balls for her and give her treats. I knew that Gage had been especially fond of her. In retrospect, knowing now what I did about the abuse Gage had suffered as a boy, I wondered if the dog's affection had helped fill a void in his life—which would have made his accidently killing her that much more tragic.

He nodded grimly. "I loved that dog and I felt just horrible about it. My only consolation was that she died instantly and didn't suffer."

I leaned back against the couch cushion and let out a

groan. Some kind of friend *I* was. How could I have been so quick to believe something so deplorable? Would Gage ever forgive me?

"Oh, Gage," I said softly. "I am so sorry."

"So, what happened?" Maureen asked. She still sounded shellshocked.

"She must have followed me," Gage said. "I don't know where she came from. She just seemed to appear out of the bushes beside the road. I couldn't stop in time..." The catch in his voice clearly expressed his remorse.

"But you wrapped her in a blanket," said Maureen. "You buried her in the woods and never told anyone."

Gage spread his hands in a supplicating gesture. "I was scared. I knew Dad would kill me." He uttered a clipped, humorless laugh. "You think I was going to tell him? Riding too fast without permission on a motorcycle that belonged to Eddie Weinstein—who Dad hated anyway—and killing somebody's dog in the process? Yeah, right."

"Where did you get the blanket?" Maureen persisted.

"Mrs. Johnson gave it to me. She was a nice lady. I didn't want her wondering what had become of her poor old dog, so I went to her and confessed the whole thing. She saw how wrecked I was about it, and she was very understanding. She thanked me for letting her know and promised she wouldn't say anything to get me in trouble. All she asked was that I bury her dog and not leave her lying there by the side of the road. She gave me the blanket, and I found a nice shady spot under the branches of a hemlock tree. I covered it with leaves, then placed a log and some rocks on it so coyotes wouldn't come along and dig it up. When Hannah disappeared Mrs. Johnson was one of the first to offer to help search. In all the chaos that followed, poor old Bonnie was sort of forgotten."

"And none of your friends said anything about it," I murmured.

Gage shrugged. "The guys all knew what an ass my stepfather could be. They all had my back. And besides, the police came around asking about a missing girl, not a dog. By that time, it just didn't seem important."

"You said the police searched the woods," I said. "Wouldn't they have noticed a freshly dug grave?"

"Sure," he said, "but if they dug it up they would only have found a dog. I left Bonnie's collar and tags on so the police could easily have tracked her to Mrs. Johnson. She would simply have told them her dog died."

"All these years…" Maureen cried. "How could you not tell me?"

"I thought you *knew*. You caught me burying her after all. Don't you remember how you screamed at me? I was consumed with guilt and I thought you despised me. Then Hannah disappeared and our parents freaked out. The whole thing was a nightmare. You became so distant…"

With a sob, Maureen leaped up and threw her arms around her brother. "Oh, Gage, I am so, *so* sorry." She pressed her face into his shoulder. "How could I have thought you killed her? How could I have ever thought you would just leave her there in the woods? I am the worst sister in the whole world."

Gage patted her on the back, murmuring comforting noises, assuring her that all was forgiven.

I felt like an intruder sitting there watching as they

held each other. *I should leave, let them work things out.* For years there had been a rift between them of pain, guilt, and suspicion. Now at last things could start to heal.

Quietly, I got to my feet and began tiptoeing toward the door. Connie had to be home by now. It wasn't late. Maybe after dinner I could take care of the grocery shopping.

"Brenna."

I turned when Gage called my name. He still held his sister against his chest, but he met my eyes over the top of her head. "We'll talk later, okay?"

There was a new softness in his eyes, a tenderness I hadn't seen before. It was like a huge weight had been lifted from his shoulders. I smiled and nodded in response.

But as I headed once more for the door, Maureen called me back. She smiled through her tears as she removed herself from Gage's arms. "Can you come back in the morning? Nick and the girls are coming around ten to work on their rugs. I thought I'd order some pizzas for lunch and we'd make a party of it." She glanced quickly at her brother. "You'll come too, won't you?"

"Of course," he said, then turned his eyes again in my direction. "What do you say, Brenna? Can we start again?"

"Connie's welcome too," Maureen hurried to interject. "Does she like pizza?"

"I'll ask her," I said, meeting Gage's look with a meaningful smile. "But I'll be here for sure."

Walking home, I marvelled at how this one tragic misunderstanding had resulted in so much misery. If only Gage and Maureen had talked years ago, cleared the air.

How different things might have been. They would probably have supported each other in the midst of the family's ordeal rather than becoming adversaries.

Suddenly, I stopped short. The ramifications hit me like a brick. Hannah. She really *had* vanished without a trace. For twenty-five years, Maureen had lived under the assumption that her younger sister lay secretly buried in the woods next door. Learning the truth now only served to re-ignite the mystery. What had happened to Hannah? Had she been kidnapped? Or had she wandered off and met with some calamitous accident?

I reached the driveway and was about to turn and head for the front porch when I looked up and saw Hannah standing at the edge of the blacktop halfway up the block in front of Prescotts' house. I froze, studying the apparition: thin, childish face covered in freckles, long blond braids hanging over her shoulders, pink jacket, blue jeans, and bare feet.

As I stood staring, I was overtaken with a sudden urge to follow her. I hesitated, twiddling my fingers uneasily. Would she lead me to where her body lay hidden? Could it really be that simple after all these years? Yet if I *did* find her, how would I ever explain how I had done it?

Suddenly my phone rang, nearly giving me a heart attack. At the same moment, Connie came out onto the porch. Without thinking, my eyes darted in my cousin's direction.

"Brenna?" she called. "Are you coming in? Dinner's almost ready."

"Just a second," I replied. I glanced back up the street but Hannah was gone. It was clear this ghost suffered no interruptions. Blowing out a quick breath, I turned back to

Connie and held up an index finger while I reached with the other hand for my phone. It was my real estate agent, probably calling to relate the results of the open house at the condo.

"Hey, Linda, any good news?"

"Hi Brenna, just wanted to let you know we had a great turnout. There was lots of interest. Everyone was very impressed. Plenty of positive comments."

"Awesome. So, did we get any offers?"

"Not yet, but I'm optimistic. It's a beautiful condo in a great location and the market is strong right now."

"Not even a nibble?"

Linda laughed. "Be patient. Most people like to go home and think things over before committing to such a big decision."

The agent sounded bubbly, but I got the impression I shouldn't hold my breath.

"Okay," I said. "I'll try to be patient. Let me know if anything happens."

I hung up feeling disappointed. I had pictured multiple offers on the spot, perhaps even a bidding war. *Give it time. It'll sell.*

I thought about Tamara whose unit was on the same floor down the hall from mine. Should I call her? She had said she would keep an eye on the comings and goings at the apartment. But realistically I doubted she could add anything to the realtor's account. Then I remembered she was working today. She might not even be home yet.

I was dying to talk to her, but not about my condo. Now that the big secret had been resolved I could once more confide in my best friend. Not only did I appreciate her novel perspective on ghostly manifestations, but I knew she'd be happy to hear that Gage was back in my good graces.

    I would call her as soon as I got the chance, but for now Connie was waiting.

Chapter Eighteen

The minute I stepped inside the house, I could tell Connie's mood had improved since getting the good news about Buster's prognosis. Some people celebrate by toasting with a hearty drink, others go out on the town. Connie cooks.

The tantalizing aroma of roast chicken steeped in rosemary and garlic set my stomach to grumbling, and reminded me that it had been hours since lunch and I'd only had a salad. I set the table while Connie finished mashing the potatoes.

"Hey, wasn't today the open house at your condo?" she asked, handing me a platter of chicken.

"Yep, the realtor just called. Nothing exciting to report I'm afraid. She said there was a good turnout, but no offers. So now I'm in 'be patient' mode." I gave a little humph of irritation. Patience is not one of my better attributes.

"For heaven's sake, Brenna," she said. "It's only been a week. Give it time."

"I know, I know." I blew out a breath and took a seat in the dining room. I reached for the bowl of green beans. "By the way, I had my first rug braiding lesson today."

"How'd it go?" Connie set the potatoes on the table then sat across from me. She took a roll and began to smear it with butter.

"It was fun. Maureen's a great teacher. I really got into it. Turns out I have more artistic talent than I thought."

"Really? Did you bring home your rug? Can I see it?"

"It's not finished. We're getting together again in the morning for our next lesson. And by *we*, I mean me, Nick Donato and his two girls."

"Nick Donato's braiding a rug?" She gave a chortle of disbelief then speared a large portion of white meat on the platter and transferred it to her plate.

I laughed. "Well, he's trying but he's pretty much all thumbs. He's there more as a cheer leader for the girls, although I kind of get the feeling there are sparks smoldering between him and Maureen."

Connie's eyes went wide. "You're kidding."

I shrugged. "He agreed to stay for lunch tomorrow after the lesson. Maureen's going to order pizza and make a party out of it."

"Right, because what's more romantic than eating pizza after a long day of rug braiding with your kids?"

"We're both invited, by the way."

She made a face. "Count me out. I was planning to go into the shop tomorrow. With Buster coming home on

Monday, I thought I could get an early start on some orders. Are you going to stay for pizza?"

"I was thinking about it." I looked down at my plate and busied myself cutting a piece of chicken. Offhandedly, I added, "Gage is going to be there too."

"Ah-ha." She smiled and gave an astute nod. "So, you're not mad at him anymore?"

I was not about to discuss ghosts with Connie nor any of the other delicate topics hashed out next door. "Let's just say I was party to a heart-to-heart discussion between Maureen and Gage and I predict things between them will be a lot better from now on."

"That'll be a nice change," Connie said, helping herself to the mashed potatoes.

As much as I loved my cousin and was deeply appreciative of all her help, I found her attitudes tended to be a tad judgmental. She took a lot after her mother, though I knew she'd deny it.

"You're working tomorrow?" I asked. "I thought you weren't open on Sundays."

"We're not, but we got a big order in today for a fiftieth anniversary party. They want six table centerpieces, a large spray for on top of a piano, and a corsage and boutonnière for the couple—all to be delivered by next Friday at noon. Pass the gravy. Thanks. Plus three bouquets for new babies need to be delivered Monday or Tuesday, and a couple of birthday party centerpieces are due on Wednesday. And that doesn't count the walk-ins." She began to mix the gravy into her potatoes until she had created a muddy-looking slurry on her plate.

"Since I want to stay home on Monday with Buster when he comes home from the vet, I thought I could get a head start. Tracy said she'd work all day Monday, but if things get busy she won't have time to do much flower arranging in the back."

I tapped a finger thoughtfully on the table. "I have an idea. Why don't I go in on Monday and help Tracy? I wouldn't do flower arranging, but I could handle the front counter if things got busy. That is, if you don't think I'd just be in the way."

Connie gave me a sideways look. "Ever operate a cash register before?"

"Back in college I worked part-time at a shoe store. I rang things up all the time, no problem."

She grinned. "Close enough. Everything's computerized now, anyway. And Tracy'll be there if you run into trouble. Maybe it'll be the start of a whole new career for you."

"I wouldn't go *that* far. But it might be fun." I smiled. "It'll give me something to do. I'll go in tomorrow and you can give me a quick lesson in the finer points of flower selling."

"Wait—what about Maureen's pizza party?" She gave me a little smirk. "You don't want to disappoint Gage."

"Don't worry about Gage. I'll go over in the morning for my rug braiding lesson, have some pizza when we break for lunch, and then leave right afterward. The party was pretty impromptu anyway. They won't mind if I take off early. I should make it to the shop a little after one. I'll bring you some pizza."

"Sounds perfect," Connie said. "I'll go early and get started on some flower arrangements. Then we'll spend the rest of the afternoon going over how to take orders and ring up sales."

Siblings and Secrets

I was clearing the table when my phone rang. It was Gage.

"Do you still have Maureen's shopping list?" he asked. "She needs a few things for tomorrow so I thought I'd head up to Brubaker's. And as long as I'm going I might as well take care of the rest of the list."

"I do. In fact, I was thinking of going up there myself. Connie needs a few things too."

The sound of his voice had set my heart palpitating. Could he tell?

"Great," he said. "Why don't I pick you up in ten minutes and we'll go together?"

"Okay, meet you out front." I expelled a deep breath as I hung up. It had been ages since I'd felt this keyed up. Sort of like when Kevin Dombrowski had asked me to my first high school dance.

Turning around, I found Connie looking at me with a shrewd smile.

"What?" I asked, as a telltale flush spread across my cheeks.

"You're blushing, so I assume that was Gage."

"I am *not* blushing," I said, pressing the back of my hand to my face. "It's warm in here. We're just going to run up to the store to get groceries."

Connie continued to smile. "Well, I guess you've answered my question."

I frowned. "What question?"

"What's more romantic than pizza and rug braiding? Apparently grocery shopping."

I grabbed my purse and headed for the front door.

"It's all right, you know," she called after me. "You could do a lot worse."

Shopping with Gage was hardly romantic, but it was fun—in a comfortable, domestic sort of way. Until now, I hadn't fully realized how lonely I'd been these past two years and how much I had missed doing mundane, everyday things with a male companion whose company I enjoyed.

Like buying toilet paper.

"Huh-uh," I said, nixing his choice of a discount brand.

"This one's cheapest."

I shook my head. "Get the two-ply. You'll thank me later."

When we got home, he grabbed two of my four grocery sacks and carried them inside for me. Arms full, we tiptoed through the living room so as not to wake Connie who was dozing on the couch in front of the TV. I set my bags on the kitchen table and took a moment to straighten the front of my shirt. Without warning, Gage caught my shoulders and spun me around to face him, planting a firm kiss on my astonished lips.

I sputtered and stumbled back. I wasn't displeased, but he'd taken me by surprise.

"Sorry. I've been wanting to do that for an awfully long time."

"You *have?*" I squeaked, dazed and a little breathless.

"Mm-hm." His eyes twinkled. "I'd say for at least twenty-seven years. That's about how long I've had a crush on you."

I would have been seven years old. And he... I did some quick calculations.

"You were ten years old," I said, narrowing my eyes at

him.

He laughed unabashedly. "What can I say? You were awfully pretty as a child. Still are."

Was he teasing me? Was he serious? I was too stunned to think straight.

"I was devastated when you moved away and never came back," he continued in a voice more earnest. "I put away my water pistol for good after that. The joy just went out of it."

From the other room I heard Connie rouse. "Brenna, is that you?" The old couch groaned as she stood up.

"I'd better go," Gage said. "See you tomorrow." Moving toward the door, he nearly ran into Connie.

"Hi, Gage," she said as he brushed past. "Bye, Gage."

As the front door swung shut, my cousin turned back to me with a lift of her brow. "Did I miss anything?"

I grabbed a bunch of bananas from the nearest shopping bag. "Just putting groceries away."

The next morning, I rang Maureen's doorbell promptly at ten. Gage opened the door with a robust smile looking invigorated, as though he had gotten his first full night's sleep in a long time. His unshaven chin and tousled hair suggested he'd stayed the night. I knew he kept his old bedroom in the house in case his sister needed him.

"Come in, come in," he said with a broad sweep of his arm toward the living room.

"You're in a good mood," I said.

"I am. Maureen and I had a long heart-to-heart last night."

What about Hannah's ghost? She wasn't gone. I had seen her just yesterday. Had they talked about that? Was Gage willing to believe in her now?

I opened my mouth to ask, but further conversation was suspended as the sound of giggling girls behind me announced the arrival of Nick Donato with Carly and Gina. Hearing the sisters, Maureen appeared from the kitchen.

"Hey, girls," she called out, motioning with a wooden spoon. "I'm making cookies to have later. You're just in time to help me spoon the dough onto trays."

With squeals of delight, the girls ran to join her.

"Hi, Nick," Maureen added almost as an afterthought, though it appeared she was blushing.

Or maybe it was the heat from the oven.

Nick returned her look with an engaging smile.

Nope, she's definitely blushing.

Pleased as I was by this budding romance, I worried it could lead to heartbreak if Nick wasn't prepared to deal with Maureen's "quirks."

Quit being such a pessimist. If it's real, they'll work it out. I caught Gage's eye and he responded with a slight pull at the corners of his mouth. If he shared my concern, he didn't show it.

Maureen turned to me. "Is Connie coming over later? There's a football game on this afternoon. We can watch it while we eat pizza."

"She sends her apologies. She wants to get a jump on things at the shop. Her dog's coming home from the vet tomorrow and she wants to stay home to keep an eye on him." I flipped a strand of hair back over my shoulder. "Actually I can't stay long, either. I'm going to leave right after we eat. Connie's going to teach me how to run the cash register so I can lend a hand at the store tomorrow while she stays home."

Maureen nodded. "That's nice of you. She's lucky to have you here."

I laughed. "Fortunately, her regular assistant will be there too, to make sure I don't mess things up too much."

"Well, we'd better hurry then," she said. "Come on, girls. Let's go finish those cookies." She motioned to Carly and Gina and the three of them disappeared into the kitchen.

"So, how 'bout those Seahawks?" Gage said to Nick. "Should be a great game today."

They started talking football stats and I pretended for a moment to understand. Finally, I left them to their guy-bonding and went into the kitchen to see how things were progressing. I found Maureen and the two little girls with their fingers in the bowl placing heaps of chocolate chip cookie dough on baking sheets.

"Miss Moreland," cried Carly, "Gina licked her fingers and put them back in the dough."

"You shouldn't eat the cookie dough, Gina," Maureen said.

"Why not?" asked the younger sister. "I like the dough best."

Well, yeah, I thought, smiling to myself. Doesn't *everybody* like the dough best? Why else would Ben & Jerry's make chocolate chip cookie dough ice cream?

"Because it has raw egg in it and that's not good for you," replied Maureen in a firm, reasonable tone.

"*Eww,*" Gina said, making a face.

I had heard the same argument from my mother. She

always tried to dissuade me with dire warnings of stomach aches and throwing up. But despite these scare tactics, I still sneak bites of dough whenever I make cookies. I don't scare easily when it comes to my sweet tooth.

"Besides, you'll put germs on the cookies," Carly said. "Right, Miss Moreland?"

Maureen inclined her head as though giving the question serious thought. "I'm not too worried about germs because the oven is very hot. The germs should all be killed when the cookies are baked."

She's a natural at this, I thought. *She really has a rapport with these children.*

Once the trays were in the oven and a timer set, we rejoined the men who were settled in the living room deep in debate over the league's best quarterbacks.

Maureen cleared her throat noisily. "We're going to head upstairs now to get back to braiding our rugs. Gage, would you please listen for the timer and take the cookies out when they're done?"

"Sure thing."

"Nick? You coming?" Maureen asked.

Nick looked up and shook his head. "Naw, you guys go on and finish your rugs. I'll stay here and keep Gage company. Mine wasn't looking so hot anyway."

Carly giggled. "Daddy's rag rug looks more like a rag than a rug."

He fake growled and reached out to box her ear, but she squealed and ran behind Maureen.

Their interaction was heartwarming. Nick obviously adored his girls and they idolized him. *Who says a single father can't be an awesome parent?* No wonder Maureen was taken with him.

"Why don't you finish it for me," Nick said, grinning at his daughter.

The girls followed Maureen to the attic and I brought up the rear. We got comfortable on the floor and Maureen brought out the boxes of half-finished rugs and fabric strips. Eagerly, we picked up where we'd left off the day before. Maureen obligingly went over the instructions again: outside strand, over, under, over, through, repeat—each strip worked into the whole.

As my rug took shape, I had to admit I was pleased with myself. This was fun. Who knew I could make something so pretty with strips of rags and my bare hands? Judging by their smiles and giggles, Carly and Gina were getting into it too. If they had a tangle or a problem braiding around a curve, Maureen was right there with a helping hand, patiently assisting them in a way that never sounded condescending.

Gage and Nick eventually came up to watch, offering their own advice and encouragement.

After an hour and a half, Maureen called a halt. The rugs were nearing completion, but the girls' giggling was giving way to complaining and it was obvious they were getting restless. Gratefully, I straightened my back and flexed my shoulders.

"Time to stand up and stretch," Maureen said. "Then we'll go order some pizzas."

Carly and Gina let loose enthusiastic yells and galloped down the stairs with Maureen and Nick close on their heels. Gage came up behind me and gave my stiff muscles a rigorous massage.

"Maureen's happy," he said, leaning close to my ear.

I nodded. "Working with the girls is good for her."

"It's more than that. Have you seen how she and Nick look at each other?"

Did he think that would solve everything? I took a step away from him and turned around. "Sure, but what happens when he asks her out? Does he know about her...illness?"

Gage gave a shrug.

"Look," I said, "I think it's wonderful that you and Maureen have straightened things out. But I don't think that's the end of it, do you?"

He took a deep breath. "We're working on it. We talked for a long time last night. I told her I didn't blame her for Hannah's disappearance and I think she's finally starting to see it wasn't her fault. I'm hoping that just being happy for a change will help."

"Well, it can't hurt. But it might be a good idea for you to talk to Nick. Give him a heads up, so you don't wind up with another Andy situation."

"You're probably right. I just don't want to scare him off."

"Well, here's something else to think about. Hannah's ghost is still making appearances. Don't laugh. I saw her yesterday."

"Brenna..." He looked pained. "I'm trying to be more understanding here, but—come on."

All I could do was keep going. I had a bombshell of my own to drop. "We still don't know what happened to her, but I think Buster knows where she's buried."

"*What?*"

"I'm almost positive he's found her. Twice now, he's gotten out of the back yard and come home all dirty, like he's been digging. And both times he's brought home a half-rotten girl's tennis shoe."

His gave me a skeptical frown. "That doesn't prove anything."

"No, but get this—the first time I saw Hannah's ghost she had shoes on, but the last couple of times she was barefoot, like she'd lost her shoes."

He threw his hands up. "Do you know how *crazy* that sounds?"

I was beginning to understand how Maureen felt, being told she was crazy all the time. "Sure," I retorted, "but I happened to save the last one. I thought the police could test it for DNA."

"Uh-huh, and what are you going to tell the police? Your dog brought home a random old shoe and you want them to spend valuable time and resources testing it, just in case it's evidence in a twenty-five-year-old cold case?"

I jammed my hands onto my hips, waiting for him to give me a lecture on why this was a bad idea.

Sure enough. "What will you say when they ask you *why* you think it's Hannah's shoe? Are you going to tell them it's because you saw her ghost going barefoot?"

Okay, put like that it did sound a bit whacked.

"And what about when they ask you where Buster found the shoe? You have no idea, do you?" Gage turned and took a few steps, his somber eyes focused on the wall. "I remember a few weeks after Hannah disappeared, this woman came forward who claimed to be a psychic. She swore she could find Hannah. The police thought she was full of crap, but she convinced my parents to let her try. She put on quite a show for them—incense, crystal ball, mystic trance—the whole circus act. She sent everyone running on a couple of wild goose chases before the cops finally threatened her with perpetrating a fraud."

"Okay, okay," I said. "Forget the police. But I'm still convinced it's Hannah's shoe and Buster knows where she's buried. It doesn't matter whether you believe me or not."

His expression softened. "Okay, just for the sake of argument, let's say you're right about this. What do you propose to do about it?"

"I'm thinking once Buster's healthy again—say in a couple of weeks—I'll leave him alone in the back yard and let him dig out under the fence like before. I'll watch him from the kitchen window and when he does, I'll follow him."

Gage looked doubtful, but the conversation ended when Maureen hollered up the stairs at us.

"*Hey*, are you guys coming? The pizza will be here any minute."

"We'd better get going," I said. "I still have to get to the flower shop to help Connie."

Chapter Nineteen

Connie's Pretty Petals Florist Shop was fifteen minutes away on Aurora Avenue, the main highway through Shoreline. She gave me a systematic tour, showing me where things like vases, ribbons, and greeting cards were kept, as well as pointing out the buckets full of different varieties of flowers she kept stored in the walk-in refrigerator in back. At first, she tried referring to the various flora by their Latin genus names, but gave up when I retaliated by calling them by their colors: "the *red* ones, the *purple* ones, the *yellow* ones."

It didn't take me long to figure out the cash register. As Connie said, it was computerized and not too complicated. In fact, most of the business was done by computer, although I found a pen and printed order pad next to the phone on a desk behind the counter. Connie said she liked to jot down notes "old school" when customers called with orders over the phone. I felt confident I could handle things for a day or two, especially with the help of Connie's assistant Tracy, and Jerry the delivery guy.

What a dream to work in such a place, surrounded by flowers. Such vibrant colors and intoxicating fragrances. What a difference from the high stress environment of a busy law firm.

Monday morning I arrived at seven thirty sharp, prepared to open the store for business precisely at eight. I rubbed my hands vigorously together to calm my first-day jitters, then dove into the preliminary procedures Connie had set out for me. Tracy arrived minutes later. She was a stout woman in her late forties with short brown hair and a pale face just beginning to wrinkle around the edges. She had a cheerful demeanor and we immediately clicked. After giving me a few pointers and some words of encouragement, she disappeared into the back to start work.

At exactly eight o'clock, the bell above the front door tinkled and my first customer strode in. Tall and blond, wearing a camel sports coat and sharply-pressed charcoal slacks, he had the lean physique of a runner. He approached the counter with an arresting smile.

My pulse quickened. *Here we go.*

"Hi," he said in a voice smooth as warm chocolate. "I'm Troy. You're new here, aren't you?"

Electric-blue eyes twinkled behind a pair of chic tortoiseshell glasses, narrow face enhanced by a trace of beard stubble on a sturdy jaw. I pegged him at somewhere in his upper thirties—one of those guys who only gets sexier with age.

"First day," I said, trying not to stare. *If all Connie's customers look like this, I may just stay on full time.*

"Nice to meet you." His smile was genuine and unguarded.

I pushed my hair back in a self-conscious gesture. "I take it you've been here before."

He laughed. "I guess you'd call me a regular. I don't live far from here. Every Monday I like to swing by on my way to work and pick up a bunch of flowers to brighten up the office."

His easy-going manner put me at ease. I came around the counter and directed him to the display case. Several bouquets of cut flowers were wrapped and set in buckets of water for easy accessibility. "I don't know what you normally get, but we have a nice selection here to choose from. Everything's fresh as of this morning. Do you need a vase?"

"No thanks, just the flowers," he said. He chose a colorful mixture of dahlias, delphinium, and sunflowers. Laying them on the counter, he fished a credit card from his wallet and handed it to me.

"That'll be twelve-fifty," I said. As I swiped his card and entered the amount into the machine, I made casual conversation. *Good customer relations. Nothing to do with the fact that he looks like a million dollar executive-cum-underwear model.* "Where do you work? Seattle?"

"University District." His lips pulled up at the corners. "Don't hate me...I'm a lawyer."

I laughed. *What were the odds?* "No problem. Some of

my closest friends are lawyers. In fact, just a couple of weeks ago, I was working for a very distinguished lawyer in Seattle."

His eyebrows rose. "Really? Which one?"

I handed him the sales slip to sign and was about to offer him a receipt when the phone next to me rang suddenly, causing me to start. My elbow bumped the display of gift cards on the counter, and it would have crashed to the floor if we hadn't both reacted and made a grab for it. Our fingers overlapped and we had a brief moment of awkwardness.

He stepped back and I righted the display, uttering a quick "thank-you" as I reached for the phone. "Pretty Petals Floral and Gifts," I chirped. Then in reply to the caller's inquiry, "Five o'clock."

I hung up and said with a nervous laugh, "Sorry about that. First day. Guess I'm still a bit jumpy."

"No problem." He smiled and tilted his head. "You were going to tell me which attorney you worked for."

"Oh, right," I said. "Ralph Murray." My old employer had been tough as gristle—irascible and uncompromising, but also brilliant and unwaveringly scrupulous. My feelings for him fell somewhere between respect and terror. One minute he'd be stubborn and unreasonable, and the next discerning and supportive. He had taught me much and I was grateful.

He nodded. "Murray, Gerber, and Hall. I'm familiar with them. Ralph retired, didn't he?"

"That's right. He said he wanted to travel."

He gave me a crooked half-smile. "So you took the opportunity to quit and pursue your life-long dream of selling flowers?" He was being tactful. He might have asked why they didn't keep me on at the firm. But that would have been awkward if I'd been let go.

I saved him the embarrassment. "They would have found me another position if I'd wanted to stay. I worked for Mr. Murray for nearly nine years. But it seemed like a good time to go. I was sick of the downtown rat race."

"What did your husband think?"

I blinked. "My husband?"

He inclined his head toward my left hand where the diamond in my ring caught the light. "Aren't you married?"

I looked down at my hand. The ring was like a part of me. "My husband died two years ago. I can't quite bring myself to take it off." One of these days I would, but not yet.

His expression sobered. "I'm sorry."

Before the conversation could go any further, the bell above the door jingled and a woman in a tailored business suit entered. She approached the display case and began to peruse the flowers behind the glass.

"I'd better be going." He grabbed the bouquet off the counter and tipped me a quick salute. "Thanks," he said. "It was nice talking to you." With that, he sauntered out the door.

I still held the signed credit card slip in my hand. I raised it to read the name. He had introduced himself when he came in, but my nerves had caused my brain to fog over and I'd forgotten what he said. I was curious to see if I recognized him. During my years working in the legal profession, I had periodically had occasion to deal with other attorneys on cases, usually over the phone or through correspondence.

The name on the slip was Troy Cavendish. It sounded vaguely familiar but I couldn't quite place it. Then I noticed something on the floor by my foot. I thought one of the gift cards from the display had fallen, but when I picked it up I gasped in horror. Somehow, between the distraction of the phone call and my jitters, I had dropped the man's credit card and he had left without realizing it. *Drat!* I rushed out the front door hoping to catch him but he had disappeared.

I had no time to berate myself. The woman in the business suit had selected half a dozen roses and brought them to the counter. I forced myself to smile and complete the sale as she carried on about stopping on her way to buy flowers for a co-worker who was celebrating a birthday.

I felt sick. As soon as she left, I intended to look up the number for Troy Cavendish's office in Seattle so that I could call to let him know I still had his credit card. Naturally, I would refund his money for the inconvenience but I hated that he should think I was incompetent. I wanted to kick myself. I *never* made this kind of mistake. In all the years I'd worked for Ralph Murray, I'd always prided myself on my efficiency; it was the quality the old attorney had most appreciated.

But it would have to wait. On the heels of the businesswoman came a young man who wanted to order a bouquet for his mother whose beloved cat had died.

"What kind of flowers does one give for a deceased feline?" he quipped.

I said the first thing that came into my head. "Pussy willows?" Connie had a small bundle in the large cooler in the back room. The slender stems were covered with the soft, silvery tufts so reminiscent of tiny cat paws. They weren't in season, but Connie told me they were grown specifically for florists in an exclusive greenhouse.

The customer laughed agreeably. "I never would have thought of that, but I like it. What else?"

Relieved that my first stab at a suggestion hadn't fallen flat, I went on. "We'll mix them with pink and white carnations to signify love and remembrance, a trio of white stargazer lilies for sympathy, and perhaps some forget-me-nots for a dash of color and nostalgia."

"Sounds perfect," he said. "Let's do it."

As I wrote up the order, I silently thanked Connie for the cheat-sheet she had given me to study the night before on the traditional meanings of flowers and what their colors stood for.

"We'll have them ready for you to pick up by three this afternoon," I said.

As he left, I exhaled deeply and thought, *That went well, maybe I'm actually getting the hang of this.*

However, not all my ideas were so well received.

"Red roses?" protested the young man who came in next. "After the first date? I don't want to *marry* her. Just, you know, keep her *happy*, if you know what I mean." He gave me a lecherous grin. Twentyish, swaggering and conceited, the gangling lout obviously considered himself a real stud.

I wanted to suggest dandelions, but reminded myself that this was a business—Connie's livelihood. I recommended a medley of carnations and white daisies. He went away happy, and all I could do was shake my head and hope the lady was smart enough to see through him.

After his departure, I finally had a break. I whipped out my phone and began to search for law offices in Seattle, Washington. Scrolling down, I finally landed on his name: Troy Cavendish, Attorney at Law, specializing in criminal defense. My eyebrows rose of their own accord. *Wow.*

I took a deep breath, steeled myself, and tapped in the number. The call was answered on the second ring by an efficient-sounding female voice. I asked to speak to Mr. Cavendish and she put me right through.

Why is it that when it's imperative you speak to someone right away, you get put on hold for an hour, but when you're not especially eager, you get connected right away?

"This is Troy Cavendish," he answered in a serious voice.

I swallowed. "Hi. This is Brenna at Connie's Pretty Petals Florist in Shoreline. We met this morning when you came in to buy some flowers."

"Of course, Brenna." His tone relaxed, becoming buoyant and friendly. "What can I do for you?"

"I guess this means you haven't realized you don't have your credit card." *Of course not or he would have called by now.* I held my breath, waiting for his reply.

"What? No. Did I leave it there?"

I grimaced and let out my breath. "I'm so sorry. I found it on the floor behind the counter after you left. Looks like I dropped it when the phone rang. My only excuse is that you were my very first customer and I was flustered."

He chuckled.

Relieved at his good humor, I responded with an

embarrassed laugh. "Thank you for being so understanding. I promise, I'm not usually this inept."

"Hey, I'm the one who walked off without it. I didn't even notice."

"Can you stop here on your way home tonight to pick it up?"

"I can't make it this evening, but how about if I come by in the morning? Will you be there?"

"Absolutely." I'd have to clear it with Connie but I didn't think she'd object. She would love having another day to stay home and care for Buster. Oddly, I found myself looking forward to seeing the man again.

I buried the card in the back of the cash register and the rest of the morning proceeded without mishap. I sold a potted cactus to a highly tattooed teenage girl with long black hair and a nose ring. I wondered why she wasn't in school but shrugged it off as none of my business.

Next, I sold a pink stuffed teddy bear and a vanilla-scented candle to a young woman deeply involved in a conversation on her cell phone. She never once made eye contact with me as she plopped her selections on the counter and dug her debit card from the depths of her over-sized purse. When the transaction was complete, she took her bag and, still glued to her phone, turned and walked out of the store without ever acknowledging my existence.

"You're welcome," I called to her disappearing back. Whatever happened to good manners? *Careful, you're starting to sound like your mother.*

At noon I called Connie.

"How's Buster doing?"

"He's glad to be home," she said. "But he's not his old

self, that's for sure. He mostly wants to sleep."

"That's probably for the best. He needs to get his strength back."

"How are things at the shop? Don't forget to eat lunch. You and Tracy can trade off."

Once a boss, always a boss. "Don't worry," I said. "We've got it covered. I'm on my break as we speak. Things haven't been too busy so far, just a nice steady stream of customers to keep things interesting. Tracy's mostly stayed in back working on those orders you were talking about, and Jerry's off making a delivery."

"So, no problems?"

"Not really," I said. I didn't want her to worry, but I also couldn't lie. "I had one little hiccup, but I took care of it."

"What happened?" There was a hint of apprehension edging her voice.

Darn, I shouldn't have said anything. Of course she's going to worry.

"It was my very first customer. One of your regulars. He stopped to pick up flowers for his office. We got to talking, then the phone rang and I got distracted. Somehow I forgot to give him back his credit card and he left without it."

Her distress was evident in the hissing noise she made through her teeth.

"But it's okay," I hurried to reassure her. "I called him right away and he was very understanding. Didn't seem upset at all. He's going to come in tomorrow and pick it up."

"Wait—first thing Monday morning? Was it Troy?"

"Yeah, nice guy." I guess it shouldn't surprise me that

she'd know the shop's regular patrons.

"One of my best customers. Been coming in every Monday for the past two years. I'm glad it was him and not somebody else."

"He said he lives not far from here and stops every week on his way to work. Did you know he's an attorney?"

Connie laughed. "Hey, there you go. Why don't you ask him for a job? Maybe he could use a new secretary."

I balked at her use of the archaic term. With my advanced training, skills, and experience, I had been so much more than a secretary. I considered myself a legal assistant, a professional, just one step away from a paralegal. But there was no point bringing this up now. "Unfortunately, I think he already has one."

"Well," she insisted, "it wouldn't hurt to give him a résumé. I think he'd be a great guy to work for."

"Yes, mother." I was being facetious, but in truth it wasn't a bad idea. *Strike while the iron is hot,* my mom used to say. Or was it *nothing ventured, nothing gained?* My mother used to drive me crazy with her unending supply of old adages, but once in a while I could see where they made sense. In this case, I figured it couldn't hurt to give Mr. Cavendish my résumé. He said his office was in the U-District, far enough north of downtown to be appealing. The worst he could do was throw it away.

Connie changed the subject. "By the way, Maureen called and wanted to know if you'd like to come over this evening and finish up that rug you were making. Nick's girls are going over after school, but I told her you might not be home till six. She said that was okay if you were up to it. Sadly, Gage won't be there. She said he had to go to work this morning and probably won't make it back out this way for the rest of the week."

"Imagine that. The poor man has a job to go to."

"Unlike some people we know."

I stuck my tongue out at the phone. "About that. I wouldn't mind staying on longer if you need me. I could even do deliveries in a pinch. That way, you can stay home a little longer to keep an eye on Buster, and Tracy can leave earlier. She told me she likes to be home when her kids get home from school."

"Uh-huh. You just want to be there when Troy comes in."

"Well, I have to be here if I'm going to give him my résumé, don't I?"

She laughed. "Touché. Fine. You go in tomorrow and I'll stay home again with Buster. But Wednesday I really think I need to come in and check on things, and give Tracy a hand."

"Sure," I said. "Meantime, I'll call Maureen and see if I can put her off till Wednesday. I'll be too frazzled to work on my rug tonight anyway, after being here all day. Now, go back to watching TV or go take a nap with Buster. I promise not to wreck your store while you're gone."

"Thanks. I appreciate that," Connie said.

The next morning promptly at eight, I was again greeted by the very dashing Mr. Cavendish. I couldn't help comparing his amiable personality to the broodiness I associated with Gage Moreland, though given the tribulations Gage had endured growing up, it didn't seem fair.

"Good morning, Brenna," he called as he strode through the door.

He remembered my name. Impressive.

"Good morning, Mr. Cavendish."

"Call me Troy," he said as he approached. I saw then that he carried two large "to go" cups from the coffee shop next door. He set one of the cups on the counter before me. Without conscious thought, my eyes strayed to his left hand and registered the lack of a ring.

"You struck me as the mocha latte type," he said with a grin. "Extra whip with chocolate sprinkles."

My eyebrows sprang up in surprise and undisguised pleasure as I inhaled the sweet, warm aroma of the coffee. "Perfect. Thank you." I raised the cup to my lips and took a tiny sip, mindful of scalding my tongue. "How much do I owe you?"

He waved a hand. "Nothing. My treat."

I laughed and set the cup down. "Well, thank you again. But after my carelessness yesterday, I ought to be the one buying *your* coffee." I opened the cash register and retrieved his credit card. "There you go. Thank you for coming by."

"Are you trying to get rid of me?" His eyes shone and he gave me a devilish smile.

He was flirting and a part of me was flattered. There was no denying he was good-looking and fun to talk to, but how far should I let this go? I didn't want to encourage him. I wasn't ready for any kind of serious relationship. But what harm could there be in a little lighthearted banter?

I thought about Gage and felt the teensiest bit of guilt.

After the stolen kiss in the kitchen and his confession of a childhood crush, I knew there was something between us. But so far our feelings had remained unspoken, which was exactly how I wanted it. We had known each other since we were kids, and I was happy for now just remaining friends, keeping things simple and uncomplicated.

I gave Troy a gracious smile. "Well, I know you're a busy man, and I don't want to hold you up."

He grinned. "You're right. Heaven forbid I should be five minutes late." He put the card in his wallet and shoved it into his back pocket.

"Oh, and I refunded the price of the flowers," I said. "It was the least I could do for making you come in here two days in a row."

He started to object and I threw my hands up to stop him.

"I insist," I said. "Store policy. I screw up, you get your money back. It's a law."

He pulled an unconvincing frown. "Well, okay," he said. "Far be it from me to break the law."

"But you *can* do me a favor." I gave him what I hoped was a winning smile, stopping just short of batting my eyelashes. *Oh god*, I thought with an inner eye roll. *The depths to which I'll stoop for a new job.*

The grin rebounded onto his face. "Anything I can do, just name it."

I reached under the counter for the envelope I had placed there that morning. I pushed it toward him. "This is my résumé. I know you're probably not looking for anybody right now, but maybe you could pass it on to a colleague. I thought you might know somebody who's looking for a good legal assistant...preferably not downtown."

He took the envelope and tucked it carefully into the inside pocket of his coat. "I don't know of anyone hiring at the moment, but I'll definitely keep it on file, just in case."

As he said this, I noticed his smile slip. I followed his gaze down to my hands, and that's when I realized I'd been fiddling with the wedding ring on my finger. It was becoming a nervous habit. *Like an unconscious ward against suitors.* Wrenching my hands apart, I made a careless swipe at my hair, pushing it back behind my ear. His expression was unreadable.

Before things could get any more awkward, the bell above the front door tinkled and a lively older couple entered the store. They began to browse through the shelves of gifts, talking loudly back and forth.

"I'd better get to the office," Troy said. "It was nice seeing you again."

"Thanks for the coffee," I called after him as he strode to the door.

Feeling oddly conflicted, I exhaled deeply as I watched him exit to the sidewalk and disappear. It seemed wrong to lead him on, yet I had to admit I enjoyed the diversion. Besides being attractive, he was smart, funny, and easy to talk to. I wondered if I would see him again.

Chapter Twenty

When I got home, Buster met me at the door, eyes bright and tail wagging. He seemed almost his old self again.

"How'd it go today?" Connie came from the kitchen, wiping her hands on a towel. "Did you get Troy all straightened out?"

"Yep, everything's fine." I yanked off my coat and went to hang it in the hall closet.

"Did you give him your résumé?"

I gave my shoulders a quick shrug. "I did, but I'm not holding my breath."

"Well, it's a start," she said. "By the way, Nancy Chumley came by this morning. She wanted to talk to you about the craft fair. The school board meeting was last night."

"Oh, that's right," I said, plopping onto the couch. I

pried off my shoes and rubbed the balls of my aching feet. I was gaining a new respect for salespeople. I didn't know how they did it, standing up all day. "They were going to vote on letting us use the school gym."

"They unanimously agreed to let us have it on the first Saturday of December." Connie bobbed her head in a self-satisfied way as though she had personally had a hand in seeing the job done.

"Did she happen to mention what it would cost? I doubt they're going to let us have it for nothing."

"Cost? I don't think she mentioned it." Her brow wrinkled in uncertainty.

"I'm sure they'll want us to pay for insurance," I said, "and maybe even janitorial services to clean up afterward. I'll check with Nancy, or better yet, maybe I'll just call the school in the morning and see what I can find out. Then you, me, and Maureen should get together to figure out what we'll have to charge each vendor for a space."

I thought for a moment. "I'll bet I can look up the standard size of an elementary school basketball court on the internet. That should give us a rough idea of the square footage of the gym, which will help us figure out how best to divide up the space. The sooner we get the cost figured out, the sooner we can start advertising to local craftspeople. We'll want to sell as many spots as possible to cover our expenses."

"Well, you have all day tomorrow," Connie said. "Weren't you planning to go to Maureen's to work on your rug? The two of you can have a meeting and figure it all out. You don't need me."

"You *are* the chairperson," I said. "I don't want you to feel left out."

She shrugged. "I'm delegating." Then her look became thoughtful. "But I *could* use your help again at the shop on Thursday if you're not busy. Tracy and I are going to have our hands full on some big orders, and I may need you to do a couple of deliveries if we get in a pinch. Jerry's got a dentist appointment and needs the day off."

"Sure," I said. "No problem. Buster's doing a lot better, and it'll give me something to do."

"Great," Connie said. "Thanks. Now I've got to get back to work on dinner. Those potatoes won't peel themselves." She turned and flitted into the kitchen with Buster hot on her heels.

I leaned back, rolling my shoulders, trying to get comfortable on the lumpy couch. I had just about reached a state of relaxed bliss when a strident rooster crow jerked me abruptly upright. *I've got to change that,* I thought. Blowing out a breath, I grabbed the phone off the coffee table where I'd left it, and read the text.

It was Tamara: *Haven't seen you in ages. I'm off tomorrow. Lunch?*

I smiled. I'd been wanting to talk to her. So much had happened since we'd last spoken. I paused for a moment, thinking. I was due at Maureen's first thing tomorrow to work on my rug. Turned out we were both early risers so she had invited me to come at eight for coffee and bagels before we got started. I figured that would also be a good time to discuss the craft fair. Plus, I wanted to call the school district to get the rental cost for the gym. I could do that from Maureen's. After that I had the whole afternoon.

I texted back a reply: *Love to. Can we do late lunch? Busy in the a.m. How about 1:30? Meet you at McGruders?*

She responded right away: *Perfect. See you then. How is the dog?*

Doing well. Almost recovered.

Good to hear. See you tomorrow.

I put down the phone and I leaned back, inhaling deeply. A delicious aroma wafted from the kitchen.

"Dinner in twenty," hollered Connie.

"Smells wonderful," I called back.

"Nothing fancy. Just a stew I threw together with odds and ends I had in the fridge."

I smiled, knowing perfectly well anything Connie "threw together" would be a culinary masterpiece. My mouth began to water. Suddenly, I was starved.

Maureen met me at the door at five minutes after eight the next morning. I couldn't get over how much her appearance had improved since the first time I saw her the night of her impromptu birthday party. Her skin had more color, her hair more bounce, and I would swear she had gained a couple of pounds.

Pizza and cookies will do that to you, I thought. But on her it looked good. Wearing a modest turquoise sweater and jeans, she looked positively svelte.

"Maureen," I said, "you look amazing."

She lowered her eyes bashfully. "You're just saying that."

I grinned. "I think Nick Donato's been a good influence on you."

Her smile widened and her whole face lit up. "I know. I can't believe it. Everything's happening so fast. First

Gage, and now Nick. I haven't been this happy in—*forever*."

"What about…" I started hesitantly, fidgeting with my hands, playing with the ring on my finger. The last thing I wanted to do was throw cold water on her exuberance, but there were issues to be faced, not the least of which was Maureen's refusal to go outside.

"Let's go eat," she said, "and we'll talk."

She led the way to the dining room where she had laid out an inviting breakfast of bagels, cream cheese, and fresh fruit, along with a pot of hot coffee. I sat down and reached for a bagel as she continued.

"Things have changed between Gage and me. No more secrets, no more suspicions. After all these years, it's like I have my brother back. You can't imagine how good that feels. We were always so close as kids. I thought we'd lost that forever."

I could almost see the joy blooming in her cheeks.

"That's awesome, Maureen," I said. "I'm so happy for both of you."

She paused and savored a bite of melon. Then she turned to face the window, gazing out at the heavily wooded lot next door where she had once thought the body of her sister lay secretly buried by her brother. With Gage exonerated, Hannah's fate was once more an unsolved mystery. When Maureen spoke again, her tone was solemn.

"What happened to Hannah was a tragedy," she said. "That won't change. But I'm starting to accept that it wasn't all my fault."

I nodded encouragement. At last, Maureen seemed to be on the road to recovery. "That's what I've been saying all along. Hannah loved you. She would never have wanted you to blame yourself." I reached across the table and took her hands. "I think Hannah's spirit came back, not to frighten you, but to let you know she's all right."

She looked down, breathing deeply, then raised her head again and met my eye. "I don't know why I still get upset when I talk about Hannah. I'm sure everything you say is true. I just have to get past these old feelings."

I bit my lower lip. "I have kind of a radical idea."

A tiny worry line appeared on her brow.

"What if you spoke to Hannah the next time she appears?" I said. "Tell her you love her, that you miss her. And then listen with your heart to see if she answers."

Maureen's mouth pulled tight and some of the color drained from her face. Her breathing became shallow and I could see that while she was making progress, she obviously wasn't there yet.

She grabbed half a bagel, tore off a piece, and began to spread it with cream cheese. Without looking up, she said, "That's a good idea. I just need to get up the courage. That's why I've decided to go back to seeing my therapist."

"Maureen, that's great," I said. "I'm so glad to hear it. When do you start? Is he coming here?"

She nodded. "I talked to him yesterday. He wants to start by coming here on Monday mornings. Then after a couple of weeks if everything goes okay, we're going to try moving to his office."

"That's wonderful," I said, beaming at her and clapping my hands together. It was the first time I'd heard her talk about leaving the house without having an anxiety attack.

She answered with a short laugh, then swallowed a bite of bagel and washed it down with a sip of coffee. "You know, Brenna, I have you to thank for all this. You're the only real friend I've had in years. The only one who listened to me and believed me. And you're the only one since your grandmother who ever wanted to spend time with me."

I shrugged, embarrassed. "Come on, we've known each other since we were kids, and I've always thought of you as a friend. Besides, I couldn't stand the thought of all your talent just sitting here going to waste." I smiled and licked a bit of cream cheese off my finger. "And on that note, we need to talk about the craft fair. Nancy says the school board has approved our use of the gym at the elementary school, so now we really have to start making plans."

"Right." She gave me an appraising look. "There's just one more thing."

"What's that?"

"I need a favor."

I laughed aloud. "So, there was a motive behind all that buttering up. How can I refuse? What do you need? Ask me anything."

"I need you to babysit Nick's kids Saturday night. I've asked him over for dinner and I'd like to be able to talk to him without the girls present. If we're going to keep seeing each other—which I hope—then he needs to know everything."

I sucked air in through my teeth. "Everything? The ghost?"

She gave a quick laugh. "Well, I won't lead with that. But he needs to know about Hannah, and my...panic attacks. I want him to know I'm seeing a therapist and why."

I gave my mouth a wry twist. "Considering how people in this neighborhood love to talk, I'd say there's a good chance he already knows."

The only way he could avoid the ubiquitous grapevine was if he never spoke to any of his neighbors. Remembering the enthusiastic greeting he'd received from the group at the meeting the other night, I was sure this wasn't the case; they'd all known him and been eager to include him in their lively circle.

"Maybe, but he needs to hear it from me. I want us to start off with everything out in the open." She shrugged. "If he doesn't run screaming, then maybe we'll have a chance."

Had Gage spoken to Nick? How well did they know each other? What kind of man was Nick Donato? From what I'd seen so far—a single dad raising two little girls—I was impressed. He seemed like an intelligent, even-tempered, fun-loving guy. And despite what he must have heard about Maureen's vanished sister, her absentee parents, and middle-of-the-night screaming fits, he appeared truly interested in her. I hoped to God he was serious and not just leading her on.

Connie had once mentioned that Nick's ex-wife was an alcoholic. That was probably why they had divorced and why he had custody of the kids. How did he feel about mental illness? What would his reaction be to Maureen's agoraphobia? Inviting him to dinner Saturday night was a good first step toward finding out. Despite my misgivings, I had to agree that talking to Nick and laying it all out on the table was the right thing to do, even though it had the potential to be heartbreaking. Maureen had come a long way. She deserved to be happy. If I could help by babysitting while they hashed things out, then naturally I would do it.

"Of course, I'll be glad to watch the girls." I picked up my coffee cup, then put it down again. I wanted to say something, to warn her not to get her hopes up too high. Nick might very well run the other way. I chewed my lip as I hesitated, not sure how to broach the subject.

She read my mind. "I know. This could backfire." She pushed a piece of fruit around on her plate, then looked up with an optimistic smile. "But we get along so well when we're together, and I know his girls like me. I'm hoping he thinks enough of me to see past this, and see how hard I'm working to get better." She shrugged. "But if not, that's okay. I prefer to know now rather than later."

"Hold on to that thought," I said. "If he doesn't see what a wonderful, caring person you are, then he's not worth it. And remember, your well-being is not dependent on him."

"I know." She gave a quick laugh. "But he *is* awfully good-looking. He *might* be worth a quick fling."

I laughed and rolled my eyes, relieved she was maintaining her humor about this. "He just might be."

She smiled then and gave my shoulder a friendly nudge. "Which reminds me, Gage has been asking about you." Her voice carried a teasing lilt.

Uh-oh, I thought. Aloud I said, "Whoa—don't go getting ideas. Gage and I are just friends, okay? What does he want?"

"He wants to see you, of course. I told him you'd been working at Connie's flower shop the last couple of days."

"And I'll be there again tomorrow for sure and possibly Friday," I said. "Things have been really busy lately."

"That's what I thought, plus I told him you'd probably be babysitting Saturday night." She paused and offered an apologetic smile. "So, he wondered if you might be free on Sunday to come over and watch the game with us. Just an informal get-together like last time."

I assumed "us" included Nick and the girls, depending on the man's reaction Saturday night to Maureen baring her soul. If he didn't turn and run, but responded with the sympathy Maureen was hoping for, then this casual gathering would be a perfect next step in their relationship. It would also be a safe, comfortable setting in which to see Gage. No expectations.

"Sure," I said, "I can do that. The game starts around one, doesn't it?"

"I think so, but feel free to come earlier. I'll make a bunch of snacks." She gave her hair a quick toss. "Now then, back to the craft fair. What do you know about this gym?"

I took a gulp of coffee and grabbed the notes I had brought with me, spreading them on the table before me. Maureen came around and sat beside me, studying the hen scratches I had made.

"This is a tentative diagram," I said. "The standard elementary school basketball court is seventy-four by forty-two. That should give us plenty of room. See here, if we divide the perimeter into six foot lengths, not counting the corners, we should be able to get ten tables down each long side and five along the ends."

She scrutinized the drawing. "Wow, you've really put

a lot of work into this."

"Thanks," I said, and for a moment wondered what in the world I had gotten myself into. With everything else I had going on—selling my condo, looking for work, helping Connie at the shop—I was beginning to worry I had taken on too much. But I had never been one to do a project halfway. *Must be in my DNA*, I thought. My mom was the same way. Once committed to a task, we were both obsessive about details and getting the job done right. I had started this venture as a means to help Maureen, and I intended to see it through.

"The numbers are all approximate," I went on, "based on the dimensions of the basketball court, not the whole gym itself."

She squeezed her lower lip between her thumb and forefinger. "This allows for thirty tables, more or less. Do you think we'll need that many? I mean, this is the first time we've ever done anything like this in this neighborhood. What if we only sell half the spaces?"

I shrugged. "Then I guess we'll spread things out—give everyone more room to display their goods. Even fifteen would be a good response for our very first craft fair. But I'm hoping to pull people in from all around the area, not just this neighborhood. I thought I'd put flyers in all the craft stores and fabric shops in the north end. If we're lucky and get a good response, there's room to put more tables down the center."

We continued this discussion for the next hour, going over ideas for advertising and for displaying our homemade rugs to best advantage. At nine thirty, I called the school district main office to find out the cost and to clarify what was needed to finalize our use of the gym.

Siblings and Secrets

The administrative assistant cheerfully answered my questions, and said she would put the rental agreement in the morning's mail so that I would have it by the next day.

After this, we moved to the attic sewing room to work on my half-finished rag rug. It didn't take me long to pick up where I'd left off. With no interruptions by the two little girls, I made quick headway, weaving the pliable fabric strips into a soft, firm mat. The warm hues—orange, yellow, moss green, and brown—mingled together, creating an abstract collage of colors that reminded me of a patch of forest floor on a sunny day.

When the oval reached the size of an average bathroom rug, Maureen showed me how to finish off the ends by tucking them in and adding a few sewn stitches to keep them from coming undone. Overall, I was pleased with the result, and unexpectedly found myself eager to do another one. Who knew making rugs could be so much fun?

At twelve thirty I thanked Maureen and helped her put away the materials. I had lunch plans downtown with Tamara and time was getting tight. But first I headed home for a quick check on Buster. He was doing much better since surviving the poison, but Connie and I had agreed that under no circumstances should he be left unsupervised for long periods in the back yard.

Chapter Twenty-One

Buster's tail wagged nonstop as I attached the leash to his collar and led him out the front door. I wanted to take him for a quick run up to the corner and back so he could stretch his legs and take care of business. After that, he'd be fine in the house for a few hours.

From the porch, I glanced left and noticed Sylvia Prescott, two doors down, emerge from her front door and storm into the middle of her front yard where she stood with arms folded as though facing off with the house across the street. I hesitated, and in that moment her husband came after her. He placed his hands on her shoulders and turned her around to face him. Their body language made it clear that heated words were being exchanged. I gave the leash a tug and trotted down the steps, making a quick right turn toward Maureen's house in the opposite direction. The last thing I wanted was to get within range of Sylvia's scathing tongue.

The Moreland house was the oldest in the neighborhood, the original farmhouse going back to the Twenties, a remnant of the hundred-year-old homestead that had been sold and parcelled off to make way for the surrounding development. Just past the house was the forest—a tract of tall conifers, leafy maples, and thick underbrush bisected by a narrow footpath.

Reaching the trees, I stopped and allowed Buster to poke his nose among the weeds at the edge of the road. The woods in daylight had been a rollicking place to run and play with friends. Even now, I could hear echoes of childish laughter reverberating through the trees, and somewhere in the distance my mother calling me to come home for lunch. As kids we had shunned the dark glades and hollows, those oppressive places where the forest grew thick and impenetrable, where imaginary bears and monsters lurked. I smiled. The very act of scaring ourselves had been a sort of game in itself.

Such a carefree time. If only those days could have gone on forever. Now the woods held for me a sort of awe. Here was an island in the city, a cool, green home to birds and small animals, surrounded on all sides by human activity. I sighed wistfully and pulled my jacket closer as a cool breeze whipped up around me. High clouds scudded across the sky, obscuring the sun and casting dense shadows beneath the trees. Fall was definitely in the air.

Discovering that Maureen owned the land had been a shock. I understood why she'd held onto it all this time, but now that reason no longer existed. I wouldn't blame her if she decided to sell the property—it had to be worth a small fortune—but I hated the thought of seeing it bulldozed and subdivided.

I narrowed my eyes as I watched Buster snuffle through the tall grass and brush. The little hound had a powerful nose, capable of tracking the faintest of scents. Had he indeed discovered where Hannah was buried? But how was it the police had failed to find her if she was someplace close by?

Suddenly, my phone rang. I snatched it out of my pocket and looked at the caller. The realtor. My pulse quickened. "Hello?"

"Brenna? It's Linda. Guess what? We've received a couple of offers on your place. Do you have a minute to talk?"

I took a hasty glance at the time. This conversation would need more than a minute, and I had to get going if I didn't want to be late meeting Tamara.

"Linda, that's great, I'm excited. But right now I'm running late for an appointment downtown. I'll be in the area, so how about if I swing by your office, say around three thirty?"

"Sure, I'll be here till five. See you then."

I let out a happy squeal as I hung up and replaced the phone in my pocket. *At last.* Things were finally moving forward. Selling the condo would free me from my monstrous monthly mortgage payment, and give me money to buy a place of my own.

Buster looked up curiously and trotted over to see what all the fuss was about. I reached down and gave him an exultant hug, then straightened and started for home. I could hardly wait to tell Tamara.

"I guess that's good news," Tamara conceded morosely, "for you. I know it's what you want. But it's miserable news for me. What if the buyers are horrible people? What if they get drunk and obnoxious? What if they're old and stinky and bad-tempered? Or worse yet, what if they play opera music real loud?"

I rolled my eyes. "Oh, *relax*. I'm sure whoever buys the condo will be perfectly nice. In fact, you'll probably become best friends with them and forget all about me."

She gave a woeful sniff. "No chance." Her luminous eyes and pouty lips took on a melancholy puppy dog expression.

I had to laugh. "Don't be so dramatic. I promise we'll stay in touch. I won't even be that far away. We can still meet on Sundays and go running or something."

"Careful, Brenna," she said with a sly smile. "I'll hold you to it."

The waitress brought our orders and Tamara took a bite of her grilled salmon, murmuring with pleasure. As usual, the restaurant's offering of fresh seafood was outstanding. The wide picture windows presented spectacular views of Lake Union, the marina, and the surrounding hills of Seattle, although typical of September, the sky was leaden with the threat of rain.

"So," Tamara said, "what have you been up to since I saw you last?"

I jabbed at my shrimp salad. "I've got so much to tell, I hardly know where to start."

"Ooh, sounds promising. Have you found a new job?"

"No, actually I've been helping my cousin at her flower

shop. But I *did* meet a lawyer while I was there and I gave him my résumé. He said he'd keep his ears open in case he heard of anyone hiring."

She leaned back and picked at her salmon again. "That's hardly earth-shattering."

"He could be a swimsuit model," I said in an offhanded way. "Tall, blond, gorgeous..."

She bolted upright. "Are you going out with him?"

"No. I told you, I just met him. But he flirted."

"Did you flirt back?"

"Yeah...well, sort of." I shrugged, amused at my friend's zeal. I knew her interest in my love life stemmed from her well-intentioned, if misguided, concern for me. "I smiled and we made small talk, but I didn't want him getting the wrong idea."

Tamara threw her hands up. "What am I going to do with you? Do you want him to offer you a job, or don't you?"

"Seriously?" I fixed her with a deadpan stare, glad no one was sitting nearby who could overhear this ridiculous conversation. We were past the lunchtime rush and the restaurant crowd was thinning out as people returned to work. "That is *not* how I intend to get a job."

"Well, a little flirting wouldn't kill you. How else do you expect to get back in the game? Tall, blond, and gorgeous sounds like the perfect combination to me."

"You know I'm not interested in snagging a new boyfriend—especially one who could potentially be my boss."

My mind flashed back to Troy's sculpted features, his striking blue eyes and dazzling smile. The truth is, I *was* attracted to him, and I *did* secretly hope to see him again, but I couldn't tell Tamara that or she'd fixate on it and never let it go.

"I know what the real problem is," she said matter-of-factly.

I cocked an eyebrow. "What's that?"

The waitress appeared just then to refill our water glasses. When she had gone, I looked at my friend expectantly. "Well?"

"You're still stuck on your neighbor's brother." She accompanied this statement with a knowing little bob of her head.

I gave a quick snort. "I am *not* stuck on him. But he *is* the one I wanted to talk to you about."

Her eyebrows shot up. "Don't tell me—you two are on again! Last time I saw you, you were ready to leave town to get away from him."

"That was before I found out the truth. Turns out he's not the villain I thought he was."

"Wait—let's order dessert," Tamara said, "and then I want you to start at the very beginning. I want to hear all the juicy details."

At last. I'd been dying to tell her everything now that it was no longer a secret. The truth came off as so bizarre, it was a relief to have someone to share it with who wouldn't think I'd gone completely off the deep end.

We both ordered a scoop of raspberry sherbet. Then, between bites, I told her the whole story...

"...and so for twenty-five years," I concluded, "Maureen believed her brother had accidently killed Hannah, and secretly buried her body in the woods."

"*Oh, my god*," Tamara gasped.

"But when I confronted him, he was shocked. Turns

out what Maureen saw him bury was a *dog*. That's what he'd hit with his friend's motorcycle when it wandered into the road. It was a terrible accident and he felt horrible about it, but he forgot about it in the face of his little sister's disappearance. It never occurred to him to connect the two. Why would he? And in all those years, Maureen never told another soul. She was determined to protect Gage and save him from going to prison."

Tamara shook her head. "No wonder she's messed up."

"Yeah, but the really messed up thing is that Gage had no idea she'd been protecting him." I let out an audible sigh, like releasing air from an over-inflated balloon. "And then she told *me*, and made me promise to keep it secret. Naturally, I was furious with Gage for letting Maureen carry the blame for Hannah's disappearance all those years. I thought he was the worst kind of coward."

I glanced around. Two men in business suits had come in and taken a table by the window; they appeared immersed in conversation. I lowered my voice and continued. "So all this time, twenty-five years, Maureen has been wracked with guilt. When she started seeing Hannah's ghost, she began having these debilitating panic attacks. She was convinced her sister blamed her. That's why she stopped going outside."

Tamara frowned. "But if she thought it was Gage who killed Hannah, why did Maureen feel so guilty?"

I patted my mouth with my napkin. "Well, first because she'd left Hannah alone in the house when she was supposed to be babysitting, and second because her silence meant that Hannah's body was never recovered, never properly laid to rest, just left there in the woods to rot." The words conjured such a horrifying picture that I couldn't help shuddering.

Tamara wrinkled her nose. "Ew, when you put it like that..."

"Exactly. And of course Gage didn't know about any of this. He always assumed Hannah had been kidnapped or something. He was a kid too, remember, and as far as he knew, the police were handling it. The sad thing is that he and Maureen never talked about it, and over the years Maureen's guilt and resentment kept growing until it destroyed the close relationship they'd once had. When their parents left, Gage got stuck taking care of his older sister, who by that time was having serious emotional issues."

"At least he *did* take care of her. A lot of guys wouldn't."

I nodded. "That's what I told Connie."

Tamara waved the waitress over and asked for coffee. Neither of us was ready to leave yet.

Suddenly, the imperative crow of a rooster erupted from the depths of my coat pocket. I threw Tamara an apologetic glance as I dug for my phone and read the text.

"Guess who?" I said.

Her eyebrows rose curiously. "Gage?"

I nodded. "He wants me to come to his office. Says he has something to show me. Probably plans for a new house he's designing."

Tamara grinned. "Sounds like he's making excuses to see you. What's that old line? 'Wanna come up and see my etchings?' Could be fun."

My face puckered in a perverse grimace. "And have him thinking I'm just sitting around all day with nothing to do but wait for him to call? Besides, after lunch I'm meeting my realtor."

I texted back: *Not today. Gotta see my realtor.*

His reply was immediate: *Tomorrow?*

Sorry. Working at Connie's all week.

I silenced the phone and stuffed it back into my pocket. "There," I said, brushing my palms together a couple of times. "Now where were we?"

It wasn't that I didn't want to see Gage. It was just that I found his nearness confounding. I wanted to keep a sort of balance between mutual attraction and casual friendship—nothing too serious. Running to him when he crooked his finger seemed contrary to that purpose and I wasn't about to fall for it. Come up and see my etchings indeed.

Tamara leaned toward me, a pair of elaborate beaded earrings dangling beneath her mass of dark hair. She spoke softly, but her words came fast. "The last time we talked, you said the ghost was real. You said you'd seen her, and you were trying to listen to her."

"I *have* seen her. She is definitely real." It still seemed incredible.

"Have you figured out what she wants?"

"I think she wants me to find her. I think her body's nearby."

Tamara sucked in a breath. "Why do you think that?"

I told her about Buster and the rotted shoes he'd brought home. Then I told her about Hannah's ghost being barefoot. "It has to mean something, don't you think?"

"So, do you think she's buried in the forest after all? I mean, just because *Gage* didn't bury her there doesn't mean someone else didn't." She shuddered.

"I don't know," I said. "It's possible, I guess, only Gage told me the police scoured those woods and determined Hannah wasn't there. It's not that big an area, really, only about an acre. He said the whole neighborhood traipsed through there and found nothing. Besides, I'm pretty sure that's not the direction Buster went."

Tamara gave me a piercing look. "You have a plan, don't you? Something stupid and dangerous."

A great vote of confidence. She sounded like my mother. I waved off her concern. "No, nothing like that. I'm just going to follow Buster one of these days and see where he goes. If he starts digging, I'll know where to look."

"Aren't you afraid the killer might still be hanging around? It could be one of the neighbors." She looked around again to make sure no one was listening.

"Yeah, right," I scoffed. "I've met most of the neighbors, and they're about as dangerous as a pack of Smurfs."

In truth, it hadn't occurred to me that there might be a killer living incognito among the mundane citizens of the neighborhood—a community full of humdrum, middle-aged suburban types.

"Besides," I said, "it's been twenty-five years. The police have never actually proven there *was* a killer. And even if there *was*, he's got to be long gone by now."

"I suppose the little girl could have fallen into a storm drain or something," Tamara said, stirring her coffee thoughtfully.

I nodded. "I can think of all sorts of scenarios that

don't involve murder. The beach is only a couple of miles away. I can imagine Hannah getting bored and trying to go there by herself. Groups of us kids used to walk there all the time with our moms. Or maybe the library. It's in the same direction and there were lots of isolated shortcuts she might have taken along the way. If she tripped and hit her head, or broke her leg, she might have lain there till she died of exposure. Or she might have been struck and killed by some horrible hit-and-run driver who just left her in a ditch and took off."

"Yeah, but think about it," Tamara said. "If her body was just lying around the neighborhood decomposing, don't you think somebody would have found it? I mean, dead bodies *stink*."

I grimaced. "That's true, and Gage told me the police used search dogs."

"Drowning and being washed out to sea seems probable, or kidnapping."

"No ransom note."

"Could have been traffickers," Tamara said. "Maybe she was sold to some foreign prince to be his sex slave. Maybe she's still alive and living in a harem on the other side of the world. I saw this movie once, where this girl—"

"Whoa," I said, "slow down. You're getting carried away. First of all, I've seen Hannah's ghost, so I know she's not still alive, and second, neither of those fits with Buster digging up her shoes." I blew a breath out through my teeth. "I'm positive she's nearby, and her ghost wants me to find her body."

She grinned. "Right. So what's your plan?"

I shrugged. "Nobody will think there's anything suspicious about me chasing after my wayward dog. I'll just follow Buster, and if I find anything, I'll call the police."

"Sounds simple enough. Why don't you ask Gage to come with you?"

"Because Gage doesn't believe in ghosts. I told him about Buster and the shoes, and he pretty much thinks I'm crazy."

Tamara chewed on her lip, then said finally, "Well, just be careful."

Chapter Twenty-Two

Leaving the restaurant, I headed straight for my realtor's office, eager to hear about the offers she had received on my condo. The office was situated on the ground floor of one of Seattle's posh downtown high-rises. Its large front windows were plastered with photos displaying to best advantage many of the properties they represented.

My agent ushered me to a private room and motioned to a chair in front of a wide chrome desk. A middle-aged woman with a square face, shrewd gray eyes, and a short, no-nonsense haircut, Linda Racine had been selling properties in the Seattle area for thirty years and had a sterling reputation.

"We have two offers," she began without preamble, perching her perfectly manicured fingers atop two sets of papers on the smooth surface of the desk. "One is for all cash, though they're offering substantially less. The other is closer to the asking price, but with contingencies."

"What kind of contingencies?" I didn't know much about real estate transactions. When Jason and I had bought the condo seven years ago, he had handled most of the negotiations. At the law firm where I'd worked, I had dealt occasionally with title searches and escrows, but always in an abstract way. I had never had reason to become personally involved with the intricacies of wheeling and dealing.

"The buyers are in the process of selling their current home in Portland," she said. "They're moving to Seattle and have just put their house on the market. They're motivated to sell and they say there has been some interest, but there are no guarantees and no telling how long it will take. And then, of course, the bank will require an inspection and an appraisal before approving their loan. This is standard procedure."

"What about the all cash offer?" I asked, feeling slightly apprehensive.

She pushed a printed form across the table for me to peruse. "He says he'll waive the inspection, so once the title search has been done he's prepared to write you a check."

I studied the offer. "This is a lot less than we discussed. We're talking about a two-bedroom condo in a prime location with water views."

I could feel the heat rising in my cheeks. This condo had been my dream home, the love nest Jason and I had worked and scraped for. It was more than just concrete and glass, it was the encapsulation of all my sweet memories. I wanted to rant, to berate this heartless, unknown buyer, and shame this cold, unfeeling agent.

"It *is* an older building," Linda pointed out reasonably. "It needs a few updates, and don't forget the pending assessment for the new roof. That could run in the thousands."

I rubbed the back of my neck. It wasn't fair to blame Linda. She was doing the job I had hired her to do, and it would be a huge relief to get out from under the enormous mortgage payments I was making, as well as the HOA fees, insurance, and taxes. I drew in a breath and blew it out again. *A bird in the hand.* Time to get over it. I needed to sell and move on.

"Would you like to make a counter offer?" asked Linda.

I thought for a moment. "Yeah, let's bump it up by fifty thousand and see what he says. I'm hoping to make enough on this sale to buy another house—anywhere but downtown. You know housing prices in Seattle are ridiculous."

"Okay." She smiled and stood, reaching across the desk to shake my hand. "I'll present it to him and we'll go from there. Shouldn't take more than a day or two to get his response."

The next morning, I followed Connie to the flower shop, taking my own car with the back seats folded up to make room in case I had to make deliveries. Connie went on and on about my PT Cruiser. She couldn't get over how much cargo space the car offered. Sort of a cross between a station wagon and a 1940's gangster car, it was the little auto's quirkiness that had drawn me to it in the first place.

My expectations of a quiet morning were thwarted when the last person I expected to see waltzed through the door precisely at eight. When the bell above the door jingled, I looked up and there was Troy Cavendish sauntering toward me wearing his customary grin.

A warm flush of pleasure wicked up my spine as he drew near. "It's not Monday," I said, meeting his smile with one of my own.

"I was hoping you'd be here," he said. "I have a job offer for you, if you want it."

For a moment I couldn't speak. *Work for Troy?* Could I do that? Did I *want* to? Wouldn't that put a crimp on any chance of dating in the future? Or was I being presumptuous? Maybe I had misread his signals. Suddenly, Gage's dark brooding eyes flashed accusingly in my mind.

"That's great," came Connie's voice at my shoulder. I hadn't realized she'd come up behind me. "Isn't it, Brenna?" She gave me a subtle nudge with her toe.

"Of course," I squeaked. I looked down at my hands on the counter, making a conscious effort not to fiddle with my ring. "In your office?"

"No," he laughed. "That would be totally inappropriate since I'm hoping to ask you out."

I let out a quick breath, feeling relieved and foolish at the same time. As I met his gaze, he cocked his head provocatively. Blue eyes shone behind the lenses of his glasses. Until that moment, I had never truly appreciated how beguiling a good pair of frames could look on a handsome masculine face.

"It's my *father* who needs a new legal assistant," he continued. "He's got a practice in Edmonds overlooking the Sound, a beautiful location. His current assistant has been out on maternity leave and just decided she doesn't want to come back to work after all. He currently has a temp working for him. I told him about you and he's eager to meet you."

So, Troy's father is also an attorney. Like father, like son. "What kind of law does he practice? Criminal defense, like you?"

He shook his head. "Huh-uh. Wills, probates, adoptions, that sort of thing. Probably a lot like what you did for Ralph Murray."

Things were looking up. First, an offer on the condo, now a promising lead on a job, right in the area I wanted. "Sounds perfect. Give me his name and number, and I'll call him to set up a time for an interview."

"His name is Ross Cavendish, and as far as an interview, would tomorrow morning be too soon? I can pick you up here and take you to his office if you like. He's looking forward to meeting you. Fact is, I'm pretty sure it's a done deal if you want it. My father knows Ralph Murray, and he's already called him about you. I guess Ralph gave you a great reference and told my dad he'd be crazy to pass up a chance to hire you."

I gave a self-conscious laugh, feeling a blush creep over my face. "That's nice to hear, but I'll have to swing it with my current boss—she's something of a slave-driver." I angled a sly look at Connie who had been standing next to me listening to the whole conversation. She chuckled as she slapped me playfully on the shoulder.

"Go," she retorted. "Get a job. You've been goofing off

far too long."

"Then it's settled," Troy said. "I'll pick you up here at eight tomorrow morning. We'll stop for breakfast on the way. I know a little place near the ferry terminal that makes the best pancakes."

I shot him a look of mock reproof. "Don't you have to work tomorrow?"

He shrugged. "My office, my rules. Besides, my assistant does most of the work anyway."

"*Ha,* I believe it."

The rest of the morning passed in a fog of euphoria, edged with a touch of nervous anticipation. Customers came and went, I answered the phone, dusted shelves, and watered the potted plants. During my morning break, I took a moment to look up Ross Cavendish. The internet described him as being a partner for over twenty years with the firm of Randall, Cavendish, and Torres in Edmonds, Washington. I couldn't help smiling at the picture on the firm's website; no question Ross was Troy's father.

Just before noon, Connie took a phone order for a rush delivery. Someone at an office in Seattle needed a bouquet of red roses delivered right away, and they were willing to pay extra for the inconvenience.

Connie handed me the order form. "It shouldn't take long to get there," she said as she pulled the long stems from the bucket in the refrigerated display case. "It's in the Wallingford District, close to the zoo. Just take the freeway to 45th and go west about half a mile. Piece of cake."

I studied the address. It was a major thoroughfare and, besides the zoo, it was near the Seattle Public Library. I'd spent a lot of time in that neighborhood during my therapy period. "No problem. I know that area pretty well."

"Why don't you grab lunch while you're out," Connie added as an afterthought.

Thirty minutes later, I entered the lobby of an imposing two-story brick building that declared itself to be the offices of Grand Designs NW, an architectural firm with a large sign over the door advertising services in residential and business innovation, custom remodeling, additions, green building, and interior design. Holding the bouquet of roses in front of me, I approached the receptionist at the front desk who watched me with a mirthful expression on her face.

"Hi," I said, feeling awkward. "My instructions were to see the receptionist. I guess that's you."

She nodded and her smile widened into a grin. "I've been expecting you. Hold on just a minute." She picked up the receiver on her desk and tapped out a number on the keypad. After a moment, she spoke into the phone, her voice rising in a cheerful lilt. "Your delivery is here."

She looked back at me. "Would you wait, please? He'll be right down. You can set those here on the desk if you like."

Gratefully, I set the box holding the glass vase gently on the corner of the desk and looked around. The lobby wasn't large, but it was bright and elegantly furnished with modern upholstered chairs, potted plants, and trendy artwork. An elevator door stood to the right. Just behind the receptionist on the wall above her head was a plaque listing the professionals who worked here. I nearly gasped out loud when I spied the name, Gage Moreland.

I should have known, I thought, resisting the urge to smack myself in the forehead. Gage was an architect. He told me he had something to show me at his office and I blew him off. So he set this whole thing up. *He certainly gets points for determination.*

At that moment, the elevator door swished open and Gage emerged looking puckishly pleased with himself. He held his hand out in a welcoming gesture. "Brenna, so glad you could make it."

"Ha-ha," I intoned. "Was Connie in on this little subterfuge?"

"I have no idea what you're talking about." His smirk was barely disguised. "Come on upstairs, I have something I've been dying to show you." As he led me to the elevator, he called over his shoulder. "Thanks, Sharon—enjoy the flowers."

On the next floor, we entered a spacious room flanked on two sides by shelves filled with books and three-ring binders. In the center was a large rectangular table on which were spread wide sheets of paper covered with incomprehensible lines and inscriptions. A young red-headed man wearing wire-framed spectacles leaned over the table with a pencil, engrossed in one of the drawings. He looked up briefly, gave us a nod, then returned his attention to the sheet he was studying.

"This is where we do layouts," said Gage, taking on the role of tour guide. It occurred to me with a pang that, in his whole career, Gage had never had any family to whom he could show off his workplace or his achievements. The schism between him and his sister had stretched over his entire adult life, and by all accounts, his absent parents had never expressed any support or encouragement.

I smiled and kept up a stream of compliments as Gage led the way down a hall, past a conference room, a materials library, and then into a large office with tall windows looking out toward the distant trees of Woodland Park.

"Nice," I said as I pivoted to take it all in. "Is this your office?" A long work table topped with paper, pens, and various unfamiliar tools of the trade stretched along one wall. On a desk sat a computer, along with two wide-screen monitors beneath a row of shelves filled with more books and binders. A large printer filled one corner, and a tall split-leaf philodendron with wide, glossy leaves added a splash of greenery. The whole effect was neat and professional.

"Uh-huh," said Gage. "This is where it all happens, although I *did* tidy up a bit before you came."

"Very impressive." I flipped my hair back with one hand. "Was there something particular you wanted to show me? A new project you're working on?"

"Behind you," he said cryptically.

I turned to find the fourth wall of the office covered in a gallery of framed, color photographs in different sizes showcasing buildings in various stages of completion. *Designs he's created,* I thought, glancing over the pictures.

"Look closer," he said. "Anything look familiar?"

As my eyes roved the wall, I was suddenly caught by the image of two deer standing in a sunlit glade. The larger, a buck with forked antlers, stood staring directly into the camera, his ears thrust forward as though riveted forever in an aspect of watchfulness.

"That's the picture I took," I said with surprise, "when we visited that house you designed on Mercer Island. Turned out pretty well."

"Yeah," he said, "you've got a good eye. If you don't find a job in a lawyer's office, you could always be a photographer."

I threw my hands up, bouncing on the balls of my feet. "I almost forgot! I got a job—as of this morning!"

He took a half step back. "Whoa, when did this happen? I didn't even know you were looking."

I laughed and said, "I wasn't. It just sort of fell into my lap."

He raised his eyebrows, giving me a quizzical stare. I waved my hands back and forth in the air, then started from the beginning. "One of Connie's regular customers at the flower shop is a lawyer—"

"And you asked for a job?"

"Sort of. Let me finish. I gave him my résumé and asked him to pass it on to anyone he knew who might be looking for a legal assistant. Turns out, his father is *also* a lawyer. The father's assistant just quit and the son gave him my résumé. He called Ralph—my old boss—who I guess he knew—who apparently told him wonderful things about me, and told him he'd be crazy not to hire me." I could hear myself rambling, but I kept on. "And tomorrow I'm going to his office to meet him." I stopped and took a breath, rubbing my hands together excitedly.

Gage nodded his head. "So, you don't *actually* have the job yet."

I gave a shrug. "Well, no, not *technically*, but Troy assures me it's a done deal if I want it."

"Troy?"

"The son."

Gage looked at me askance. "The lawyer you met at the flower shop."

"Right." For a fleeting moment, an image of Troy's lean, blond, good looks rose up in my mind, and I couldn't help comparing him to Gage's dark, hunky features—a greyhound next to a timber wolf. I pushed the thought away. "The father practices the same sort of law they did at the office where I used to work, so it sounds like a perfect fit. I can sure use the job."

Gage's face softened and he cracked a smile. "You'll get it. No problem."

"Hopefully, I'll know after tomorrow." I glanced at the time on my watch. "So, you want to get a sandwich or something? Then I need to get back."

We walked around the corner to a fast-food place where we picked up burgers and fries. Sitting at a table in the corner, we talked while we ate. I told him about the offers on my condo and my visit with Maureen.

"She's so much better since you two cleared the air—happier, more upbeat, definitely healthier-looking," I said. "She told me she's going to start seeing her therapist again. I think she's really set on getting better."

"A lot of that is thanks to you," Gage said with a warm smile. He unwrapped his hamburger, lifted the top bun, and began picking off the pickles.

"She just needed someone to talk to." I brushed a crumb off the table, then leaned over and pilfered his discarded pickles. "Speaking of which, I think things are heating up between her and Nick Donato."

Gage's expression was serious. "Yeah, and she tells me

you're babysitting Nick's kids on Saturday while she has him over for dinner to"—he paused for effect—"tell him *everything*." His mouth twisted sarcastically. "What could possibly go wrong?"

"I know, but don't you think it's a good idea for her to be honest with him? Tell him about her illness and how she's planning to see a therapist? Besides, considering how gossipy the neighborhood is, he probably knows most of it already."

"Sure, but what happens when she tells him about being haunted by Hannah's ghost? A lot of people would call that certifiable. Nick had a lot of issues with his ex-wife. I doubt he'll want to go through *that* again. He's got those two girls to think about." He opened a ketchup packet and spread it on his hamburger.

I fumed, fearing he might be right. But I was banking on the chemistry I'd seen between them, trusting that Nick was as good a guy as I believed him to be. I stuffed my mouth full of French fries while I sorted out my thoughts. Lots of people believed in the lingering spirits of departed loved ones, and they weren't declared crazy. I often thought of my father and imagined him watching over me.

"You do remember that *I've* seen Hannah's ghost too, right?"

A woman at a nearby table shot me a curious glance but I ignored her.

Gage allowed himself a half smile. "You always did have a wild imagination—but I haven't seen you getting all hysterical, either."

"Ha-ha," I retorted without humor. "The difference is that Maureen suffered years of anguish and guilt thinking everyone around her blamed her. I'm no psychiatrist, but

I'm pretty sure that would be traumatic for any fifteen-year-old." I crumpled my hamburger wrapper into a ball. "She didn't just wake up one day and decide to develop agoraphobia. She needs our support if she's going to get well, but it's not going to happen *poof*, like that."

Gage reached across the table and took my hand, his somber eyes full of contrition. "You're amazing, you know that? And you're right. So, how can I help? You want me to talk to Nick?"

I pulled back my hand, suppressing the fluttery feeling aroused by his touch. "I *did*, but now I'm thinking we shouldn't interfere. Nick seems like a standup guy, and I think maybe it would be good for Maureen to explain everything to him in her own words."

"And if he rejects her? Won't that cause a setback? I remember how depressed she was after she and Andy broke up."

I wiped my fingers on a paper napkin. "I don't think so. She seemed prepared to accept Nick's reaction, whatever it might be."

I saw Gage tighten his jaw. He clearly expected the worse.

"It's not just Nick," I said. "All of this—talking it out with you, opening up to friends, helping with the craft fair—it's all part of her healing process. She kept everything bottled up inside for so long. Now it's like a huge weight has been lifted and she can start forgiving herself. We just have to be there for her."

He gave a thoughtful nod.

I leaned across the table and wagged a finger in his face. "So you've got to quit telling her she's crazy—and mean it."

Gage threw his hands up in defeat. "I know, I know, the ghost is real." His voice didn't hold much conviction.

"The ghost *is* real," I said. "And it's time we found out what she wants."

He nearly choked as he bit off a laugh and rolled his eyes. "And how do you propose we do that? Have a séance?"

The word conjured an image of a dark, eerie room lit by candles with the three of us, Maureen, Gage, and me, holding hands around a small table uttering strange incantations. Something right out of a 1930's horror movie. How would that play to Maureen's already fragile mind and her terror of being haunted?

"No," I hissed, glancing around to see if anyone was listening. Thankfully, the nosy lady had departed. Still, I lowered my voice and leaned forward with my arms on the table. "You just have to listen with an open mind. I think what Hannah wants is for us to find her and lay her to rest properly. That's the only thing I can think of that might bring her peace."

Gage rubbed a hand over his face. His expression definitely read skeptic, but he didn't interrupt.

"I'm convinced Buster, Connie's dog, knows where Hannah's body is buried," I said. "In fact, I believe Hannah's spirit has a way of calling him, calling any of us actually, if we only listen. I intend to let him out in the back yard and see where he leads me."

Gage swept up the empty wrappers and paper cups, and piled them on the plastic tray in front of him. "Fine," he said. "Do what you want, but I think you're wasting your time. I think Hannah was kidnapped, killed, and dumped somewhere far away from here. If her body was buried close by, somebody would have found it long ago."

Chapter Twenty-Three

As promised, Troy picked me up at the flower shop at eight the next morning and took me to breakfast before my interview, though I was too nervous to eat.

He smiled as he watched me pick at my pancakes. "Relax, Brenna. I told you, Ralph Murray gave you a great reference and that was enough for my dad. This interview is really nothing more than a formality."

I set my shoulders and returned his smile. I was grateful for this opportunity. The job sounded perfect and I was determined to get it. I'd been loafing too long, coasting on Connie's generosity.

The law offices of Randall, Cavendish, and Torres were located in a large refurbished two-story house on a hill overlooking Puget Sound. It was painted cornsilk yellow with dark brown shutters, and tastefully landscaped with ferns, pink heather, and rhododendrons. A Japanese maple spread vermillion foliage over one corner of a compact lawn.

Troy gave a friendly greeting to the receptionist sitting at a desk in what once must have been the living room of the old house. She gave him a perfunctory nod and he led the way up a wide carpeted stairway to the next floor. He rapped on the door at the top of the stairs, then waited only a moment before pushing inside.

The office was orderly and professional. Tall shelves displayed rows of legal tomes while mahogany paneling, dark leather furnishings, and a massive oak desk imbued the room with a dignified, venerable authority. Wide windows across one wall afforded expansive views of the town and waterfront.

The man behind the desk looked up, raised his index finger in a *just a second* gesture, and returned his attention to something he was studying intensely on the desk in front of him. From where I stood, it appeared to be the newspaper's daily crossword puzzle. I had to smile. This was a good omen. Mr. Murray had always done the crossword too, and we had often collaborated on solving difficult clues.

"Dad..." began Troy impatiently.

The older gentleman raised his craggy head and eyed me with studied scrutiny. Without preamble, he said, "Young lady, if you can give me a ten letter word starting with 'c' meaning 'keeper of the keys,' you've got the job."

"*Dad*..." Troy groaned in the long suffering tone of one accustomed to coping with the annoying eccentricities of an older person.

I put a confident hand on Troy's arm. "It's okay—I've got this."

Thanks to all those romance novels I'd read in high school, I knew the answer. Every good Gothic manor had a housekeeper, a dependable servant charged with keeping the keys. Leveling my gaze at the elder Cavendish, I said, "*Chatelaine*. Would you like me to spell it?"

The lines of his face deepened as his mouth spread in a crafty smile. "Ralph said you were good."

I returned the wry look, appreciating of his sense of humor. "Why do I get the feeling you already knew the answer?"

He laughed aloud. "I had to give you a test, didn't I? I've already checked your background, and gotten a reference from your previous employer. You've got the job if you want it. The temp I've got wants to work to the end of the month if that's all right with you. So you'd start October first. How does that sound?"

Just over a week and still so many things to be done for the craft fair: posters, media advertising, sign-up sheets, maybe a website... Suddenly, I felt cornered.

Stop! I gave my shoulders a vigorous mental shake. *You have plenty of time, and there are lots of willing neighbors happy to help out. You can do this—and you need this job. It's perfect.*

"October first sounds great."

Next to me, Troy beamed like he'd just brokered world peace.

The icing on the cake came shortly after I got home that evening. Linda Racine called to tell me my counter-offer had been accepted and she was in the process of drawing up the paperwork. By this time next month, the sale would be complete and I would have a check in hand.

Things were happening fast.

But there was still one thing I wanted to do.

Monday morning I watched from the kitchen window as Buster wandered aimlessly around the back yard. He stopped here and there to sniff at some noteworthy scent, then after a few minutes, found a shady patch under a tree and settled down to chew on a stick he had unearthed in the grass.

As I watched, my mind drifted back to Saturday night. Sitting with Carly and Gina had been easy, they were such amiable kids. I taught them to play Old Maid, and we had spent the evening laughing and vying together in good-natured competition. Nick hadn't returned until well after the girls were in bed, which I took as a good sign. He had kept his feelings close to his chest, but as I prepared to go, he had thanked me and said, "Guess I'll see you tomorrow. You're going over to Maureen's to watch the game, aren't you?"

I pulled a chair over to the window and leaned my elbows on the sill. Maybe my great idea wasn't going to work after all. Buster seemed totally uninterested in breaking out of the yard today. He just lay in the grass chewing his stick, occasionally snapping at flies.

Again, my mind wandered. I thought about my conversation with Maureen during the football game yesterday when I had finally managed to get her alone in the kitchen. The girls had gone out to play in the back yard while Gage and Nick were fixated on the television in the living room.

Siblings and Secrets

I asked her how it went with Nick Saturday night since he obviously hadn't run for the hills. Her answer had been a secretive little smile and a shrug. "We talked," she said. "I told him everything—*almost* everything—and he listened. We're still friends."

A positive response under the circumstances. *One day at a time.*

I had been sitting at the kitchen window for over an hour now and was about to give up and abandon my position, when the beagle looked up and stared toward the Chumleys' as though someone had called him. He dropped the stick and loped toward the edge of the yard, diving beneath the same rhododendron where he had previously dug out under the fence.

I slipped out through the rear door, catching sight of Buster as he made a beeline across Chumleys' back yard toward the Prescotts' whose property was circled by a high privacy fence built of vertical cedar boards. Once Buster dug underneath that, I would no longer be able to see where he went.

There was only one house beyond Prescotts' before the intersection at the end of the block. Fortunately, the house on the corner had no fence, so if I hurried, I could catch up to Buster as he tunneled out of Prescotts' back yard. I didn't know the family who lived there, but Connie had told me once that the husband and wife both worked and their kids were in high school. With any luck, they wouldn't be around on a weekday.

I trotted up the street and around the corner, slowing as I approached the yard where I expected to see Buster surface. The manicured landscape was neatly arranged with flower beds and ornamental shrubs, but nothing so bushy as to block my view. I leaned against a shade tree by the side of the road, positioning myself at the back corner of the fence in case Buster's escape route angled sharp west toward the house abutting the rear of Prescotts' yard. No matter where he emerged under the fence, I should be able to spot him right away.

I scanned the bottom of Prescotts' fence, looking for telltale signs of digging. I didn't know how long it would take the little hound to work his way under the bottom board, but figured that since he had done this before, it wouldn't take long.

As I waited, I contemplated what I would find at the end of this search—not Hannah, not the friend I remembered, but a decayed corpse. The grisly thought made me shudder. But I steeled myself; if finding Hannah's body would bring her peace, I was determined to keep going.

What was taking Buster so long? Maybe I should sneak a peek over the fence. I glanced up and down the block to see if anyone was about. I didn't want to arouse suspicions, have some neighbor ask what I was doing snooping around. But the street was empty. People were at work, children were at school. I took a deep breath and hurried across the lawn.

Using a large, conveniently placed rock as a step, I grasped the top of the solid, six-foot fence and pulled myself up to peer over the top into Prescotts' back yard. I was surprised to see a large, unkempt enclosure overrun with weeds and tall grass. What a contrast to the tidy yard and gardens in the front. At the back of the property was a weather-beaten shed the size of a small garage.

Both Bill and Sylvia were retired, and apparently had

money if the tales of Sylvia's father were to be believed. The least they could do was hire someone to mow the grass.

A movement in the weeds caught my eye. A section of tall grass was rustling at the base of what looked like a small, tumbledown gazebo nearly hidden within a patch of thistles and overgrown morning glory.

Buster? A moment later, the white tip of his tail, waving like a signal flag, became visible when his hind end backed into view. After a breath, he nosed once more into the brush, disappearing in the tangle of foliage growing around the crumbling structure.

He must be chasing a rabbit. I scanned the area. All I needed was for Sylvia to spot the dog messing about in her back yard. *It's not like he's trampling her flower beds,* I thought wryly, *but there's no sense giving the woman more reason to dislike me.*

Then a chilling thought occurred to me. Overgrown weeds. Dilapidated shed. Rats and mice would flourish here in these dark hidey-holes. It must have been Bill Prescott who put out the poisoned bait that had nearly killed Buster. I had to get the dog out of there.

But how? Even if I could somehow scale the fence, there was no way I could safely climb back over while carrying Buster. I would have to grab him and sneak past the side of the house to the street out front. Then maybe I could lead him up around the corner and encourage him to pick up where he'd left off before he became distracted.

Or maybe this was a wild goose chase. Either way, I had to remove Buster from Prescotts' yard without being seen.

I dropped back to the ground and looked around for

something I could use to help me get over the fence. I was neither a gymnast nor a pole vaulter. No suitable tree grew close enough to climb, and no handy ladder lay nearby. I blew my breath out, feeling defeated. Then I spied a metal garbage can near the back of the house where I stood. *That'll work.*

I dragged it the length of the yard and set it close to the fence. I took another careful look around to make sure the coast was clear, then clambered up and hoisted myself over, tumbling inelegantly into the long grass on Prescotts' side.

I rolled onto my knees, calling in a low voice. "*Buster!* Come here, boy."

He ignored me and continued his pursuit of whatever he had chased underneath the decaying gazebo. "*Better not be a skunk,*" I muttered under my breath.

Crouching low, I sprinted through the weeds till I reached him tussling in the brambles. He was digging—quite determinedly. The whole front half of his body had burrowed out of sight under the rotted floor boards. Loose dirt flew everywhere.

"*Buster,*" I hissed. "Come out of there." I knelt next to him and reached into the hole, feeling along his body until I caught hold of his collar. After a couple of good tugs, he backed out, covered with dirt and holding tightly onto a tattered hunk of cloth.

I wrinkled my nose as I wrested it away from him. "What have you got there?"

It definitely wasn't a rabbit. I held it up, and my breath caught. Even crusted with years of dirt and mildew, it was identifiable as a pink jacket.

It had to be Hannah's. But this was unthinkable.

Siblings and Secrets

Here? In Prescotts' back yard? Three houses down from where she had lived? The hairs on my arms rose and my hands began to tremble. *Hannah's remains were right here in this hole, within reach of my fingertips.* My heart began to pound like a riot of jackhammers.

Tail whipping side to side, tongue lolling, Buster kept his eyes riveted on the ragged jacket. Then, like a rainbow taking form in the mist, Hannah materialized in front of me, an arm's length away, shimmering, translucent in the sunlight, hovering in the trodden weeds above the place Buster had been digging. She held my eyes for an instant, then faded away.

My brain felt like pudding. I could scarcely think. My first impulse was to call Gage, but he was at his office in Wallingford. It would take him at least half an hour to get here.

I needed the police. I felt for my phone, then realized like an idiot I'd left it in my coat hanging on a kitchen chair back at the house. I rubbed my forehead to clear my head. *Just take Hannah's jacket and get the hell out of here.*

I glanced toward the house. No sign of anyone. Prescotts must be gone.

I wadded the filthy cloth into a ball intending to smuggle it out under my arm. As I did, something fell and struck me on the knee. I reached to pick it up and realized it was a gold locket on a chain. It wasn't corroded which meant it was real gold and not some cheap metal. *Interesting piece of jewelry for an eight-year-old.* Perhaps a gift from her father. It must have been in the pocket of the jacket. Given the length of chain, it had probably hung down to her belly button. I gave my hands a quick swipe on my jeans, then carefully pried it open.

Inside were two miniature photos. On the left side, cut in a tiny circle to fit the locket, was a picture of my mother—younger, but unmistakable. And on the right was a picture of *me* at about seven years old. It looked like my first grade school photo. I gaped in confusion. Why these pictures? Where had Hannah gotten them? Had I given her the pictures when we were children? I couldn't remember.

Buster was getting restless. He swung his head to look at something over my shoulder and his tail began to wag. Before I could turn around, I caught a movement out of the corner of my eye and something hard whacked me in the back of the head. Pain clouded my vision as I pitched forward into the dirt and weeds. The last thing I heard was Buster's frantic barking.

Chapter Twenty-Four

I woke slowly, a fierce pain in my head. When I tried to move I found I was lying on my side, ankles tied and hands bound behind my back with cord that cut painfully into my wrists. My hip and shoulder ached from pressing against a cold, unforgiving concrete floor; a coarse, oily-tasting rag stuffed into my mouth nearly caused me to choke.

I forced my eyes open, squinting through my eyelashes into a dim, cobwebby space cluttered with shovels, rakes, hoses, and other garden implements. It reeked of fuel and fertilizer, the caustic chemicals burning my nose. Besides one small, grimy window, the only light came from a single bulb hanging from the ceiling. This had to be the shed I had noticed in the back of Prescotts' yard. It had looked deserted and I'd paid it little attention.

In the shadows behind me, a man and woman stood

arguing.

"What have you done?" the man bawled.

Was that Bill Prescott? He sounded horrified.

"Keep your voice down," hissed the woman. "I hit her with the back of the shovel. She was digging around the gazebo with that blasted dog."

Sylvia? The puny housewife with the horn-rimmed glasses? Fear took hold of me, twisting my gut like the coils of a snake. I flexed my wrists, testing the bonds. The rope was tough and fibrous, like nylon clothesline wrapped around several times and cinched tight.

"You didn't have to *hit* her," Bill exclaimed. "She wasn't hurting anything."

A shuffling step scraped against the concrete floor behind me and I tensed, waiting.

"Keep away from her," Sylvia snarled abruptly, "or I'll hit you too."

"But Sylvia, that's *Brenna*."

What does he care? If he killed Hannah, why would he hesitate to kill me?

"I don't care *who* she is," spat his wife. "She found the body."

"*What* body? What are you talking about?" His voice rose in alarm.

Sylvia kept talking, her words firing rapidly. "She had a piece of the clothing, so you know she found it. I couldn't catch the dog—he was too fast—but I poisoned him once and I can do it again. This time I'll use antifreeze—he won't recover from that."

So, it was *Sylvia* who had given Buster the poisoned meat. She had tried to kill him. Obviously, she had been complicit in Hannah's murder, but why did Bill sound so bewildered? I kept listening, trying to make sense of it all while surreptitiously tugging at the ropes holding my wrists. They wouldn't budge and I was losing feeling in my fingers.

Quick footsteps paced on the hard floor. Sylvia was becoming more agitated. "She had the locket too. *See?*" The word was sharp, like an accusation.

"The locket?" Bill's murmur was barely audible. "I haven't seen that in years. Where did Brenna get it?"

"Off the body, you moron," said Sylvia. "Haven't you been listening?"

This was followed by the metallic *chink* of something hitting the concrete.

"That little girl had it," Sylvia continued. "She must have taken it that day. Don't you remember? She came over to see the kittens. The kitchen door was open and she walked right in, the little brat. She found me in the bedroom, crying—as if you cared—because I had just discovered that stupid locket in the back of your sock drawer. A pretty unoriginal place to hide it, I must say."

I was struck by the spitefulness in Sylvia's voice. Why did Bill put up with his wife talking to him that way? How had they stayed married so long? But more importantly, what was Bill Prescott doing with a locket containing pictures of me and my mother?

"Sylvia..." he said in a conciliatory tone.

"That's when I knew she was yours," Sylvia blurted. "I suspected it for years. I saw how you looked at that little hussy, how you slobbered over her baby. It wasn't natural. But then I found that locket and I *knew*."

Motionless, I lay on the floor of the shed trying to hear over the thunderous pounding of my heart. My picture.

My mother's picture. Was Sylvia saying that Bill Prescott was my *father?*

"It was nothing," Bill said. "A passing fling. It was a long time ago."

"Who gave you the locket?" persisted Sylvia. "That slut, your teenage lover? Or her interfering mother, Arlene? I hated that woman—always so righteous, looking down her nose at me like I was trash."

Arlene had been my *grandmother*. So, it was *true?* My head throbbed. This was almost more than my muddled brain could handle.

Bill ignored the question. Instead he said, "Brenna doesn't know anything. You have to let her go, she may have a concussion. She needs a doctor."

"Didn't you hear me?" Sylvia screeched in a shrill, frenzied voice. "She found the body. She had the girl's jacket. She knows *everything*. You have to help me get rid of her. It'll be easy. I did it once before, and no one ever suspected. Together, we can do it again. *You owe me.*"

My heart catapulted into high gear. I could hear the blood rushing in my ears. Sylvia had just confessed to killing Hannah—and she planned to do the same to me. Only Bill stood in her way. *My father*. Would he protect me?

"You killed that little girl?" Bill asked in a labored voice.

"It wasn't my fault. How was *I* supposed to know she was hiding in the bushes when I threw that rock? It was *you* I was trying to hit."

Bill ignored the gibe. "But where did you bury her? How come I never knew?"

"Don't you remember that day?" Sylvia snapped. "We

were in the back yard. We had a huge fight and you roared off on your motorcycle—didn't come back till after dark. I wasn't sure you were ever coming back. For all I knew, you'd run off to be with your girlfriend and your precious love child."

"But the little girl...?" he pressed. It sounded like he was speaking through clenched teeth.

"She was hiding in the bushes by the back porch, listening to us argue," Sylvia said. "She must have heard everything. I was furious with you, and I threw a big rock."

"I remember." Bill said. "I ducked."

"Yeah, but *she* didn't." Sylvia gave a chilling little laugh. "It hit her in the head—must have killed her instantly. I found her there after you left. I didn't know she'd taken the locket, but it wouldn't have changed anything. I panicked. So I buried her under the floor of your new gazebo where I didn't think anyone would look. And I was *right*." Her voice went soft and syrupy, mimicking a simpering damsel: "Nobody *ever* suspects a meager wisp of a *girl*—which is what I was back then."

An icy tremor ran up my spine. Listening to this exchange, I was convinced Sylvia was more than a little insane. I flexed my wrists, painfully twisting to work the ropes loose. My captors were so absorbed in each other, they were paying no attention to me.

"Under the gazebo?" Bill croaked. "*How?*"

"You had just started working on it. You only had the basic frame assembled. The floorboards weren't nailed down yet. You had them all measured and cut, but they were just lying on the joists. It was easy enough to move the boards, dig a hole, bury the body, and put the boards back in place."

She sniggered contemptuously. "If you hadn't come back, I was prepared to put the whole thing together myself. My dad taught me how. He thought every girl should at least know how to use a hammer. Lucky for me you did return, and the next time you went out to work on it, you nailed the floorboards over the grave and no one was ever the wiser."

"That's why you never went near the gazebo after I finished it," Bill murmured, letting out a sigh. "I built that for you, you know. I thought you'd like it, maybe grow some flowers around it."

Sylvia broke in. "We're wasting time. We have to dispose of your bastard troublemaker or she'll spoil everything."

Terrified, I redoubled my efforts, struggling as the ropes cut into my flesh. But they felt looser now. I pulled harder. If only I could get my hands free. I refused to go down without a fight.

"No, Sylvia," Bill said firmly. "The first one was an accident. You never meant to kill that girl. But what you're talking about now is cold-blooded murder."

"We *have* to kill her," Sylvia declared. "Don't you see? She'll tell the police. They'll arrest me. They'll send me to prison."

"We'll explain to them what happened," he said. "I'm sure they'll understand." He spoke slowly, reasonably, as though to an obstinate child.

"I'll tell them it was *you*," cried Sylvia, her voice escalating maniacally. "*You* killed her. They'll believe me. You already have two strikes against you. I won't go to prison. I *won't*."

"Tell them what you like—I don't care." Bill's deep voice was resolute. "I can't allow you to harm her. Brenna's my daughter, the only child I'll ever have."

"*And whose fault is that?*" Sylvia's screaming accusation was heartrending. "If you hadn't been drinking that night..."

Suddenly, Bill was on his knees behind me, prying at the knots holding my wrists. "I'm sorry, Brenna. I'm so sorry." His voice was choked with remorse. "You never should have come here. You should have stayed in Arizona with your mother. You were safe there. Sylvia's not well—she doesn't know what she's doing."

My body trembled with relief as a flood of adrenaline kicked in. *Everything will be all right now. I have a father, and he's going to save me.* I could feel the ropes loosening.

But in an instant, my euphoria changed to horror as I heard muffled footsteps behind me, and the *clang* of the shovel connecting violently with Bill's skull. He toppled unconscious onto the floor next to me. I tried to cry out, but my mouth was still gagged and the only sound I could make was a strangled screak in my throat.

I wriggled around to face my assailant. Sylvia stood over me wielding the shovel. Light reflected off her glasses lending a murderous gleam to her eyes. With her wildly teased hair and ill-fitting clothes, she could have been a mad fishwife out of some dark medieval folktale.

"You thought you could come back here and take him from me," she hissed. "You filthy whore. Parading up the street in those tight pants, seducing my husband with your shameless tricks. But I'm on to you. You'll never have him."

She's confusing me with my mother, I thought wildly. *Or*

any of the other girls in Bill's reckless past.

My hands were almost free. The knots were undone and now it was just a matter of disentangling my wrists from the coils of rope. I struggled frantically.

She raised the shovel.

Just another second...

At that moment, a jumble of garden tools leaning against the wall—hoe, pick, spade, axe, rake, and pitchfork—spontaneously fell, colliding with two rusty bicycles, knocking them like dominoes into a stack of oil cans, flower pots, and apple crates. The whole lot tumbled to the floor with a clangorous crash.

Sylvia wheeled, brandishing the shovel against this new threat. She turned this way and that, poised to strike, but nothing was there.

Seizing the opportunity, I leaned back on my elbows, lifted my legs—still tied together at the ankles—bent my knees, and kicked out with all my might. I struck Sylvia hard in the back of her thighs, propelling her forward into the wall of the shed. Dropping the shovel, she reeled back, stumbled and fell, striking her head against the corner of a large metal tool box. She let out a cry, then lay still.

I shook the rope off my wrists and yanked the rag out of my mouth. Spitting and coughing, I began feverishly untying my ankles. A glance at Sylvia told me she was breathing, but I was more concerned with Bill. I crawled to where he lay motionless on the hard floor. A quick check of his pulse confirmed he was alive, but a bleeding gash and dark swollen contusion on the side of his head urged me to get help as quickly as possible.

I staggered to my feet and pressed my hands against my temples to stem the throbbing in my head. I looked around, searching the shadows for the exit, eager to escape this nightmare. That's when I saw the locket lying near the jumble of tools on the floor. Its shiny surface glinted in the dim light cast by the single bulb overhead. I picked it up and stuffed it into my pocket.

The exit was near the front corner of the shed. I would have to step over Sylvia's sprawled body to get there. How long would she remain unconscious? I hesitated, imagining her waking suddenly and grabbing my ankle.

I took several deep breaths to steady myself, then hopped over her and hurried to the door. I yanked it open and rushed outside, running straight into—*Maureen*. Buster was with her, dashing about, keeping up a steady cacophony of excited barks.

"Are you all right?" she cried, sounding breathless like she'd been running. Her face was flushed and creased with worry. She threw her arms around me.

Too shocked to speak, I nodded and let her lead me away from the shed. After a few paces, I stopped and stammered, "Maureen, what are you doing here? How did you find me?"

"It was Hannah." She smiled weakly. "I did what you said. I listened to her—and she told me you were in danger." Bewildered, she looked around. "What *happened?* Why are you here?"

I swallowed, attempting to quell my nerves and stop the shaking that threatened to overwhelm me. I faced her and took hold of her hands.

"I found her," I blurted out. "Hannah. She's been buried here this whole time, under that gazebo."

Incredulous, Maureen's mouth flew open and she turned to stare wide-eyed at the decaying structure overgrown with weeds. "Bill Prescott?" she murmured. "Bill Prescott killed Hannah?" Her eyes welled with tears.

"No," I said. "It was *Sylvia*. I'll explain everything later, but first we need to call 911. Do you have your phone? We need the police and an ambulance."

Within minutes, the Prescotts' back yard was swarming with police and paramedics. The onslaught of sirens and flashing lights roused the quiet community and gave them a show like they'd never seen before.

I told the police I'd followed my wandering dog into the yard and found him digging under the gazebo. I showed them the filthy pink jacket I'd unearthed, then described how I was struck from behind, tied up in the shed, and nearly murdered by Sylvia Prescott. They were particularly interested in the details of her confession, and called for a forensics team to investigate.

Paramedics brought Bill Prescott out of the shed on a gurney. He was awake, his head wrapped in bandages. I hurried to his side. There was so much I wanted to say, but I was overcome by a barrage of emotions and the words caught in my throat.

Instead, he took my hand and murmured, "I'm so sorry, Brenna, so sorry—for everything."

We watched as paramedics brought Sylvia from the shed and attempted to treat her. She screamed and fought like a wildcat until they were finally forced to sedate her. The police handcuffed her to a gurney, and she was taken away in an ambulance.

Bill dropped his eyes to our hands clasped together on

the edge of the gurney. "Sylvia wasn't always like this," he said in a halting voice. "It's my fault. There was an accident...years ago...I'd been drinking." He looked away as though shying from a bad memory. "So reckless and stupid. I hit a patch of ice...lost control of the car. Sylvia was badly injured. Afterwards, she couldn't have children. She never got over it, never forgave me."

Then I remembered something Sylvia had said: *You owe me.*

He looked up, his eyes full of tears. "She was so jealous, so resentful—knowing I had a daughter, seeing you here in the flesh. But I never thought she'd go this far."

I squeezed his hand and gave him a kiss on the forehead, then stood back while the paramedics loaded him into an ambulance and whisked him away to the hospital.

I declined a ride in an ambulance, but was checked over by a paramedic who applied an ice pack to the goose egg on the back of my head. He advised me to go home and get plenty of rest, and see a doctor if I developed any adverse symptoms. The police also informed me that I would have to come down later to the station to give a formal statement.

Buster, meanwhile, ran around sticking his nose into everything, making a nuisance of himself until a length of rope was located in Prescotts' shed by one of the officers. I attached it to the beagle's collar and hauled him out of the way while the detectives proceeded with their investigation.

During this flurry of activity, Maureen had stood aside and listened, then silently watched as the forensics team began to dismantle the floor of the gazebo. As soon as I could, I went to her and said, "You probably shouldn't watch. Let's go back to my house and talk."

Keeping her eyes straight ahead, Maureen spoke in a soft voice. "It was like you said. She got into my head. I couldn't ignore her. I was scared—*so scared*—but she told me you were in danger and needed my help." She turned and looked at me then, giving a weak laugh. "I didn't know what the danger was, but I was afraid I wouldn't get here in time. I'm not even sure how I got here. Somehow, she led me."

Despite everything that had happened, my face broke into a smile. I grasped her hands. "And look at you now—you're *outside*. You overcame your fear to save me. I'll be forever grateful."

She nodded slowly, her eyes meeting mine. "I still don't completely understand what happened, but in the end, it looks like you saved yourself. I think I got here a minute late."

"It was close," I said, shuddering as I recalled how near to death I had come. "But Hannah helped. She created a diversion when I needed it. Let's go home and I'll explain everything."

As we started across the yard we were suddenly confronted by Gage running toward us, his face charged with worry. "What's going on?" he cried. "Are you all right? There's police everywhere."

He pulled us both into a protective hug as he gaped at the throng of uniformed officers. I leaned my head against his chest, listening to the rapid beat of his heart, grateful he was there.

He studied us in turn, searching anxiously for answers.

His eyes narrowed on his sister. "When I came home and couldn't find you, I was scared to death. I knew it had to be something colossal to get you out of the house."

He looked up then and stared at the work progressing at the gazebo. Two men wielded shovels, and a man wearing coroner's coveralls knelt beside a pile of freshly dug dirt. Gage glanced down at Buster lying at my feet, seeming to notice the beagle for the first time.

He stepped back and gave me a pointed look. "You did it, didn't you? You found Hannah. You followed the dog and he led you to her. Just like you said."

I nodded. "There's so much I have to tell you."

His face wore a contemplative expression. "I think she may have come to me this morning. I worked hard to block her out, but she was persistent. That's why I came home. I couldn't shake the feeling that something was wrong." He gave Maureen a crooked smile. "I'm sorry."

"So now you believe," I said.

"Let's say I'm keeping an open mind."

Maureen turned once more to gaze at the spot where her sister's remains had been discovered. The forensics team was working carefully now with trowels and brushes. Suddenly, she let out a gasp and reached for her brother, clutching at the sleeve of his coat for support. Buster, too, leaped to his feet, barking excitedly in the direction of the gazebo. Gage and I both swung around to look.

A bright light shimmered over the excavation site. A spectral form coalesced briefly within the light—the perfect body of a young girl—then gradually dissolved, leaving behind a faint ethereal afterglow that drifted away on the breeze. Oblivious, the police continued their work.

"Did you see her?" cried Maureen.

Gage nodded slowly. "I saw...something."

I brushed a wisp of hair behind my ear. "This time was different. I don't think we'll see her again."

I remembered what my friend Tamara had said. She thought the little girl's ghost had waited all these years for the right person to come along, someone with a connection, an affinity with Hannah, and a willingness to listen. Now that she'd been found, her spirit could move on. With a catch in my throat, I whispered, "Good-bye, Hannah."

Just then, the coroner got up and went to confer with one of the detectives, a graying, heavyset man in a dark suit. After a few minutes, the man approached. "You're the Morelands?" he asked. "I'm Detective Hatcher."

Gaged nodded. "I'm Gage Moreland, this is my sister Maureen, and our neighbor Brenna Wickham. Our parents moved out of state."

"I worked your sister's case when she first disappeared," said the detective. "All these years, it's never been far from my mind."

"It's Hannah," Maureen blurted. Not a question, but a statement.

He gave her a solemn look. "The coroner confirms that the remains buried here are those of a child. He'll run DNA tests to be sure, but given the location and condition of the bones, I think we can safely say that your sister has been found. I'll let you know in a few days when the report comes back."

"Thank you," Gage said as the detective turned to rejoin his team.

"Let's go," Maureen said. She wiped tears off her face,

then gave her brother a sober look. "We have to call Mom and Dad."

Gage expelled a long audible sigh. Then he held his arms out to us and we each took an elbow, walking three abreast past the Prescotts' house. Further talks would be had between us, but for now there were phone calls to be made. I could only image the bittersweet conversation destined for the Moreland family, but after twenty-five years of not knowing, the news would have to bring some kind of relief.

At the street, we encountered a police barricade and a crowd of gawkers. Keeping our heads down, we pushed through the gauntlet of curious neighbors and hurried on.

I thought about my own upcoming phone call to my mother. I could hardly wait to tell her what I had learned. I smiled to myself and gave a soft, inward laugh. She had a lot of explaining to do.

END

Watch for Book Two in the
Brenna Wickham Haunted Mystery series

FAMILIES and FELONS

<u>An excerpt:</u>

I was suddenly startled by a muffled metallic jangling. My first impulse was to jump up and grab my cell phone off the desk. With a start, I realized the sound wasn't coming from there. The old rotary phone in the closet was ringing again.

For a moment I sat dumbstruck, but on the third ring I bounced off the bed and made a leap for the closet. I threw the door open and fell to my knees, grabbing for the handset. "Hello?"

I pressed my ear to the receiver, bracing myself. Again, a faint male voice was barely discernible through the static. Outside, the bushes beneath my window rattled in the wind making it impossible to hear. The dark, moonless night heightened the gloom and increased my feelings of foreboding.

Finally, the phone went silent and I found myself holding nothing but a cold, inanimate hunk of old plastic. I pulled in a deep breath, striving to slow my racing heart. For a full minute, I sat staring at the old telephone. *Please, God, not another ghost!*

Hands shaking, I replaced the handset and shoved it once more into the closet.

A true denizen of the Pacific Northwest, Kathleen loves deep blue water, tall green trees, and The Seattle Seahawks. She can often be found with her husband on their boat cruising the San Juan Islands of Washington State. She is the author of the *Brenna Wickham Haunted Mystery* series, and a member of the Puget Sound Chapter of Sisters in Crime.

News about upcoming books in the *Brenna Wickham Haunted Mystery* series can be found at www.kathleenjeasley.com

Printed in Dunstable, United Kingdom